DANGEROUS

DIANA PALMER

DANGEROUS

**Doubleday Large Print
Home Library Edition**

This Large Print Edition, prepared especially for Doubleday Large Print Home Library, contains the complete, unabridged text of the original Publisher's Edition.

HQN™

ISBN 978-1-61664-451-2

DANGEROUS

This is a work of fiction. Names, characters, places and incidents are either the product of the author's imagination or are used fictitiously, and any resemblance to actual persons, living or dead, business establishments, events or locales is entirely coincidental.

This edition published by arrangement with Harlequin Books S.A.

This Large Print Book carries the Seal of Approval of N.A.V.H.

To Cindy Angerett, 9-1-1 dispatcher,
Beaver County, Pennsylvania,
and to Emergency Services Personnel
everywhere, who give their time generously,
both on and off the clock,
to help someone in need.

A Note from the Author

Dear Reader,

Of all the books I've written in recent months, this one has taken the biggest toll on me, emotionally. I knew from *Heart of Stone* that some of Kilraven's family had been murdered. I knew from *The Maverick* that his little three-year-old girl was one of the victims. But actually dealing with the emotions that arise from such tragedy, even in a novel, can be difficult.

I have, thank God, never lost a child. But as I wrote the scenes dealing with Kilraven's loss, I developed a whole new relationship with boxes of tissues. This seemingly steel-hard man has a very soft center, and discovering it was fascinating.

I also dealt with an unexpected and shocking reality when I got to the last few chapters. The man I had fingered as the murderer informed me quite bluntly that he had nothing to do with it. (Men with nets are not approaching, characters do take on lives of their own.) So I had to go back and rethink my strategy, and my plot. I didn't really mind. It was kind of fun.

Winnie started out as a meek woman who wouldn't even stand up to her own brother. During the course of this book, in which she works as a 9-1-1 operator, she became a fountain of calm and quiet knowledge, and the courage she had always possessed was revealed to her. She did in fact become a "little blonde chainsaw," as her new mother-in-law dubbed her.

I had a lot of help with this novel from a lovely lady who actually is a 9-1-1 operator, Cindy Angerett. She gave me great insight into the job, and I have dedicated the book to her in gratitude. Please note that I do make mistakes, more than ever these days as my mind ages with me. But the mistakes are my own, and I take full responsibility for any you may find. I owe my life to a diligent 9-1-1 operator. They are a gift from God in times of great danger. I love them all.

Thank you all, again, for being so kind and so loyal for all these years. The greatest joy I have in my profession is the friends I make in the course of following it—not only in my publisher and editors, art, marketing and publicity people, booksellers and wholesalers, but in the readers who have become my extended family.

Love to all from your greatest fan,

Diana Palmer

1

Kilraven hated mornings. He especially hated mornings like this one, when he was expected to go to a party and participate in Christmas gift-giving. He, the rest of the police, fire and emergency services people in Jacobsville, Texas, had all drawn names around the big Christmas tree in the EOC, the 911 emergency operations center. Today was the day when presents, all anonymous, were to be exchanged.

He sipped black coffee in the Jacobsville Police Station and wished he could get out of it. He glared at Cash Grier, who smiled obliviously and ignored him.

Christmas was the most painful time to him. It brought back memories of seven years ago, when his life had seemed to end. Nightmarish visions haunted him. He saw them when he slept. He worked his own shifts and even volunteered to relieve other Jacobsville police officers when they needed a substitute. He hated his own company. But he hated crowds far more. Besides, it was a sad day, sort of. He'd had a big black Chow keeping him company at his rental house. He'd had to give it away because he wasn't allowed to keep animals at his apartment in San Antonio, where he would be returning soon. Still, Bibb the Chow had gone to live with a young boy, a neighbor, who loved animals and had just lost his own Chow. So it was fated, he guessed. He still missed the dog, though.

Now, he was expected to smile and socialize at a party and enthuse over a gift that would almost certainly be a tie that he would accept and never wear, or a shirt that was a size too small, or a book he would never read. People giving gifts were kind-hearted, but mostly they bought things that pleased themselves. It was a rare person who could observe someone else and give just the right present; one that would be treasured.

At his job—his real job, not this role as a small-town police officer that he'd assumed as part of his covert operation in south Texas near the border with Mexico—he had to wear suits from time to time. Here in Jacobsville, he never wore a suit. A tie would be a waste of money to the person who gave him one for Christmas. He was sure it would be a tie. He hated ties.

"Why don't you just string me up outside and set fire to me?" Kilraven asked Cash Grier with a glowering look.

"Christmas parties are fun," Cash replied. "You need to get into the spirit of the thing. Six or seven beers, and you'd fit right in."

The glare got worse. "I don't drink," he reminded his temporary boss.

"Now isn't that a coincidence?" Cash exclaimed. "Neither do I!"

"Then why are we going to a party in the first place, if neither of us drink?" the younger man asked.

"They won't serve alcohol at the party. And for another, it's good public relations."

"I hate the public and I don't have relations," Kilraven scoffed.

"You do so have relations," came the tongue-in-cheek reply. "A half brother named Jon Blackhawk. A stepmother, too, somewhere."

Kilraven made a face.

"It's only for an hour or so," Cash said in a gentler tone. "It's almost Christmas. You don't want to ruin the staff party now, do you?"

"Yes," Kilraven said with a bite in his deep voice.

Cash looked down at his coffee cup. "Winnie Sinclair will be disappointed if you don't show up. You're leaving us soon to go back to San Antonio. It would make her day to see you at the party."

Kilraven averted his gaze to the front window beyond which cars were driving around the town square that was decorated with its Santa, sled and reindeer and the huge Christmas tree. Streamers and colored lights were strung across every intersection. There was a tree in the police station, too, decked out in holiday colors. Its decorations were, to say the least, unique. There were little handcuffs and toy guns and various emergency services vehicles in miniature, including police cars. As a joke, someone had strung yellow police tape around it.

Kilraven didn't want to think about Winnie Sinclair. Over the past few months, she'd become a part of his life that he was reluctant to give up. But she didn't know about him, about his past. Someone had hinted at it because her attitude toward him had suddenly changed. The shy smiles and rapt glances he'd been getting had gone into eclipse, so that now she was formal and polite when they spoke over the police band while he was on duty. He rarely saw her. He wasn't sure it was a good idea to be around her. She'd withdrawn, and it would be less painful not to close the distance. Of course it would.

He shrugged his broad shoulders. "I guess a few Christmas carols won't kill me," he muttered.

Cash grinned. "I'll get Sergeant Miller to sing you the one he composed, just for us."

Kilraven glared at him. "I've heard it, and please don't."

"He doesn't have a bad voice," Cash argued.

"For a carp, no."

Cash burst out laughing. "Suit yourself, Kilraven." He frowned. "Don't you have a first name?"

"Yes, I do, but I don't use it, and I'm not telling it to you."

"I'll bet payroll knows what it is," Cash mused. "And the bank."

"They won't tell," he promised. "I have a gun."

"So do I, and mine's bigger," Cash returned smartly.

"Listen, I have to do concealed carry in my real job," he reminded the older man, "and it's hard to fit a 1911 Colt .45 ACP in my waistband so that it doesn't show."

Cash held up both hands. "I know, I know. I used to do concealed carry, too. But now I don't have to, and I can carry a big gun if I want to."

"At least you don't carry a wheel gun, like Dunn does." He sighed, indicating Assistant Chief Judd Dunn, who was perched on the edge of his desk talking to a fellow officer, with a .45 Ruger Vaquero in a fancy leather holster on his hip.

"He belongs to the Single Action Shooting Society," Cash reminded him, "and they're having a competition this afternoon. He's our best shot."

"After me," Kilraven said smugly.

"He's our best resident shot," came the reply. "You're our best migrating shot."

"I won't migrate far. Just to San Antonio." Kilraven's silver eyes grew somber. "I've enjoyed my time here. Less pressure."

Cash imagined part of the reduced pressure was the absence of the bad memories Kilraven still hadn't faced, the death of his family seven years ago in a bloody shooting. Which brought to mind a more recent case, a murder that was still being investigated by the sheriff's department with some help from Alice Mayfield Jones, the forensic expert from San Antonio who was engaged to resident rancher Harley Fowler.

"Have you told Winnie Sinclair about her uncle?" Cash asked in a hushed tone, so that they wouldn't be overheard.

Kilraven shook his head. "I'm not sure that I should at this stage of the investigation. Her uncle is dead. Nobody is going to threaten Winnie or Boone or Clark Sinclair because of him. I'm not even sure what his connection to the murder victim is. No use upsetting her until I have to."

"Has anyone followed up on his live-in girlfriend?"

"Not with any more luck than they had on the first interview," Kilraven replied. "She's so stoned on coke that she doesn't know the time of day. She can't remember anything that's of any use to us. Meanwhile, the police are going door to door around that strip mall near the apartment where the murder victim lived, trying to find anybody who knew the guy. Messy murder. Very messy."

"There was another case, that young girl who was found in a similar condition seven years ago," Cash recalled.

Kilraven nodded. "Yes. Just before I. . . lost my family," he said hesitantly. "The circumstances are similar, but there's no connection that we can find. She went to a party and disappeared. In fact, witnesses said she never showed up at the party, and her date turned out to be fictional."

Cash studied the younger man quietly. "Kilraven, you're never going to heal until you're able to talk about what happened."

Kilraven's silver eyes flashed. "What use is talk? I want the perp."

He wanted vengeance. It was in his eyes, in the hard set of his jaw, in his very posture. "I know how that feels," Cash began.

"The hell you do," Kilraven bit off. "The hell you do!" He got up and walked off without another word.

Cash, who'd seen the autopsy photos, didn't take offense. He was sorry for the other man. But there was nothing anybody could do for him.

KILRAVEN DID GO TO the party. He stood next to Cash without looking at him. "Sorry I lost my temper like that," he said gruffly.

Cash only smiled. "Oh, I don't get ruffled by bad temper anymore." He chuckled. "I've mellowed."

Kilraven turned to face him with wide eyes. "You have?"

Cash glared at him. "It was an accident."

"What was, the pail of soapy water, or the sponge in his mouth?"

Cash grimaced. "He shouldn't have called me a bad name when I was washing my car. I wasn't even the arresting officer, it was one of the new patrol officers."

"He figured you were the top of the food chain, and he didn't like people seeing him carried off from the dentist's office in a squad car," Kilraven said gleefully.

"Obviously, since he was the dentist. He put one of his prettier patients under with laughing gas and was having a good time with her when the nurse walked in and caught him."

"It does explain why he moved here in the first place, and settled into a small-town practice, when he'd been working in a major city," Cash mused. "He'd only been in practice here for a month when it happened, back in the summer."

"Big mistake, to start raging at you in your own yard."

"I'm sure he noticed," Cash replied.

"Didn't you have to replace his suit. . .?"

"I bought him a very nice replacement," Cash argued. "The judge said I had to make it equal in price to the one I ruined with soap and water." He smiled angelically. "She never said it had to be the same color."

Kilraven grimaced. "Where in hell did you even find a yellow and green plaid suit?"

Cash leaned closer. "I have connections in the clothing industry."

Kilraven chuckled. "The dentist left town the same day. Think it was the suit?"

"I very much doubt it. I think it was the priors I pulled up on him," Cash replied. "I did just mention that I'd contacted two of his former victims."

"And gave them the name of a very determined detective out of Houston, I heard."

"Detectives are useful."

Kilraven was still staring at him.

He shrugged.

"Well, I'm never talking to you when you're washing your car, and you can bet money on that," Kilraven concluded.

Cash just grinned.

The 911 operations center was full. The nine-foot-tall Christmas tree had lights that were courtesy of the operations staff. The LED bulbs glittered prettily in all colors. Underneath, there was a treasure trove of wrapped packages. They were all anonymous. Kilraven glared at them, already anticipating the unwanted tie.

"It's a tie," Kilraven muttered.

"Excuse me?" Cash asked.

"My present. Whoever got me something, it will be a tie. It's always a tie. I've got a closet full of the damned things."

"You never know," Cash said philosophically. "You might be surprised."

Amid the festive Christmas music, the staff of the operations center welcomed their visitors with a brief speech about the hard work they put in all year and listed some of their accomplishments. They thanked all the emergency services personnel, including EMTs, fire and police, sheriff's department and state police, Texas Rangers and state and federal law enforcement for their assistance. The long refreshment tables were indicated, and guests were invited to help themselves. Then the presents were handed out.

Kilraven was briefly stunned at the size of his. Unless it was a very large tie, or camouflaged, he wasn't sure what he'd snagged here. He turned the large square over in his hands with evident curiosity.

Little blonde Winnie Sinclair watched him out of the corner of her dark eyes. She'd worn her blond, wavy hair long, around her shoulders, because someone had said Kilraven didn't like ponytails or buns. She wore a pretty red dress, very conservative, with a high neckline. She wished she could find out more about their enigmatic officer.

Sheriff Carson Hayes had said some of Kilraven's family had died in a murder years before, but she hadn't been able to worm any more information out of him. Now they had a real, messy murder victim—actually their second one—killed in Jacobs County, and there was a rumor around law enforcement circles that a woman in San Antonio had known the victim and died for it. There were even more insistent rumors that the cold case was about to be reopened.

Whatever happened, Kilraven was supposed to leave and go back to his federal job in San Antonio after Christmas. Winnie had been morose and quiet for days. She'd actually drawn Kilraven's name for that secret present, although she had a hunch her coworkers had arranged it. They knew how she felt about him.

She'd spent hours trying to decide what to give him. Not a tie, she thought. Everybody gave ties or handkerchiefs or shaving kits. No, her gift had to be something distinctive, something that he wouldn't find on any store shelf. In the end, she put her art talent to work and painted him a very realistic portrait of a raven, surrounded by colorful beads as a border. She didn't know why. It seemed the perfect subject. Ravens were loners, highly intelligent, mysterious. Just like Kilraven. She had it matted at the local frame shop. It didn't look bad, she thought. She hoped he might like it. Of course, she couldn't admit that she'd given it to him. The gifts were supposed to remain anonymous. But he wouldn't know anyway because she'd never told him that she painted as a hobby.

Her life was magic just because Kilraven had come into it. Winnie came from great wealth, but she and her brothers rarely let it show. She enjoyed working for a living, making her own money. She had a little red VW that she washed and polished by hand, bought out of her weekly salary. It was her pride and joy. She'd worried at first that Kilraven might be intimidated by her monied background. But he didn't seem to feel resentment, or even envy. In fact, she'd seen him dressed up once for a conference he was going to. His sophistication was evident. He seemed at home anywhere.

She was going to be miserable when he was gone. But it might be the best thing.

She was crazy about him. Cash Grier said that Kilraven had never faced his demons, and that he wasn't fit for any sort of relationship until he had. That had depressed Winnie and affected her attitude toward Kilraven. Not that it squelched her feelings for him.

While she was watching him with helpless delight, he opened the present. He stood apart from the other officers in his department, his dark head bent over the wrapping paper, his silver eyes intent on what he was doing. At last, the ribbon and paper came away. He picked up the painting and looked at it, narrow-eyed, so still that he seemed to have stopped breathing. All at once, his silver eyes shot up and pierced right into Winnie's dark ones. Her heart stopped in her chest. He knew! But he couldn't!

He gave her a glare that might have stopped traffic, turned around and walked right out of the party with the painting held by its edge in one big hand. He didn't come back.

Winnie was sick at heart. She'd offended him. She knew she had. He'd been furious. She fought tears as she sipped punch and nibbled cookies and pretended to be having a great time.

KILRAVEN WENT THROUGH the motions of doing his job until his shift ended. Then he got into his own car and drove straight up to San Antonio, to the apartment of his half brother, Jon Blackhawk.

Jon was watching a replay of a soccer match. He got up to answer the door, dressed in sweatpants and nothing else, with his loosened black, thick hair hanging down to his waist.

Kilraven gave him a hard stare. "Practicing your Indian look?"

Jon made a face. "Getting comfortable. Come in. Isn't this a little late for a brotherly visit?"

Kilraven lifted the bag he was carrying, put it on the coffee table and pulled out the painting. His eyes were glittering. "You told Winnie Sinclair about the raven pictures."

Jon caught his breath when he saw the painting. Not only was it of a raven, Melly's favorite bird, but it even had the beadwork in the same colors framing it against a background of swirling oranges and reds.

He realized, belatedly, that he was being accused. He lifted his dark eyes to his
brother's light ones. "I haven't spoken to
Winnie Sinclair. Ever, unless I'm mistaken.
How did she know?"

The older man's eyes were still flashing.
"Somebody had to tell her. When I find out
who, I'll strangle him."

"Just a thought," Jon pondered, "but
didn't you tell me that she called for backup
on a domestic dispute when you didn't call
and ask for it?"

Kilraven calmed down a little. "She did,"
he recalled. "Saved my butt, too. The guy
had a shotgun and he was holding his wife
and daughter hostage with it because the
wife was trying to get a divorce. Backup
arrived with sirens and lights blaring.
Diverted him just long enough for me to
subdue him."

"How did she know?" Jon asked.

Kilraven frowned. "I asked. She said
she had a feeling. The caller hadn't told
her about the shotgun, just that her estranged husband had walked in and made
threats."

"Our father used to have those flashes
of insight," Jon reminded him. "It saved his

life on more than one occasion. Restless feelings, he called them."

"Like on the night my family died," Kilraven said, sitting down heavily in an easy chair in front of the muted television. "He went to get gas in his car for the next day when he had a trip out of town for the Bureau. He could have gone anytime, but he went then. When he came back. . ."

"You and half the city police force were inside." Jon winced. "I wish they could have spared you that."

Kilraven's eyes were terrible. "I can't get it out of my mind. I live with it, night and day."

"So did Dad. He drank himself to death. He thought maybe if he hadn't gone to get gas, they'd have lived."

"Or he'd have died." He was recalling Alice Mayfield Jones's lecture of the week before. "Alice Jones read me the riot act about that word *if*." He smiled sadly. "I guess she's right. We can't change what happened." He looked at Jon. "But I'd give ten years of my life to catch the guys who did it."

"We'll get them," Jon said. "I promise you, we will. Had supper yet?" he added.

Kilraven shook his head. "No appetite."

He looked at the painting Winnie had done. "You remember how Melly used her crayons?" he asked softly. "Even at the age of three, she had great talent. . ." He stopped abruptly.

Jon's dark eyes softened. "That's the first time I've heard you say her name in seven years, Mac," he said gently.

Kilraven grimaced. "Don't call me. . .!"

"Mac is a perfectly nice nickname for McKuen," he said stubbornly. "You're named for one of the most famous poets of the seventies, Rod McKuen. I've got a book of his poems around here somewhere. A lot of them were made into songs."

Kilraven looked at the bulging bookcases. There were plastic bins of books stacked in the corner. "How do you ever read all those?" he asked, aghast.

Jon glared at him. "I could ask you the same question. You've got even more books than I have. The only things you have more of are gaming discs."

"It makes up for a social life, I guess," he confessed with a sheepish grin.

"I know." Jon grimaced. "It affected us both. I got gun-shy about getting involved with women after it happened."

"So did I," Kilraven confessed. He studied the painting. "I was furious about that," he said, indicating it. "The beadwork is just like what Melly drew."

"She was a sweet, beautiful child," Jon said quietly. "It isn't fair to put her so far back in your memories that she's lost forever."

Kilraven drew a long breath. "I guess so. The guilt has eaten me alive. Maybe Alice is right. Maybe we only think we have control over life and death."

"Maybe so." Jon smiled. "I've got leftover pizza in the fridge, and soda. There's a killer soccer match on. The World Cup comes around next summer."

"Well, whoever I root for will lose, like always," he replied. He sat down on the sofa. "So, who's playing?" he asked, nodding toward the television.

WINNIE WAS SICK AT heart when she left after the party to go home. She'd made Kilraven furious, and just before he was due to leave Jacobsville. She probably wouldn't ever see him again, especially now.

"What in the world happened to you?"

her sister-in-law, Keely, asked when she came into the kitchen where the younger woman was making popcorn.

"What do you mean?" Winnie asked, trying to bluff it out.

"Don't give me that." Keely put her arms around her and hugged her. "Come on. Tell Keely all about it."

Winnie burst into tears. "I gave Kilraven a painting. He wasn't supposed to know it was me. But he did! He looked straight at me, like he hated me." She sniffed. "I've ruined everything!"

"The painting of the raven?" Keely recalled. "It was gorgeous."

"I thought it looked pretty good," Winnie replied. "But he glared at me as if he wanted to tear a hole in me, and then he just walked out of the party and never came back."

"Maybe he doesn't like ravens," the other woman suggested gently. "Some people are afraid of birds."

Winnie laughed, nodding thankfully as Keely put a paper towel in her hands. She dried her eyes. "Kilraven's not afraid of anything."

"I suppose not. He does take chances,

though." She frowned. "Didn't you send backup for him after some attempted shooting lately? They were talking about it at work. One of our girls is related to Shirley, who works with you at the 911 operations center," she reminded her.

Winnie grimaced. She took her purse off her shoulder, tossed it onto the bar and sat down at the table. "Yes, I did. I don't know why. I just had a terrible feeling that something bad was going to happen if I didn't. The caller didn't say anything about the perp having a gun. But he had a loaded shotgun and he was so drunk, he didn't care if he killed his estranged wife and their little girl. Kilraven walked right into it."

They were both remembering an earlier incident, when Winnie was a new dispatcher and she'd failed to mention a gun involved in a domestic dispute. Kilraven had been involved in that one, and he'd given her a lecture about it. She was much more careful now.

"How did you know?" Keely persisted.

"I really couldn't say." Winnie laughed. "I've had feelings like that all my life, known things that I had no reason to know. My grandmother used to set the table for

company when we didn't even know anybody was coming. They'd show up just
when she thought they would. The second
sight, she called it."

"A gift. I've heard them say that Cash
Grier's wife, Tippy, has it."

"So have I." Winnie shrugged. "I don't
know, though. I just get feelings. Usually
they're bad ones." She looked up at Keely.
"I've had one all day. I can't shake it. And I
don't think Kilraven's reaction to my gift
was the reason. I wonder . . ."

"Who's that coming up the driveway?"
Boone Sinclair asked, joining them. He
brushed a kiss against Keely's mouth. "Expecting someone?" he asked her, including Winnie in the question.

"No," Winnie said.

"Me, either," Winnie replied. "It isn't
Clark?"

He shook his head. "He flew up to Dallas this morning for a meeting with some
cattle buyers for me." He frowned as he
went to the window. "Old car," he remarked.
"Well kept, but old. There are two people
in it." His face tautened as a woman got
out of the driver's seat and went around to
the passenger side. She stood in the edge

of the security lights because it was already dark. Boone recognized her just from the way she walked. She spoke to someone in the car, was handed a brief-case out the window. She smiled, nodded, and turned toward the house. She hesi-tated just for a minute before she started up the steps to the front door. Boone got a good look at her, then. She was, he thought, the spitting image of Winnie. His face went harder.

Keely knew something was going on from their expressions. Winnie was staring out the window next to Boone, her dark eyes flashing like sirens. Before Keely could ask a single question, Winnie exploded.

"Her!" she exclaimed. "How dare she come here! How dare she!"

2

Winnie stormed out into the hall. Her face was taut with anger.

"Who is she?" Keely asked Boone, concerned.

His own face had gone hard. "Our mother," he said bitterly. "We haven't seen her since she left. She ran away with our uncle and divorced our dad to marry him."

"Oh, dear," Keely said, biting her lip. She looked up at his angry expression. "I think I'll go on upstairs. It might be better if the two of you saw her alone."

"I was thinking the same thing myself. I'll

tell you all about it later," Boone said gently, kissing her.

"Okay."

WINNIE HAD ALREADY thrown open the front door. She looked at the older version of herself with seething hatred. "What do you want here?" she demanded hotly.

The woman, tall and dignified, her blond hair sprinkled with gray but neatly combed, wearing a dark pantsuit, blinked as if the assault was unexpected. She frowned. "Winona?" she asked.

Winnie turned and stormed back into the living room.

Boone's eyes narrowed. "If you're here looking for money," he began in a cold tone.

"I have a good job," she replied, puzzled. "Why would I want money from you?"

He hesitated, but only for a moment. He stood aside, stone-faced, and let her in the door. She was carrying a briefcase. She looked around, as if she didn't recognize her surroundings. It had been a very long time since she'd lived here.

She turned to Boone, very businesslike and solemn. "I have some things for you. They belonged to your father, but your uncle took them with him when he. . .when he and I," she corrected, forcing the words out through her teeth, "left here."

"What sort of things?" Boone asked.

"Heirlooms," she replied.

"Why didn't our uncle come with you?"

Her eyebrows arched. "He's been dead for a month. Didn't anyone tell you?"

"Sorry," he said stiffly. "It must be sad for you."

"I divorced your uncle twelve years ago," she said flatly. "He's been living with a woman who makes her living as a low-level drug dealer, selling meth on the streets. She's an addict herself." She indicated the briefcase. "I told her these things belonged to her boyfriend's family and that legal proceedings might ensue if she didn't hand them over." Her expression was determined. "They belong here."

He motioned her into the living room. Winnie was sitting stiffly in an armchair, as welcoming as a cobra.

The older woman sat down gracefully on the sofa, her eyes going to the mantel, over which hung a painting of Boone and Winnie and Clark's late father. Her gaze lingered on it sadly, but only for seconds.

She put the briefcase on the coffee table and opened it. She drew out several items, some made of gold, including pieces of jewelry that were worth a king's ransom.

"These belonged to your great-grandmother," she told the other occupants of the room. "She was a high-born Spanish lady from Andalusia who came here with her father to sell a rancher a prize stallion. Your great-grandfather was a ranch foreman who worked for the owner. He had very little money, but grand dreams, and he was a hard worker. She fell in love with him and married him. It was her inheritance that bought this land and built the house that originally sat on it." She smiled. "They said she could outride any of the cowboys, and that she once actually fought a bull that had gored her husband, using her mantilla as a cape. Saved his life."

"There's a painting of her in the upstairs guest bedroom," Boone said quietly, lifting one of the brooches in his strong, dark hands.

"Why did you bother to bring them back?" Winnie asked coldly.

"They'd have been sold to buy drugs," she replied simply. "I felt responsible for them. Bruce took them when we left." Her face hardened. "He felt that he was deliberately left out of your grandfather's will. He was furious when your father inherited the ranch. He wanted to get even."

"So he corrupted you and forced you to run away with him," Winnie said with an icy smile.

"I wasn't forced," the older woman said kindly. "I was naive and stupid. And I don't expect to be welcomed back into the family because I returned a few heirlooms." She picked up her briefcase and stood up. Her eyes went from her son to her daughter. "Is Clark here?"

Boone shook his head. "On a date."

She smiled sadly. "I would like to have seen him. It's been so long."

"Your choice, wasn't it?" Winnie demanded. She stood up, too, dark eyes blazing. "Dad hated you for leaving, and I look like you, don't I? I paid for his pain. Paid for it every miserable day he was alive."

"I'm sorry," the older woman said haltingly.

"Sorry. Sorry!" Winnie jerked up her blouse and turned around. "Want to see how sorry you should really be?"

Boone caught his breath at the marks on her back. There were scars. Two of them. They ran across her spine in white trails. "You never told me he did that!" Boone accused, furious.

"He said that if I told, you and Clark would have similar souvenirs," she bit off, pulling her blouse down.

The older woman winced. So did Boone.

"I've wanted to see you for years," Winnie said, reddening. "I wanted to tell you how much I hated you for running off and leaving us!"

She only nodded. "I don't blame you, Winona," she said in a steady, calm voice. "I did a terrible thing, to all of you." She drew in a long breath and smiled sadly. "You won't believe it, but there was a price that I had to pay, too."

"Good," Winnie bit off. "I'm glad! Now please leave. And don't come back."

She whirled and ran up the staircase.

Boone walked his mother to the door and opened it for her. His expression was unrelenting. But his eyes were curious, especially when he saw that she had a passenger in her car. It wasn't a new car, but it was well kept. He noted her clothing. Not from upscale stores, but serviceable and not cheap. Her shoes were thick soled and laced up. She was immaculately clean, even her fingernails. He wondered what she did for a living. She seemed a sensible woman.

"Thank you for bringing the heirlooms home," he said after a minute.

Gail Rogers Sinclair looked up at him with quiet pride. "You look like your father, as he did when we were first married." She frowned. "Didn't I read that you married this year?"

"Yes. Her name is Keely. She works for a local vet."

She nodded. "Her mother was killed."

He blinked. "Yes."

"At least that crime was quickly solved," she replied. "This new murder in Jacobsville is getting a lot of attention from the Feds. I don't think it's going to be as easy to catch the perpetrator." She searched his eyes. "There may be a tie from the case to your uncle," she said calmly. "I'm not sure yet, but it could mean some bad publicity for all three of you. I'll try to keep it quiet, but these things have a way of getting out. There's always some resourceful reporter with a reputation to build."

"That's true." He was curious about her familiarity with the case. "How are you involved?" He wanted to know.

"That's need to know, and you don't," she said, gentling the words with a smile. "I understand that Winnie works as a dispatcher with emergency services. I'm very proud of her. It's a generous thing she does, working for her living. She would never have to."

"Yes. How is our uncle concerned with the murder?"

"I don't know that yet. It's still under investigation. Messy," she added. "Very, very messy, and it may involve some important people before it's over. But it shouldn't cause any problems for you three," she added. "The murderer doesn't have anything to fear from you." She glanced at her watch. "I have to go. I came down to confer with a friend, and I'm late. I'm sorry I didn't get to see Clark. What does he do?"

"He works with me on the ranch," Boone said. He was adding up her attitude and her indifference to their wealth and her sadness. "Someday," he said, "maybe we need to talk."

She smiled at him with quiet eyes. "There's nothing more to be said. We can't change the past. I made mistakes that I can't ever correct or atone for. Now, I just get on with my job and try to help where I can. Take care. It was very good to see the two of you, even under the circumstances." She looked at him for a moment more, so much pain in her eyes and in her face that it made him feel guilty.

Finally, she turned and walked down the steps toward the car. Boone watched her, scowling, his hands in his pockets. She got into the car, spoke to a shorter person in the passenger seat, started the engine and slowly drove away.

Winnie came back down after the car was gone. Her eyes were wet, her face red with bad temper despite Keely's comforting upstairs. "She's gone, then. Good riddance!"

Boone was pensive. "I wish you'd told me what Dad did to you."

She managed a wan smile. "I wanted to.

But I was afraid of what he might do. He really hated me. He said that I was the image of my mother, but he was going to make sure that I never wanted to follow in her footsteps."

"He kept you in church every time it was open," he replied quietly.

"Yes." She wrapped her arms around herself. "And threatened every boy who came here to see me. I ended up with a non-existent social life." She sighed. "I suppose I'm very repressed."

"You're also very nice," Boone said. He put his arms around her and hugged her fondly. "You know, despite the misery of our childhoods, we've done pretty well, haven't we?"

"You certainly have," she said, wiping away the tears. She smiled. "I love Keely. She's not only my best friend, now she's my sister-in-law."

He was somber. "You saved her life after the rattlesnake bit her," he said quietly. "She would have died, and I would have been responsible." His face hardened. "I can't imagine why I believed such lies about her."

"I'm sure your ex-girlfriend's detective was convincing," she said. "You shouldn't look back. Keely loves you. She never stopped, not even when she thought you hated her."

He smiled. "I was a hard case."

"Well, we're all victims of our childhood, I suppose. Dad was tough on you, too."

"He couldn't beat me down," he recalled. "He got furious at me, but he respected me."

"That was probably what saved you from the treatment I got." She sighed. "It was twelve years ago when she left. I was ten. Ten years old."

"I was technically an adult," he recalled. "Clark was in junior high." He shook his head. "I still don't understand why she left Dad for our uncle. He was a shallow man, no real character and no work ethic. It's no surprise to me that he was dealing drugs. He always did look for the easy way to get money. Dad bailed him out of jail more than once for stealing."

"Yes." She looked at the heirlooms lying on the coffee table. "It's surprising that our mother brought those back. She could have sold them for a lot of money."

"Quite a lot of money," Boone said. He frowned, recalling what she'd said about their uncle's possible connection to people suspected in the local murder. He looked at Winnie, but he didn't say anything about it. She was too shaken already. It could wait. "I wonder who she had with her in the car?" he added suddenly.

She turned. "A boyfriend, maybe," she said curtly. "I could tell he was male from upstairs. But he looked pretty short."

"Not our business," Boone said. He picked up a brooch with a tiny painting of a beautiful little Spanish girl, in her middle to late teens by the look of her, dressed all in black with a mantilla. Her red lipstick and a red rose in her hair under the black lace mantilla were the only bright things in the miniature. Her hair was long, black and shiny. She had a tiny, strange little smile on her lips. Mysterious. He smiled, just looking at it. "I wonder who she was?" he mused aloud.

"Turn it over. Maybe there's initials or something," she suggested, dabbing at her eyes with a handkerchief.

He did. He frowned. "It's labeled with a piece of tape. Señorita Rosa Carrera y Sinclair." He whistled. "This was our great-grandmother, when she was first married!

I should have known, but the portrait of her upstairs was painted when she was older."

Winnie looked at it, took it from his hands and studied the lovely face. "She was very beautiful." She laughed. "And she fought bulls with a mantilla! She must have been brave."

"If what I remember hearing from Dad about our great-grandfather is accurate, she had to be brave."

"Truly." She put the brooch down and looked at the other treasures. "So many rubies," she mused. "She must have loved them."

"You should pick out some of those to wear," he suggested.

She laughed. "And where would I wear expensive jewelry like this?" she chided. "I work for Jacobs County dispatch. Wouldn't the girls have a hoot seeing me decked out in these? Shirley would fall out of her chair laughing."

"You should get out more," he said somberly.

She gave him a long, sad look. "I'll never get out, now. Kilraven is leaving after Christmas," she said. Her face fell. "I gave him the raven painting at the party. He glared at me as if I'd committed murder under his nose and stormed out without even speaking to me." She flushed. "Nothing that ever happened to me hurt so much."

"I thought the presents were anonymous."

"They were. I don't know how he knew it was me. I've never told him that I paint."

"He's a strange bird," Boone commented. "He has feelings. Sort of like you do," he added with a grin. "Sending backup when you thought he was going to a routine domestic fight with no weapons involved."

She nodded. "He was furious about that, too. But it saved his life."

"You really ought to see Cash Grier's wife, Tippy. She has those intuitions, too."

"She knows things," Winnie replied. "Whatever sort of mental gift this is, I don't have her accuracy. I just feel uncomfortable before something bad pops up. Like today," she said quietly. "I felt sick all day. Now I know why."

"You do look like her." He was going to add that their mother used to have odd feelings about things that later happened, but he didn't.

"Yes," she said curtly. She looked at the jewelry. "I shouldn't have been so mean. She did a good thing. But it will never make up for leaving us."

"She knows that. She said she didn't come for forgiveness."

She frowned. "Why did she come?"

"She's meeting someone."

"A boyfriend here in Jacobs County?" she asked curtly.

"No, she said it was business." He frowned, too. "You know, she seems to know a lot about that recent murder here."

"Why would she?"

Boone grimaced. "I wasn't going to tell you, but it seems our uncle may have had ties to the case."

She let out a breath. "Oh, that's great. Now he's not just the man who stole our mother, he's a murderer!"

"No, not that sort of involvement," he replied. "I think he might have had some connection to the people involved. From what she said, he was a heavy drug user."

"Not surprising. I never liked him," she confessed. "He was always picking on Dad, trying to compete with him in everything. It was sort of sad to me at the time because anybody could see he wasn't the equal of our father at business or ranching or anything else."

"Our father had some good qualities. Hitting you like that wasn't one of them," he added coldly, "and if I'd known about it, I'd have knocked him through a wall!"

"I know that. It was only the one time," she said quietly, "and he'd been drinking. It was just after he and our mother met that time, when he thought she wanted to come back. It wasn't long after she'd gone away with our uncle. He came back home all quiet and furious, and he drank like a fish for about two months. That was when he hit me. He was sorry afterward, and he promised never to do it again. But he hated me, just the same, because I looked like her."

"I'm sorry."

"Me, too," she said with a sigh. "It sort of turned me against men, at least where marriage was concerned."

"Except with Kilraven."

She flushed and glared at him. "He'll probably never speak to me again, after what happened at the party. I don't understand why he was so angry." She sighed. "Of course, I don't understand why I painted a raven for him, either. It's not one of my usual subjects. I like to do flowers. Or portraits."

"You're very good at portraits."

"Thanks."

"You could have made a name for yourself as a portrait artist, even an illustrator."

"I never had the dedication," she replied. "I really do love my job," she added.

"So does Keely," he replied with an indulgent smile. "It's not a bad thing, working when you don't have to."

"You'd know," she accused, laughing. "You work harder on the ranch than your men do. That reporter for *Modern Ranching World* had to learn to ride a horse just to interview you about your new green technology because he could never find you unless he went out on the ranch."

"They're putting me on the cover," he muttered. "I didn't mind doing the article—I think it helps ranching's public image. But I don't like the idea of seeing myself looking back at me from a magazine rack."

"You're very good-looking," she said.

"And it is good PR. Not that you'll ever sell the idea of humane beef cultivation to vegetarians," she added with a chuckle.

He shrugged. "As long as people want a nice, juicy steak at a restaurant, there's not much chance that ranchers are going to turn to raising house cattle."

"Excuse me?"

"Well, you could put a diaper on a calf and bring him inside . . ."

She hit him. "I'm going to bed," she said. "And when I get upstairs, I'm going to tell Keely what you just said."

"No!" he wailed. "I was only kidding about it. She'd actually do it!"

She laughed. "There wouldn't be room. Bailey's as big as a calf."

The old German Shepherd looked up from his comfortable doggy bed by the fireplace and wagged his tail.

"See?" she asked. "He knows he's a calf."

He shook his head. He bent to ruffle the dog's fur. He glanced at Winnie. "You going to be okay?"

"Sure." She hesitated. "Thanks."

"For what?"

"Being my brother. Don't leave the jewels lying around," she advised. "If Clark comes home and sees them, he'll beg some of them for whatever girl he's crazy over at the moment."

"Good thought," he said, grinning. "I'll put them in the safe and drive them to town Monday and lodge them in the safe-deposit box."

"She could have sold them and we'd never have known," she replied quietly. "I wonder why she didn't? She's not driving a new car. Her clothes are nice, but not expensive."

"There's no telling why," he said.

"Did she say anything about where she was going?"

He shook his head. "Just that she was meeting a friend."

"At this hour? I wonder who she knows here?" she mused. "She used to be friends with Barbara, who runs the café. But Barbara told me years ago that she hadn't heard a word from her."

"It might be some newcomer," Boone said. "Not our business, anyway."

"I guess. Well, I'm going to bed. It's been a very long day."

"For you, it sure has," he said sympathetically. "First Kilraven, now our mother."

"Things can only get better, right?" she asked, smiling.

"I hope so. Tell Keely I'm going to make a couple of phone calls, and I'll be up. You sleep well."

She smiled. "You, too."

KILRAVEN HAD JUST pulled up in the driveway of his remote rental house in Comanche Wells when he noticed a sedan sitting there. Always overly cautious, he had his .45 automatic in his hand before he opened the door of his car. But when he got out and saw who his visitor was, he put it right back in the holster.

"What the hell are you doing out here at this hour of the night?" he asked.

She smiled. "Bringing bad news, I'm afraid. I couldn't get you on your cell phone, so I took a chance and drove down."

He paused by the car. "What's wrong, Rogers?" he asked, because he knew it had to be something major to bring her from San Antonio.

She didn't correct him. Her last name had been Sinclair, but she'd taken her maiden name back after she divorced Bruce Sinclair. Now she went by the name

Gail Rogers. She leaned against the car and sighed, folding her arms over her chest. "It's Rick Marquez," she said. "Someone blindsided him in an alley near his apartment and left him for dead."

"Good Lord! Does his mother know?"

She nodded. "She's at the hospital with him. Scared her to death. But he looks worse than he is. Badly bruised, and a fractured rib, but he'll live. He's mad as hell." She chuckled. "Whoever hit him is going to wish they'd never heard his name."

"At least he'll walk away," Kilraven said. He grimaced. "This case just keeps getting more and more interesting, doesn't it?"

"Whoever's behind these murders seems to feel that the body count no longer matters."

"He's feeling cornered and he's desperate," Kilraven agreed. His eyes narrowed. "You watch your back. You're in as much danger as Marquez. At the very least, they should put you on administrative until we get some sort of lead on what's happening."

"I won't sit at a desk and let everyone around me take risks," she replied calmly.

"Still. . ."

She held up a hand. "Give up. I'm stubborn."

He sighed. "Okay. But be extra cautious, will you?"

"Of course. Has forensic turned up anything interesting about the DB down here?" DB referred to dead body.

"Alice Jones is handling the case. She's got a piece of paper that they're teasing secrets out of, but she hasn't told me anything new. Senator Fowler's actually cooperating, though. It shook him up when one of his female employees turned up dead. Somebody tried to make it look like suicide, but they didn't do their homework. Had the pistol in the wrong hand."

"I heard about that," she said. "Sloppy. Real sloppy."

"That's what worries me." He bit his lower lip. "I'm going to ask for some time off to work this case. Now that our newest Junior Senator Will Sanders has stopped putting obstacles in our path, maybe we can catch a break. With Marquez sidelined, you're going to need some help. And I have good contacts."

"I know." She smiled. "We might actually solve your case. I hope so."

"Me, too." His face was taut with pain. "I've spent the last seven years waiting for something to help crack the case. Maybe this latest murder is it."

"Well, it's going to be slow," she said. "We're no closer to the identity of the man found dead in Jacobs County, or to the people who killed Senator Fowler's employee. Now we've got Marquez's attack to work on, as well." She shook her head. "I should have gotten a job baking cakes in a restaurant."

He gave her a look of mock surprise. "You can cook?"

She glared at him. "Yes, I can cook. On my salary who can afford to eat out?"

He laughed. "Come work for me. I have an expense account."

"No, thanks," she said, holding out both hands, palm up. "I've heard about some of your exploits."

"Lies," he said. "Put out by jealous colleagues."

"Hanging out of a helicopter by one hand, firing an automatic weapon, over an *ocean*," she related, emphasizing the last word.

"I did not," he said haughtily.

She just stared at him.

"Anyway, I was not hanging on by my hand." He hesitated. Then he grinned. "I wrapped one of my legs around a piece of cargo netting and held on that way!"

"I'm going home," she said with a laugh.

"Keep your doors locked," he advised firmly.

"You bet."

She climbed in under the wheel and shut the door. Beside her, a shadowy figure waved. He waved back. He wondered who her companion was. He couldn't see him clearly in the darkness, but he looked young. Maybe a trainee, he thought. He turned back toward his house.

3

Kilraven felt uncomfortable when he remembered how upset Winnie Sinclair had
been at the Christmas party. When he got
over his initial anger, he realized that she
couldn't possibly have known about his
daughter's fascination with ravens. After
all, who could have told her? Only he and
Jon knew. Well, his stepmother—Jon's
mother—knew. But Cammy had no contact with Winnie.

There was another thing. How had he
known that Winnie had painted the picture
for him? It was all secret. It was disturbing

that he'd felt it so certainly, and that he'd
been right. Her tears at the sight of his
angry face had made the connection for
him. He was sorry about his behavior. The
deaths were still upsetting for him. He
couldn't find peace. In seven years, the pain
hadn't eased.

Winnie had feelings for him. In another
time, another place, that would have been
flattering. But he had no interest in women
these days. He'd dated Gloryanne Barnes
before she'd married Rodrigo Ramirez, but
that had been nothing more than friend-
ship and compassion. Winnie, though, that
could be a different matter. It was why he
tried not to let his attraction to her show. It
was why he avoided her. If only, he thought,
avoiding her had kept him from wanting to
get closer to her.

He was going back to San Antonio soon.
He was going to take a leave of absence
and try to help solve the cold case that
had haunted him for seven long years.
Perhaps he might finally have peace, if the
killer could be brought to justice.

It was good that Senator Fowler and his
protégé, Senator Sanders, had stopped
fighting them about reopening the case. It

was bad that some powerful politician might be involved, even on the fringes of the crime. Their names would make it a high-profile case, and the tabloids would have a field day. He cringed at the thought of seeing the autopsy photos while he was standing in line at the supermarket, where the tabloids were displayed at the checkout counter. These days, some reporters thought nothing of the family's right to privacy. After all, a scoop was still a scoop.

He put the case to the back of his mind, as he tried to most every day. He only had a few days left in Jacobsville. He was going to do his job and then pack up and go home. In between, he was going to try to explain to Winnie Sinclair why his attitude toward her had been so violent at the Christmas party. He didn't want to encourage her, but he couldn't leave with the image of her hurt expression in his mind.

WINNIE HAD JUST SPENT a harrowing half hour routing two police cars to a standoff at a convenience store. In fact, it was one of only three convenience stores in the entire county. The perpetrator, a young husband with a history of bad decisions, had gotten drunk and decided to get some quick cash to buy a pretty coat for his wife. When the clerk pulled out a shotgun, the young man had fired and hit the clerk in the chest. He'd holed up in the store with the wounded man when patrons had called the police.

Winnie had dispatched a Jacobsville police officer to the scene. Another officer had called in to say he was going to back up the first officer. It was a usual thing. The officers looked out for each other, just as the dispatchers did.

There was no hostage negotiator, as such, but Cash Grier filled the position for his department. He talked the young man out of his gun. Thank God, the boy hadn't been drunk enough to ignore the chief and come out shooting. Cash had disarmed him and then had Winnie tell the paramedics to come on in. It was routine for paramedics to be dispatched and then to stage just outside the scene of a dangerous situation until law enforcement made sure it was safe for them to go in. It was just another example of how the emergency services looked out for each other.

THE CLERK WAS BADLY INJURED, but he would live. The young man went to the detention center to be booked and await arraignment. Winnie was happy that they were able to avert a tragedy.

She drove her little VW back to the ranch, and she felt happy. It was hard to go through the day after Kilraven's pointed snub at the Christmas party. She was still stinging, and not only from that. Her mother's visit had unsettled her even more.

When she got home, she found Keely and Boone waiting for her in the living room.

"There's a carnival in town. We're going," Keely said, "and you're going with us. You need a little R & R after all that excitement at work."

"How did you know. . .?" Winnie exclaimed.

"Boone has a scanner," Keely pointed out, grinning.

Boone grinned, too.

Winnie laughed, putting the coat she'd just shrugged out of back on. "Okay, I'm game. Let's go pitch pennies and win plates."

Boone threw up his hands. "Honey, you could buy those plates for a nickel apiece at the Dish Barn downtown!"

"It's more fun if you win them," Winnie said primly. "Besides, I want cotton candy and a ride on the Octopus!"

"So do I," Keely said. "Come on, sweetheart," she called to Boone as they went through the back door. "The cotton candy will be all gone!"

"Not to worry," he said, locking up. "They'll make more."

THE CARNIVAL WAS LOUD and colorful and the music was heady. Winnie ate cotton candy and went on the Octopus with Keely, laughing as the wind whipped through their hair and the music warbled among the bright lights.

Later, ankle deep in sawdust, Winnie stood before the penny pitching booth and the vendor gave her a handful of change in exchange for her two dollar bills. She was actually throwing nickels or dimes, not pennies, but she always thought of it in terms of the smaller bits of change. Just as she contemplated the right trajectory to land a coin on a plate, she spotted Dr. Bentley Rydel standing very close to Cappie Drake. Behind them, and closing in, was Officer

Kilraven, still in uniform. Winnie paused to look at him. He spoke to the couple and laughed. But then he saw Winnie over their heads and his smile faded. He turned abruptly and walked right out of the carnival. Winnie felt her heart sink to the level of the ground. Well, he'd made his opinion of her quite clear, she thought miserably. He hadn't forgiven her for the painting. She turned back to the booth, but not with any real enthusiasm. The evening had been spoiled.

CASH GRIER CALLED Kilraven a few days later and asked for his help. Cappie Drake and her brother were in danger. Her brother had been badly beaten by Cappie's violent ex-boyfriend, just released from jail on a battery conviction stemming from an attack on her. Now he seemed to be out for blood. Eb Scott had detailed men to watch Cappie, but Kell was going to need some protection; he was in a San Antonio hospital where he'd just undergone back surgery to remove a shifted shrapnel sliver that had paralyzed him years ago. Cash asked Kilraven to go up and keep an eye on Kell until San Antonio police could catch the perp.

Kilraven went gladly. It was a relief to get out of town, even for a couple of days. But it was soon over, and he was back in Jacobsville again, fighting his feelings for Winnie. He was still no closer to a solution for his problem. He didn't know how he was going to deal with the discomfort he felt at leaving Winnie Sinclair behind forever. And there was still that odd coincidence with the painting. He really needed to know why she'd painted it.

In the meantime, Alice Jones had called him with some shocking news. The bit of paper in the dead man's hand in Jacobsville had contained Kilraven's cell phone number. Now he knew he'd been right to ask for that time off to work on his cold case. The dead man had known something about the murders and he'd been trying to contact Kilraven when he'd been killed. It was a break that might crack the case, if they could identify the victim and his contacts.

THE NEXT WEEK, WINNIE worked a shift she wasn't scheduled for, filling in for Shirley, who was out sick. When she got off that afternoon, to her surprise, she found Kilraven waiting for her at the door.

She actually gasped out loud. His silver eyes were glittery as he stared down at her.

"Hello," she stammered.

He didn't reply. "Get in your car and follow me," he said quietly.

He walked to his squad car. He was technically off duty, but still in uniform. Officers in Jacobsville drove their cars home, so that they were prepared any time they had to be called in. He got in his car and waited until Winnie fumbled her way into her VW. He drove off, and she drove after him. Glancing to one side, she noted two of the operators who were on break staring after them and grinning. *Oh, boy,* she thought, *now there's going to be some gossip.*

Kilraven drove out of the city and down the long, winding dirt road that led to his rental house. The road meandered on past his house to join with a paved road about a mile on. His house was the only one on this little stretch. *He must like privacy,* Winnie thought, *because this certainly wasn't on anybody's main route.*

He pulled up at the front door, cut off the

engine and got out of his car. Winnie did the same.

"I'll make coffee," he said after he unlocked the door and led her into the kitchen.

She looked around, curious at the utter lack of anything personal in the utilitarian surroundings. Well, except for the painting she'd done for him. It was lying on the counter, face up.

She felt uncomfortable at his lack of small talk. She put her purse on the counter near the door that led down the hall to the living room. "How's Kell Drake?" she asked.

He turned, curious.

"We heard about it from Barbara last week," she said, mentioning the café where everybody ate. Barbara was the adoptive mother of San Antonio homicide detective Rick Marquez. "She has Rick at home. He's getting better, but he sure wants to find whoever beat him up," she added grimly.

"So do we. He's one tough bird, or he'd be dead. Somebody is really trying to cover up this case," he added.

"Yes. Poor Rick. But what about Kell?"

"That ended well, except for his bruises. He's going to walk again," he said. "I guess you also heard that they caught Bartlett in the act of knocking Cappie Drake around," he added. "It seems that Marquez and a uniformed officer had to pull Dr. Rydel off the man." He chuckled.

"We, uh, heard that, too," she said, amused. "It was the day before Rick was jumped by those thugs. Poor Cappie."

"She'll be all right. She and Rydel are getting married in the near future, I hear."

"That's fast work," she commented.

He shrugged. "Some people know their minds quicker than other people do." He finished putting the coffee on and turned to glance at her. "How do you take it?"

"Straight up," she said.

His eyebrows lifted.

"I don't usually have a lot of time to stand around adding things to it," she pointed out. "I'm lucky to have time to take a sip or two before it gets cold."

"I thought Grier gave you one of those gadgets you put a coffee cup on to keep it hot," he said. "For Christmas."

"I don't have a place to put it where it wouldn't endanger the electronics at my station," she said. "Don't tell him."

"I wouldn't dream of it." He set out two

mugs, pulled out a chair at the table and motioned her into another one. He straddled his and stared at her. "Why a raven?" he asked abruptly. "And why those colors for beadwork?"

She bit her lower lip. "I don't know."

He stared at her pointedly, as if he didn't believe her.

She blushed. "I really don't know," she emphasized. "I didn't even start out to paint a raven. I was going to do a landscape. The raven was on the canvas. I just painted everything else out," she added. "That sounds nuts, I guess, but famous sculptors say that's how they do statues, they just chisel away everything that isn't part of the statue."

He still didn't speak.

"How did you even know it was me?" she asked unhappily. "The gifts were supposed to be secret. I don't tell people that painting is my hobby. How did you know?"

He got up after a minute, walked down the hall and came back with a rolled-up piece of paper. He handed it to her and sat back down.

Her intake of breath was audible. She

held the picture with hands that were a little unsteady. "Who did this?" she exclaimed.

"My daughter, Melly."

Her eyes lifted to his. He'd never spoken of any family members, except his brother. "You don't talk about her," she said.

His eyes went to the picture on the table. They were dull and vacant. "She was three years old when she painted that, in pre-school," he said quietly. "It was the last thing she ever did. That afternoon, she and her mother went to my father's house. They were going to have supper with my father and stepmother. My father went to get gas for a trip he was making the next day. Cammy hadn't come home from shopping yet."

He stopped. He wasn't sure he could say it, even now. His voice failed him.

Winnie had a premonition. Only that. "And?"

He looked older. "I was working under-cover with San Antonio PD, before I became a Fed. My partner and I were just a block from the house when the call came over the radio. I recognized the address and burned rubber getting there. My partner tried to stop me, but nobody could have.

There were two uniformed officers already on scene. They tried to tackle me." He shrugged. "I was bigger than both of them. So I saw Melly, and my wife, before the crime scene investigators and the coroner got there." He got up from the table and turned away. He was too shaken to look at her. He went to the coffeepot and turned it off, pouring coffee into two cups. He still hesitated. He didn't want to pick up the cups until he was sure he could hold them. "The perp, whoever it was, used a shotgun on them."

Winnie had heard officers talk about their cases occasionally. She'd heard the operators talk, too, because some of them were married to people in law enforcement. She knew what a shotgun could do to a human body. To even think of it being used on a child. . . She swallowed, hard, and swallowed again. Her imagination conjured up something she immediately pushed to the back of her mind.

"I'm sorry," she said in a choked tone.

Finally, he picked up the cups and put them on the table. He straddled the chair again, calmer now. "We couldn't find the person or persons who did it," he said curtly. "My father went crazy. He had these feelings, like you do. He left the house to get gas. It could have waited until the next morning, but he felt he should go right then. He said later that if he'd been home, he might have been able to save them."

"Or he might have been lying right beside them," Winnie said bluntly.

He looked at her in a different way. "Yes," he agreed. "That was what I thought, too. But he couldn't live with the guilt. He started drinking and couldn't stop. He died of a heart attack. They said the alcohol might have played a part, but I think he grieved himself to death. He loved Melly." He stopped speaking and drank the coffee. It blistered his tongue. That helped. He hadn't talked about it to an outsider, ever.

Her soft, dark eyes slid over his face quietly. "You think this may be linked to the body they found in the river," she said slowly.

His dark eyebrows lifted. "I haven't said that."

"You're thinking it."

His broad chest rose and fell. "Yes. We found a small piece of paper clenched in the man's fist. It took some work, but Alice

Jones's forensic lab was able to make out the writing. It was my cell phone number. The man was coming here to talk to me. He knew something about my daughter's death. I'm sure of it."

His daughter's death. He didn't say, his wife and daughter. She wondered why.

His big hands wrapped around the hot white mug. His eyes had an emptiness that Winnie recognized. She'd seen it in military veterans. They called it the thousand-yard stare. It was the look of men who'd seen violence, who dealt in it. They were never the same again.

"What did she look like?" Winnie asked gently.

He blinked. It wasn't a question he'd anticipated. He smiled faintly. "Like Jon, actually, and my father," he said, laughing. "She had jet-black hair, long, down to her waist in back, and eyes like liquid ebony. She was intelligent and sweet natured. She never met a stranger. . ." He stopped, looked down into the coffee cup, and forced it up to his lips to melt away the hard lump in his throat. Melly, laughing, holding her arms out to him. "I love you, Daddy! Always remember!" That picture of her, laughing, was overlaid by one of her, lifeless, a nightmare figure covered in blood. . .

"Dear God!" he bit off, and his head bent.

Winnie was wary of most men. She was shy and introverted, and never forward. But she got up out of her chair, pulled him toward her and drew his head to her breasts. "Honest emotion should never embarrass anyone," she whispered against his hair. "It's much worse to pretend that we don't care than to admit we do."

She felt his big body shudder. She expected him to jerk away, to push her away, to refuse comfort. He was such a steely, capable man, full of fire and spirit and courage. But he didn't resist her. Not for a minute, anyway. His arms circled her waist and almost crushed her as he gave in, momentarily, to the need for comfort. It was something he'd never done. He'd even pushed Cammy away, years ago, when she offered it to him.

She laid her cheek against his thick, soft black hair and just stood there, holding him. But then he did pull away, abruptly, and stood up, turning away from her.

"More coffee?" he asked in a harsh tone.

She forced a smile. "Yes, please." She moved to the table and picked up her own cup, deliberately giving him time to get back the control he'd briefly lost. "It's gone cold."

"Liar," he murmured when she joined him at the coffeepot and he took the cup from her. "You'd blister your lip if you sipped it."

She looked up at him with a grin. "I was being politically agreeable."

"You were lying." He put the cup on the counter and gathered her up whole against him. "What a sweetheart you are," he ground out as his mouth suddenly ground down into hers.

The force of the kiss shocked her. He didn't lead up to it. It was instant, feverish passion, so intense that the insistence of his mouth shocked her lips apart, giving him access to the heated sweetness within. She wasn't a woman who incited passion. In fact, what she'd experienced of it had turned her cold. She didn't like the arrogance, the pushiness, of most men she'd dated. But Kilraven was as honest in passion as he was otherwise. He enjoyed kissing her, and he didn't pretend that he didn't. His arms forced her into the hard curve of his body and he chuckled when he felt her melt against him, helpless and submissive, as he ground his mouth into hers.

Her arms went under his and around him. The utility belt was uncomfortable. She felt the butt of his automatic at her ribs. His arms were bruising. But she didn't care. She held on for all she was worth and shivered with what must have been desire. She'd never felt it. Not until now, with the last man on earth she should allow herself to feel it for.

He felt her shy response with wonder. He'd expected that a socialite like Winnie would have had men since her early teens. The way of the world these days was experience. Virtue counted for nothing with most of the social set. But this little violet was innocent. He could feel it when she strained away from the sudden hardness of his body, when she shivered as he tried to probe her mouth.

Curious, he lifted his head and looked down into her flushed, wide-eyed face. Innocence. She couldn't even pretend sophistication.

Gently, he eased her out of his arms. He smiled to lessen the sting of it. "You taste of green apples," he said enigmatically.

"Apples?" She blinked, and swallowed. She could still taste him on her mouth. It had felt wonderful, being held so close to that warm strength. "I haven't had an apple in, well, in ages," she stammered.

"It was a figure of speech. Here. Put on your coat." He helped her ease her arms into it. Then he handed her the cup.

"Am I leaving and taking it with me?" she asked blankly.

"No. We're just drinking it outside." He picked up his own cup and shepherded her out of the door, onto the long porch, down the steps and out to a picnic table that had been placed there, with its rude wooden benches, by the owner.

"We're going to drink coffee out here?" she asked, astonished. "It's freezing!"

"I know. Sit down."

She did, using the cup for a hand warmer.

"It is a bit nippy," he commented.

A sheriff's car drove past. It beeped. Kilraven waved. "I'm leaving next week," he said.

"Yes. You told us."

A Jacobsville police car whizzed by, just behind the sheriff's car. It beeped, too.

Kilraven threw up his hand. Dust rose and fell in their wake, then settled.

"I had some sick leave and some vacation time left over. I can only use a little of it, of course, for this year, because it's almost over. But I'm going to have a few weeks to do some investigating without pay." He smiled. "With the state of the economy what it is, I don't think they'll mind that."

"Probably not." She sipped coffee. "Exactly what do you do when you aren't impersonating a police officer?" she asked politely.

He pursed his lips and his silver eyes twinkled. "I could tell you, but then I'd have to—"

A loud horn drowned out the rest. This time, it was a fire truck. They waved. Kilraven waved back. So did Winnie.

"Have to what?" she asked him.

"Well, it wouldn't be pretty."

"That's just stonewalling, Kilraven," she pointed out. She frowned. "Don't you have a first name?"

"Sure. It's—"

Another loud horn drowned that out, too.

They both turned. Cash Grier pulled up beside the picnic table and let down his window on the driver's side. "Isn't it a little cold to be drinking coffee outside?" he asked.

Kilraven gave him a wry look. "Everybody at the EOC saw me drive off with Winnie," he said complacently. "So far, there have been two cop cars and a fire truck. And, oh, look, there comes the Willow Creek Police Department. A little out of your jurisdiction, aren't you?" he called loudly to the driver, who was from northern Jacobs County. He just grinned and waved and drove on.

Winnie hadn't realized how much traffic had gone by until then. She burst out laughing. No wonder Kilraven had wanted to sit out here. He wasn't going to have her gossiped about. It touched her.

"If I were you, I'd take her to Barbara's Café to have this discussion," Cash told him. "It's much more private."

"Private?" Kilraven exclaimed.

Cash pointed to the road. There were, in a row, two sheriffs' cars, a state police vehicle, a fire and rescue truck, an ambulance and, of all things, a fire department ladder truck. They all tooted and waved as they went by, creating a wave of dust.

Cash Grier shook his head. "Now, that's a shame you'll get all dusty. Maybe you should take her back inside," he said with an angelic expression.

"You know what you can do," Kilraven told him. He got up and held out his hand for Winnie's cup. "I'm putting these in the sink, and then we're leaving."

"Spoilsport." Cash sighed. "Now we'll all have to go back to work!"

"I can suggest a place to do it," Kilraven muttered.

Cash winked at Winnie, who couldn't stop laughing. He drove off.

Winnie got up, sighed and dug in her coat pocket for her car keys. It had been, in some ways, the most eventful hour of her life. She knew things about Kilraven that nobody else did, and she felt close to him. It was the first time in their turbulent relationship that she felt any hope for the future. Not that getting closer to him was going to be easy, she told herself. Especially not with him in San Antonio and her in Jacobsville.

He came back out, locking the door

behind him. He looked around as he danced gracefully down the steps and joined her. "What, no traffic jam?" he exclaimed, nodding toward the deserted road. "Maybe they ran out of rubberneckers."

Just as he said that, a funeral procession came by, headed by none other than the long-suffering Macreedy. He was famous for getting lost while leading processions. He didn't blow his horn. In fact, he really did look lost. The procession went on down the road with Winnie and Kilraven staring after it.

"Don't tell me he's losing another funeral procession," she wailed. "Sheriff Carson Hayes will fry him up and serve him on toast if he does it again."

"No kidding," Kilraven agreed. "There's already been the threat of a lawsuit by one family." He shook his head. "Hayes really needs to put that boy behind a desk."

"Or take away his car keys," she agreed.

He looked down at her with an oddly affectionate expression. "Come on. You're getting chilled."

He walked her back to her car, towering over her. "You've come a long way since that day you went wailing home because you forgot to tell me a perp was armed."

She smiled. "I was lucky. I could have gotten you killed."

He hesitated. "These flashes of insight, do they run in your family?"

"I don't know much about my family," she confessed. "My father was very remote after my mother left us."

"Did you have any contact with your uncle?" he asked.

She gaped at him. "How do you know about him?"

He didn't want to confess what he knew about the man. He shrugged. "Someone mentioned his name."

"We don't have any contact at all. We didn't," she corrected. "He died a month ago. Or so we were told."

"I'm sorry."

Her dark eyes were cold. "I'm not. He and my mother ran away together and left my father with three kids to raise. Well, two kids actually. Boone was in the military by then. I look like my mother. Dad hated that. He hated me." She bit her tongue. She hadn't meant to say as much.

But he read that in her expression. "We all have pivotal times in our lives, when a decision leads to a different future." He smiled. "In the sixteenth century, Henry VIII fell in love with a young girl and decided that his Catholic wife, Catherine of Aragon, was too old to give him a son anyway, so he spent years finding a way to divorce her and marry the young girl, whom he was certain could produce a male heir. In the end, he destroyed the Catholic Church in England to accomplish it. He married Ann Boleyn, a protestant who had been one of Catherine's ladies, and from that start the Anglican Church was born. The child of that union was not a son, but Elizabeth, who became queen of England after her brother and half sister. All that, for love of a woman." He pursed his lips and his eyes twinkled. "As it turned out, he couldn't get a son from Ann Boleyn either, so he found a way to frame her for adultery and cut off her head. Ten days later, he married a woman who could give him a son."

"The wretch!" she exclaimed, outraged.

"That's why we have elected officials instead of kings with absolute power," he told her.

She shook her head. "How do you know all that?"

He leaned down. "You mustn't mention it, but I have a degree in history."

"Well!"

"But I specialized in Scottish history, not English. I'm one of a handful of people who think James Hepburn, the Earl of Bothwell, got a raw deal from history for marrying Mary, Queen of Scots. But don't mention that out loud."

She laughed. "Okay."

He opened her car door for her. Before she got in, he drew a long strand of her blond hair over his big hand, studying its softness and beautiful pale color.

Her eyes slid over his face. "Your brother wears his hair long, in a ponytail. You keep yours short."

"Is that a question?"

She nodded.

"Jon is particularly heavy on the Native American side of his ancestry."

"And you aren't?"

His eyes narrowed. "I don't know, Winnie," he said quietly, making her name sound foreign and sweet and different. "Maybe I'm hiding from it."

"Not you," she said with conviction. "I can't see you hiding from anything."

That soft pride in her tone made him feel taller. He let go of her hair. "Drive carefully," he said.

"I will. See you."

He didn't say anything else. But he did nod.

With her heart flying up in her throat, she got in and drove away. It wasn't until she got home that she realized, she still didn't know his first name.

4

Winnie was back at work the next morning almost walking on air. Kilraven had kissed her. Not only that, he seemed to really like her. Maybe San Antonio wasn't so far away. He might visit. He might take her out on a date. Anything was possible.

She put her purse in her locker and went to her station. It was in the shape of a semicircle, and contained a bank of computers. Directly in front of her was a keyboard; behind it was a computer screen. This was the radio from which she could contact any police, fire or EMS department, although her job was police dispatch.

There were separate stations for fire, police and EMS. Fire had one dispatcher, EMS had two. She, along with Shirley at a separate console, handled law enforcement traffic on her shift for all of Jacobs County. Beside her was a screen for the NCIC, the National Crime Information Center. Behind the computer screen, on a shelf, sat three other computer screens. One, an incident screen, noted the location of the units and their current status. The middle was CAD, or computer aided dispatch, which featured a form into which information such as activity code and location were placed; typing in the location brought up such data as prior calls at the residence, the nearest fire hydrant in case of fire, the name and address of a key holder and even a box to fax the incident to the police department. It also had screens for names and numbers of law enforcement personnel, including cell phone and pager numbers. There was a mobile data terminal from which dispatch could send messages to law enforcement on their laptops in their cars. The third computer screen was the phone itself, the heart and soul of the operation, through which desperation and fear and panic were heard daily and gently handled.

This information came through two call takers. Their job was to take the calls as they came in, put them into the computer and send them to the appropriate desk: fire, police or EMS. Once the location and situation were input, the computer decided which was the appropriate agency or agencies to be dispatched. For a domestic incident with injuries, police were sent first to secure the scene, and an ambulance would stage in the area until it was deemed safe for the EMS personnel to enter the house to assist the injured. Often the perpetrator was still inside and dangerous to anyone who attempted to help the victim. More police officers died responding to domestic disputes than almost any other job-related duty.

Winnie had just dispatched a police officer to the scene of a motor vehicle accident, along with fire and rescue, and was waiting for further information.

In between the calls, Shirley leaned over while the supervisor was talking to a visitor. "Did you hear about the break in the murder case?"

"What break?"

"They found Kilraven's cell phone number clenched in the victim's hand."

"Oh, that. Yes, Kilraven told me."

Shirley's eyes twinkled. "Did he now? Might one ask what else he told you, all alone at his house?"

"How do you know we went to his house?" Winnie asked, blushing.

"A few people told us. There was a sheriff's deputy, Chief Grier, a fireman, a funeral director. . ."

Winnie laughed. "I should have known."

"They did all just mention that you and Kilraven were drinking coffee at a picnic table, outside in the freezing cold," Shirley added.

"Well, Kilraven felt that we shouldn't start gossip."

"As if." Shirley chuckled. "What were you talking about?" she added slyly.

"The murder case," Winnie said with a grin. "No, really, we were," she added when she saw her coworker's expression. "You remember Senator Fowler's kitchen help died mysteriously after she gave some information to Alice Jones, the coroner's investigator from San Antonio, about the victim? Now there's gossip the murder might be linked to other murders in San Antonio." It was safe to tell her that. No way was she going to add that Kilraven's family might be involved.

"Wow," Shirley exclaimed softly.

"Heads up," Winnie whispered, grinning and turned away before Maddie Sims came toward them. The older woman never jumped on them about talking because they only passed remarks back and forth during lulls in the operations, but she did like them to pay attention on the job. She would know what they did anyway because everything was recorded when they were working. Maddie would be diplomatic about it, though.

Winnie smiled as Maddie passed. A message from the police officer responding to the wreck was just coming in, requesting a want and warrants on a car tag. She turned back to her console and began typing in the numbers.

IT WAS A BUSY NIGHT. There was an attempted suicide, which, fortunately, they were able to get help dispatched in time. There were assorted sick calls, one kitchen fire, several car versus deer reports, two domestic calls, a large animal in the road and three drunk driver reports, only one of which resulted in an arrest. Often a drunk driver was reported on the highway, but no good description of the vehicle or direction of travel was given and it was a big county. Occasionally, an observant citizen could provide a description and tag number, but not always. Unless a squad car was actually in the area of the report, it was difficult sometimes to pursue. You couldn't pull an officer off the investigation of an accident or a burglary or a robbery, she mused, to go roaming the county looking for an inebriated driver, no matter how much the officers would like to catch one.

At break, she and Shirley worried about the assault on Rick Marquez.

"I hope he's not going to be attacked again, when he goes back to work. Somebody wants this case covered up pretty badly," Shirley said.

"Yes," Winnie agreed, "and it looks like this is only the tip of the iceberg. We still have that mangled murder victim in our county. Senator Fowler's hired help told

Alice Jones something about him and the poor woman was murdered in a way that made it look like suicide. Now there's an attempt on Rick, who's been helping investigate it."

"He's lucky he has such a hard head," Shirley said.

"And that his partner went searching for him when he didn't turn up to look at some paperwork she'd just found. Yes, I heard about that from Keely," Winnie said. "Sheriff Hayes," she added with a grin, "is Boone's best friend, so they know more than most people about what's going on. Well, except for us," she added wryly. "We know everything."

"Almost everything, anyway. You know, we used to live in such a peaceful county." Shirley sighed. "Then Keely lost her mother to a killer who was friends with her father. Now we get a murder victim dead in our river and his own mother wouldn't recognize him. This is a dangerous place to live."

"Every place is dangerous, even small towns," she replied with a smile. "It's the times we live in."

"I guess so."

They had homemade soup with corn-
bread, courtesy of one of the other dispatchers. It was nice to have something besides
takeout, which got old very quickly on ten-
hour shifts. The operators only worked four
days a week, not necessarily in sequence,
but they were stress-filled. All of them loved
the job, or they wouldn't be doing it. Saving
lives, which they did on a daily basis, was a
blessing in itself. But days off were good so
that they had a chance to recover just a little
bit from the nerve-racking series of desperate situations in which they assisted the
appropriate authorities. Winnie had never
loved a job so much. She smiled at Shirley,
and thought what a nice bunch of people
she worked with.

KILRAVEN WAS PUMPING his brother for information. It was, as usual, hard going. Jon
was even more tight-lipped than Kilraven.

"It's an ongoing murder investigation,"
he insisted, throwing up his hands. "I can't
discuss it with you."

Kilraven, comfortably seated in the one
good chair in Jon's office, just glared at
him with angry silver eyes. "This is your

niece and your sister-in-law we're talking about," he said icily. "I can help. Let me help."

Jon perched on the edge of his desk. He was immaculate, from his polished black shoes to the long, elegant fingers that were always manicured. His black hair was caught in a ponytail that hung to his waist. His face grew solemn. "All right. But if Garon Grier asks me, I'm telling him that you stood on me in order to get this information."

Kilraven grinned. "Should I stand on you, just for appearances?" He indicated his big booted feet. "I'm game."

"I'd like to see you stand on me," Jon shot back.

"Come on, come on, talk."

Jon sighed. "I don't have much, but I'll share." He punched the intercom. "Ms. Perry, could you bring me the Fowler file, please."

There was a pause. A light, airy, sarcastic feminine voice answered. "Hard copy is kept in your filing cabinet, Mr. Blackhawk," she said sweetly. "Lost our password again, have we?"

Jon's face tautened. "What I am losing, rapidly, is my patience. For your information, Garon took out the files to show Agent Simmons. They're in your filing cabinet."

There was a dead silence. A filing cabinet was opened and then closed, and impatient high-heels came marching into Jon's office with a pleasant face, blue eyes and jet-black hair, cut short.

She put a file on the desk. "We do have electronic copies of this, password-protected, if your password ever presents itself again," she said sweetly.

Jon glared at her. "You were an hour late for work two mornings this week, Ms. Perry," he said, his tone as bland as her own. "So far, I haven't reported it to Garon."

She stiffened. Her blue eyes had blue shadows under them. She didn't shoot back an excuse.

"Perhaps it would help your present attitude if you knew that Ms. Smith has an extensive rap sheet, of which my mother is unaware. With your, shall we say, proclivities for sneaking in the back door of protected files, I should think you could dig out the rest of the information all by

yourself. If," he added with dripping sarcasm, "you can manage to keep your
present job long enough to look for it."

She reddened. Her blue eyes shot ice
daggers at him, but her voice was even
when she spoke. "I'll be at my desk if you
need anything further, Mr. Blackhawk."
She left, without even looking at Kilraven.
Her back was as stiff as her expression.

Jon got up and closed the door behind
her with a little jerk. His own eyes, liquid
black, were smoldering. "Ever since my
mother sent Jill Smith in here to vamp me,
it's been like this."

"You did have Ms. Smith arrested for
harassment," Kilraven pointed out with
barely suppressed amusement. "And taken
out in handcuffs, if I recall?"

Jon shrugged. "A man isn't safe alone
in his own office these days."

"You're safe from that particular woman,
I'll bet," Kilraven replied, nodding toward
the direction Joceline Perry had taken.

"Most men are."

"Care to say why?"

Jon went back to the desk and picked
up the file folder. "She has a little boy,
about three years old. His father was killed

overseas in the military. She can freeze a man from half a block away."

"Not necessary in your case, bro, you're already frozen."

Jon glared at him. "Don't call me that disgusting nickname, if you please."

"Excuse me, your grace."

Jon glared even more.

Kilraven sobered. "All right, I'll try to act with more decorum. Is Mom still speaking to you?"

"Only to tell me how poor Ms. Smith is suffering from my rejection. I've tried to tell her that her newest candidate for my affections is one step short of a call girl, but she won't listen. Ms. Smith's mother is her best friend, so naturally the daughter is pure as the driven snow."

"She might not be, but you certainly are." His brother grinned.

Jon's black eyes narrowed. "And you certainly would be, if you hadn't been conned into marrying Monica."

Kilraven's amused expression fell. "I guess so. I never planned to get married in the first place, but she knew her way around men. Funny, I never even wondered why, until we were already married and she was pregnant with Melly. She had boyfriends that actually showed up at the house from time to time to see her."

"Which didn't go over well."

"I was young and jealous. She was experienced, but I wasn't." He gave his brother a quiet appraisal. "You could still charm unicorns. Don't you think you're old enough to consider getting married?"

"No woman could live with me. I'm married to my job. And when I'm not at work, I'm married to the ranch."

"I miss it from time to time," Kilraven mused. "I guess I'll forget how to ride a horse eventually."

"That's a joke. You've got more trophies than I have."

They were both expert horsemen. In their youth, they participated in rodeo and stood undefeated at bulldogging in southern Oklahoma until they retired from the ring.

"But all this is beside the point," Jon said. He handed the file to Kilraven. "You'll have to read it here and you can't have photocopies."

"Fair enough." He started reading. Jon took a phone call. By then, Kilraven had

enough information to form an uncomfortable hypothesis.

"Senator Fowler's protégé, Senator Will
Sanders, has a brother, Hank, one of the
more dangerous career criminals and a
man who has his hands in every illegal operation in the city," Kilraven murmured as
he read. "Two attempted murder charges,
both dropped for lack of evidence to convict, and at least one accusation of rape."

"For which he drew a suspended
sentence when the lady recanted." Jon's
eyes narrowed thoughtfully. "In fact, his
brother, Senator Sanders himself, has a
statutory rape charge that was dropped
for lack of evidence. He has a taste for vir-
gins, and since a good many women are
experienced even by their mid-teens, he's
looking for them younger and younger."

"Pervert," Kilraven muttered. "The victim
in this case was fourteen. Fourteen years
old! He gave her an illegal substance and
had her in a guest bedroom in his own
house. He even filmed it for the amusement of his friends." He frowned. "There
was a dead teenage girl seven years ago,
remember? It was just before Melly. . ." He
cleared his throat. "The girl was found in a

similar condition to our murder victim in Jacobsville. I've always felt there was a connection, but we were never able to put our finger on one."

"Just coincidence, probably," Jon agreed. "They do happen."

Kilraven tossed the file back onto Jon's desk with utter disdain. "He filmed himself assaulting a fourteen-year-old. And they couldn't prove it? There was film!"

"It's not called film anymore, it's digital imaging, but I get your meaning. No, they couldn't prove it. The camcorder was erased in the police property room, by persons unknown, conveniently before arraignment. We can't accuse anybody, but Senator Sanders has a longtime employee who did hard time for a violent crime. He's violently protective of both brothers, and he has a cousin who works for SAPD."

"How convenient. Can we put some pressure on the cop?" Kilraven asked.

Jon gave him a wry look. "We've got enough problems. We're having him watched by internal affairs. That will have to do. Now, to get back to the case involving the living fourteen-year-old, the assistant D.A. in the case was hopping up and down and using language that almost got *him* arrested in his own office when they told him. That was just after the girl's parents called and said they were refusing to let her testify."

"They didn't want the creep prosecuted?" Kilraven exclaimed.

Jon's expression was eloquent. "The week after that, the girl's father was driving a new Jaguar, one of the high ticket sports models, and he paid off all his gambling debts at once."

Kilraven was quiet. "Those cars run to six figures. The file says the father worked as a midlevel accountant."

"Exactly."

"If Melly had been fourteen, and someone had done that to her, I'd have moved heaven and earth to put the man away for life. If I didn't break his neck first."

"Same here. Money does talk, in some cases."

"In a lot of them." Kilraven was thinking. "The senator's wife started divorce proceedings a few years ago, and then stopped them and started drinking. Her husband still has lovers and she can't seem to get away from him. They have a beach house in Nassau where she spends a lot of time."

"And the senator's family has a ranch one property over from our own near Lawton," Jon replied, naming the Oklahoma town where both boys were born.

"Maybe the wife knows something about her brother-in-law that she'd be willing to share," Kilraven thought out loud.

"Don't go harassing the senator or his wife," Jon said firmly. "We've finally got something that might give us a clue to our own cold case. Garon Grier has someone working undercover on this, as well. If you put somebody's back up, we could lose all the ground we've gained. Not to mention that we could be facing some real heat from higher up."

"I'm on leave of absence," Kilraven pointed out.

"Yes, but you still have a boss who won't like your involvement in a case that isn't connected to your present employment."

"I have a great boss. He'd understand."

"Sure he would, but he'd still fire you."

"I've been fired before."

"You've been reprimanded, too. Don't pile up too many demerits, boy scout," Jon teased. "You'll get yourself kicked out of any federal work."

Kilraven sighed and stuck his big hands in his pockets. "I guess I could be a small-town cop in Jacobsville for life if I had to."

"You'd never manage it. Cash Grier told Marquez that he's already one step closer to nailing you in a barrel and sending you down the Rio Grande."

"He'd have to get me in the barrel first and drive me all the way to the Rio Grande. By the time he got there, I'd have extricated myself from the barrel, appropriated his truck and had local authorities arrest him for kidnapping."

Jon didn't say anything. He just smiled. He knew his brother well enough to believe it.

"That said, he's a good man to work for. He goes to the wall for his officers."

"So does Garon Grier, here."

Kilraven nodded. "They're both good men." He frowned. "Don't they have two other brothers?"

"Yes. One of them is also in law enforcement."

"Like the Earp brothers," Kilraven mused.

"There were five of them. There are only

four Grier brothers." He got up. "We're still running down leads on the murder victim," he said. "I've got Ms. Perry checking parole files to see if we can find a match there. Maybe the victim was just out of prison and between jobs when he was wasted."

"If he has a rap sheet, he'll be easier to identify," Kilraven agreed. "And if they cheek-swabbed him, which I imagine they did, Alice Jones can use all that high-tech stuff at the forensic lab to discover his identity."

Jon nodded. "DNA is a blessing in cases like this where the DB is unidentifiable under conventional means."

"Makes our job easier," was the bland reply, "but good police work still largely consists of wearing out shoe leather. Speaking of which, I want to have a talk with Marquez. He might have gotten a look at his attackers."

"We've already asked. He didn't."

"I want to talk to him anyway."

"He isn't back on the job yet. He'll be at his mother's house in Jacobsville."

"Thanks," Kilraven said drily. "I did know that, living in Jacobsville myself."

Jon's black eyes twinkled. "I understand

that you had a visitor recently at your house. A blond one."

"Good Lord. You heard that all the way up here?"

"You were seen by a substantial number of uniformed people."

"Who drove by my house just to spy on me," Kilraven said with mock disgust. "What is the world coming to when a man can't have a cup of coffee with a guest?"

"A cup of coffee at a picnic table, outdoors, in freezing temperatures. Something wrong with the sofa in your living room?"

"If people can't see you, they guess what's going on and they're usually wrong. I didn't want Winnie subjected to gossip," he added quietly. "She's an innocent."

Jon's eyebrows went up over twinkling eyes. "And how would you have found that out?"

Kilraven glowered at him. "In the usual way."

Jon pursed his lips. "Imagine that!"

"It's not serious," came the short reply. "She's a friend. Sort of. But I asked her to the house because I wanted to know why she painted that picture that was a dead-ringer for Melly's raven drawing."

Jon sobered at once. He remembered his brother's visit that night with the painting. "And?"

"She said she started to paint a landscape," Kilraven replied with a puzzled expression. "She didn't know why she painted a raven, or those colors on the beads. She didn't know how I knew it was her, either. I've never even told her that our ranch is called 'Raven's Pride.'"

"We have those flashes of insight because it runs in our family," Jon reminded him. "Our father had a cousin who was notorious for his very accurate visions of the future."

Kilraven nodded. "I wonder where Winnie's gift comes from. She doesn't know. Funny," he added, "but Gail Rogers, the detective who's helping me with our case, has those premonitions. She gets some gossip when she pegs a suspect that nobody else connected with a case."

The intercom buzzed. Jon answered it.

"Agent Wilkes is on his way in with Agent Salton, and you're all due for a meeting in ASAC Grier's office in ten minutes," Joceline said in a voice dripping with sugar. "Would you like coffee and donuts?"

Jon looked surprised, as he should have. Ms. Perry never volunteered to fetch snack food. "That would be nice."

"There's a Dunkin' Donuts shop around the corner," she reminded him. "If I were you, I'd hurry."

"I'd hurry?" he repeated.

"Yes, because my job description requires me to type and file and answer phones. Not be a caterer," she added, still sugary. She hung up.

"One day, so help me, she'll drive me to drink and you'll have to bail me out of some jail where I'll be surrounded by howling mad drug users," Jon gritted.

Kilraven patted him on the shoulder. "Now, now, don't let your blood pressure override your good sense."

"If I had good sense, I'd ask for reassignment to another field office, preferably in the Yukon Territory!" he said loud enough for Ms. Perry to hear him as he opened his office door.

"Oooh, polar bears live there," she said merrily. "And they eat people, don't they?"

"You wish, Ms. Perry," he shot back.

"Temper, temper," she chided.

Jon was almost vibrating, he was so angry. Kilraven smothered laughter.

"I'll call you," he told his brother. "And thanks for the information."

"Just don't go off half-cocked and get in trouble with it," Jon said firmly.

"You know me," Kilraven said in mock astonishment. "I never do anything rash!"

Before Jon could reply, Kilraven walked out the door.

RICK MARQUEZ STILL had his arm in a sling and he was like a man standing on a fire ant hill. "They won't let me come back to work yet," he complained to Kilraven. "I can shoot with one hand!"

"You haven't had to shoot anybody in years," Kilraven reminded him.

"Well, it's the point of the thing. I could sit at a desk and answer phones, but oh, no, I have to be at 100 percent before they'll certify me fit for duty!"

"You can use the free time."

"Yeah? For what? Watering Mom's flowers?"

Kilraven was studying the dead bushes at the front porch. "They look dead to me."

"Not those ones. These ones." He let Kilraven into the living room, where huge potted plants almost covered every wall.

Kilraven's eyebrows lifted. "She grows bananas and coffee in the house?" he exclaimed.

"Now how do you recognize coffee plants?" Marquez asked with evident suspicion. "Most people who come in here have to ask what they are."

"Anybody could recognize a banana plant."

"Yes, but not a coffee plant." Rick's eyes narrowed. "Been around coffee plants somewhere they don't grow in pots?"

Kilraven grinned. "Let's just say, I'm not a stranger to them, and leave it at that."

Rick was thinking that coffee grew in some of the most dangerous places on earth. Kilraven had the look of a man who was familiar with them.

"I know that expression," Kilraven said blandly, "but I've said all I'm going to."

"I know when I'm licked. Coffee?"

"I'd love some." He gave Rick a wry glance. "Going to pick the beans fresh?"

Rick gave the red berries a curious look. "I do have a grinder somewhere."

"Yes, but you have to dry coffee beans and roast them before you can use them."

"All right, now you're really making me curious," Rick told him.

Kilraven didn't say a word. He just kept walking.

They went into the kitchen where Rick made coffee and Kilraven fetched cups. They drank it at Barbara's kitchen table, covered by a red checkered cloth with matching curtains at the windows. The room was bright and airy and pretty, like Barbara herself.

"Your mother has good taste," Kilraven commented. "And she's a great cook."

Rick smiled. "Not a bad mother, either," he chuckled. "I'd probably be sitting in a cell somewhere if she hadn't adopted me. I was a tough kid."

"So was I," Kilraven recalled. "Jon and I kept our parents busy when we were boys. Once, we got drunk at a party, started a brawl and ended up in a holding cell."

"What did your parents do?"

"My stepmother was all for bailing us out. Our father, however, was an FBI agent," he added quietly. "He told her that rushing to our defense might make us think we could get away with anything and we might end up in more serious straits. So he left us there for several days and let us sweat it."

"Ouch," Rick said, wincing.

"We were a lot less inclined to make trouble after that and I only recall getting drunk and going on a bender once in my adult life." That had been after he found his wife and child dead, but he didn't elaborate. "Of course, we were really mad at Dad. But now, looking back at it, I'm sure he did the right thing."

"Life teaches hard lessons," Rick agreed.

Kilraven nodded. "And one of those lessons is that we don't go alone to a meeting with a potential informer. Ever."

Rick flushed. "First time it ever came down like that," he said, defending himself.

"There's always a first time. When I was just a kid, during my first month with San Antonio P.D., one of the detectives went to a covert meeting with a crime boss and ended up in the morgue. He was a friend of my father's."

"It does happen. But if we don't take chances from time to time, we don't get clues."

"True enough."

"Not that I mind the company—I'm going stir crazy down here—but why are you here?"

Kilraven glanced down at the coffee cup. "Two reasons. First, I want to know if you got a look at your attackers."

"They blindsided me," Rick said with disgust. "I don't even know if it was one guy or two. I woke up in the hospital." He raised his eyebrows. "Second reason?"

"I want to know what you know about Senator Will Sanders's brother, Hank."

"Him." Rick sat back in the chair. "He was a navy SEAL. Decorated, in Operation Desert Storm," he said, surprising Kilraven. "Since he got out, however, he's made real strides in taking over mob territory in San Antonio. But his brother, the senator, is the real weird one."

"Weird, how?"

Rick's dark eyes twinkled. "Well, he's about one beer short of a six-pack."

"Crazy?"

Rick shook his head. "Stupid," he corrected. "He doesn't seem to be malicious, but he's protective of his younger brother and it's always a frame. The police don't like Hank, that's why they keep arresting him for things he didn't do."

"Give me a break!"

"From what I gather, the senator uses his brother for menial tasks like intimidating other politicians or enticing teenage girls to his house to meet the senator. The amazing thing is that he's never been charged with anything," he added, "except the one statutory rape offense, which was dropped."

"Jon told me about that one. How is it that he hasn't become a media feeding frenzy?"

"The senator employs an older former gangster who, in turn, employs professional bouncers. One was sent to make veiled threats about the journalists' families."

"That's low," Kilraven said coldly.

"Sure is, but it works. We've tried to co-operate with journalists to catch the guy at it, but it's hard to find a journalist who's willing to risk his family in order to put the senator's right-hand man away. You might notice just recently what happened to that young woman who worked for Senator Fowler when she divulged information to Alice Jones about the Jacobsville murder victim. Nobody's been charged in that case yet, and probably won't be."

"I heard that Senator Sanders was at that party at Senator Fowler's house when Alice Jones asked the questions," Kilraven said. "He probably figured what was going on. He may be stupid, but he's also shrewd."

"Most politicians are. I think we're going to find that Senator Sanders's younger brother is up to his ears in this case, somehow. What I don't know, yet, is exactly how."

"Winnie Sinclair's late uncle has been mentioned as having some peripheral involvement."

Rick nodded. His eyes narrowed on Kilraven's bland expression. "I haven't said anything about it. The detective we're working with on the case mentioned it to me."

"She came to see me recently."

Rick's face was thoughtful. "I hope she's not in any danger," he said. "She's been closer to the investigation than I have, spent a lot of free time going over records, looking for clues. She's angry that she was taken off the case and demoted to traffic."

"Senator Fowler intervened to get her reinstated, to his favor," Kilraven replied. "And he talked to his protégé, Senator Sanders, about the political dangers of trying to stifle a murder investigation, regardless of whether or not his younger brother was involved."

"I just hope she doesn't push too hard," Rick said. "Gail's a fine detective, with an honorable record in the department. She's had a lot of personal problems, but it's never affected her job performance."

"We all have a lot of personal problems."

Rick pursed his lips. "Yours seems to be blond."

Kilraven glared at him. "She is not a personal problem. She's a friend."

"If you say so."

"I do." He sipped his coffee. "I'm taking some time off to work on the cold case. I thought I might go up to San Antonio and see her."

"Give her my regards, and tell her I swear I'll never try to meet with any more so-called informants in any alleys late at night," Rick advised, indicating his arm in the sling.

Kilraven chuckled. "I'll do that."

5

Jon was in the middle of a long telephone call about a pending case when Joceline stuck her head in the door. Her blue eyes had some sparkle in them, rare for her these days, but when she saw that he was on the phone, she held up a hand and went back out.

Curious, he ended the conversation and walked into the outer office.

"Something?" he asked.

She grinned, holding out a sheet of paper.

He took it. His eyebrows lifted in surprise. "Dan Jones?" He stared at her. "Who is

Dan Jones and why am I reading his rap sheet?"

"He's your DB in the Little Carmichael River in Jacobsville," she said. "I checked the state records for anyone recently paroled, narrowed it down to ten possibles who haven't checked in with their parole officers lately, and requested DNA evidence to be sent to Alice Jones to compare with the DNA they pulled off the victim. And there he was. Dan Jones."

He smiled. It was rare for him to do it and extraordinary that he smiled at Joceline, who was his nemesis. She stared at him as if she didn't recognize him; the smile made him look so different. His black eyes sparkled. His white, perfect teeth gleamed.

"Remind me to put in a request for a raise in salary for you, Ms. Perry," he said. "I'll note your contribution to the case, as well."

"Thanks," she stammered.

"Dan Jones." He turned and went back into his office, his mind working in overdrive. "Get my brother on the phone, will you?"

"Yes, sir."

KILRAVEN WAS ON FIRE with the news, once he got it. He spent the next two hours trying to track down Rick Marquez's partner, Gail Rogers. She'd gone to the scene of a suicide, dispatch said, and gave him the address after he told them, not quite truthfully, that he was working the case with her. The uniformed officers at the apartment door tried to stop Kilraven, but he just waved his federal badge at them and kept walking.

The victim was lying facedown on the sofa. There was a very large knife sticking out of his back.

Kilraven glanced at the female detective sergeant. "I thought they said you were at the scene of a suicide, Rogers," he remarked.

"Sure. Suicide. He obviously stabbed himself in the back." She rolled her eyes.

"Sure. You can do that, you just have to have really long arms," Alice Jones—whose last name was now Fowler—told her, walking into the room with an evidence bag she'd just collected. Behind her was the photographer who was recording the scene. Another crime scene technician was using a vacuum collection system to suction possible trace evidence in the form of hair and fiber from the carpet around the body, and still another had an ultraviolet flashlight with which he was searching for traces of blood and bodily fluids on nearby surfaces. "What are you doing in here messing up my crime scene, Kilraven?" she added with a grin. "This isn't a federal suicide."

"From where I'm standing, this isn't a suicide, period," Kilraven returned.

"His wife says it is," Alice murmured. "In fact, she saw him do it."

His eyes narrowed. "She did."

"Yes. That was just before the two-headed cat flew in the window and attacked her."

He whistled.

"They took her down to county," the detective said, "by way of the hospital."

"For a psych evaluation?" he asked.

"For detox. She'd snorted enough meth to put two men in the morgue, from the look of it."

"People who make meth should be hung up by their noses and left to rot," he said coldly.

"Create a need, and then supply it, that's

how the song goes," Gail said solemnly. Her dark eyes were cold. "My ex-husband knew every drug known to man, and used most of them. I had no idea until we were on our honeymoon and he tried to get me to shoot up. I left him that very week."

"Love does blind us," Alice interjected.

"You'd know, Newly-Married Alice," he teased.

She grinned. "Harley and I have calves," she said. "His boss, Cy Parks, gave us a seed bull and several heifers, and they were filled ones."

Kilraven blinked. "Excuse me?"

"Well, if a heifer is open when she's not pregnant, doesn't it make sense that she's filled when she is?" she asked.

Kilraven just shook his head. "We learn something new every day."

"Know what the difference is between a bull and a steer?" she continued with a cocky grin.

He gave her a droll look. "I own half of the biggest cattle ranch in Lawton, Oklahoma, Alice. I grew up on a horse."

"Did you really?" she exclaimed.

"My brother just called me with the news

about Dan Jones," Kilraven told her. "Nice work."

"I told you I had skills," Alice reminded him. "It's amazing to me that I'm not in demand as technical advisor to any number of programs about autopsies on television." She frowned thoughtfully. "Heck, I'm amazed that they aren't after me to star in one of them. I'm young, I'm gorgeous, I'm. . .is anybody listening to me?" she opened her arms wide.

"We're trying not to, Alice," Kilraven said with a wry grin.

"Fine. I'll just go about solving crimes on my own, unappreciated, unloved. . ."

"Shall I tell Harley you said that?" he asked.

She made a face at him and left the room.

"That DNA match was really good work, Alice," he called after her.

"No need trying to butter me up, Kilraven, I'm not listening!"

"It was good work, but it doesn't help much, yet," Detective Rogers said a minute later. "We have a name and a rap sheet, but there's a lot of work left to do in order to connect him with anybody."

"We'll get there. I wanted to know if you've had any luck questioning witnesses around the motel where the victim lived."

"Nobody knows anything." She sighed. "Well, let me rephrase that, nobody knows anything for free and I'm broke until payday."

"I can bankroll you, if you're willing to go back," he said.

"I hate paying informants, but I can't really see any straight-up way to get information in this case. And I'm not really sure that they'll say anything if we pay for it," she added. "One of the guys I talked to said we were sticking our noses in places even cops shouldn't go."

"That sounds interesting."

"I'd take bullets, if I went," Alice suggested from the other room.

"I always take bullets," Kilraven informed her.

"When I finish up here," Rogers said, "we can go back to the motel and see if a few photos of Ben Franklin on currency will open any mouths."

"You're on. See you, Alice!" he called to the woman in the other room, who waved a hand in his general direction.

THE MOTEL WHERE DAN had been living was a seedy, sad little affair on the wrong side of town. Its one enticement to the poor was the low cost of housing. On the other hand, customers had to share space with any number of small furry rodents or long-legged bugs.

There were five men living in the motel, only two of whom were longtime residents. One of them knew Dan Jones, but it took several photos of Ben Franklin to get inside his room and several more to overcome his survival sense.

He was elderly, looked half-starved and wore glasses so thick Kilraven was dubious about his ability to even see his visitors.

"Bad people he was mixed up with," the old man told them. "Real bad. He said he couldn't stay anyplace long, because they were trying to shut him up. He knew things, see. He wouldn't say what, but he said he wanted to go straight and they weren't going to let him. He had a girl, nice girl, he said. She was real religious and wanted him to go to church with her. He liked it. Said he thought he could make up for some of the things he did." He shook his head. "I knew he'd never live. Once he said that name, I knew they'd kill him." He gave Kilraven a hard look. "You just make sure you say I never told you nothing, or they'll find me in some alley."

"I won't tell anyone," Kilraven promised. "What name did he say?"

He hesitated.

"What name?"

He sighed. "Hank Sanders," he said finally.

Kilraven's jaw tautened. "Senator Sanders's little brother," he muttered.

"That's the one. Law can't touch him. He's got powerful friends. You watch, they'll never get the guys who killed Dan. They can cover up any crime they want to. You just watch your own backs, or they'll get you, too."

"Nobody smart kills a cop," Kilraven told him.

"Yeah, well, these guys don't build rockets," came the wry reply.

Kilraven handed him another Franklin and walked out with the detective.

"Now what?" she asked with a sigh.

"Now what, indeed. How do we investigate the brother of a senator for a possible homicide?"

"Call some reporters . . . ?"

"Oh, no," he interrupted. "I'm not going to be a nightly news snack. Once they latch on to this cold case, there will be autopsy photos of my wife and child on every tabloid from here to New York City," he added grimly. "No, we have to play this close to the chest. I'll see what I can dig up on the senator's brother. Suppose you see if any of your informants know anything about Dan Jones and his pals."

"I'll do that." She was quiet and thoughtful for a minute. They stood just outside the motel in the chilly night air with the neon sign missing two letters of the word *motel.* It seemed to emphasize the hopelessness of the building, old and in need of much repair that the owner obviously couldn't or wouldn't effect.

"I hope I never end up in a place like this," Kilraven said glumly.

"Me, too, although I've lived in worse places in years past," she said with a soft laugh. She looked up at the night sky. "I want to do something dangerous."

"Like dive off a building or something?" he asked with a twinkle in his eyes.

She shook her head. "No. I mean, I want to reopen the case of that teenager who was found in a similar condition to our Jacobsville murder victim seven years ago."

He was instantly somber. "You think there may be a link to our cold case?"

She nodded. "Just a hunch. I don't have inside information or anything, but I've got a feeling. . ."

"I have a friend in Jacobsville who has those same hunches. Saved my life once," he recalled, thinking about Winnie.

"Mine might end in tragedy," she said with a sudden flash of insight. "It's very risky. But I think it might be a piece in the puzzle."

His eyes narrowed. "You think there may be a tie to the senator."

"I don't have a scrap of evidence that points to him. Just a hunch. She was very young," she recalled. "She went off supposedly to meet a boy she was dating and turned up dead in an unspeakable condition, just before you lost your family, and looking like our mysterious Dan Jones when his body was found. It may be a co-incidence. On the other hand. . ."

"It never hurts to play the odds," he agreed.

"I'll get right on it. You watch your back," she added with a grin. "I'd hate to have to identify you by your DNA."

"So would my brother," he replied, smiling.

She nodded. "I'll be in touch."

WINNIE KNEW SOMETHING was going on with Kilraven, but she didn't know exactly what. He'd gone to San Antonio to see his brother and Marquez's female partner. Before that, he'd spent time with Rick at his house. She wished she knew Kilraven well enough to ask him what was happening. They weren't getting any inside information at dispatch and that alone was disturbing. They usually had some tidbits about any case that was being worked, even ones up in San Antonio.

She was still floating on air from that hard, sweet kiss, and hoping it wasn't going to be an isolated incident. He was the first and only man she'd ever had such feelings for. She'd hoped that he felt the same way. But he hadn't phoned her or looked in at Barbara's Café where she had lunch most days. In fact, he was conspicuous by his absence.

The holidays were over. She and Keely had taken down the beautiful old Christmas ornaments and packed them away, along with the other decorations and the tree. The house looked cold and bare. Jacobsville still had its tinsel and bells and Christmas trees on light poles, along with garlands of fir and holly. But those artificial leftovers generally didn't come down until the middle of January. They made Winnie sad. She'd hoped she might see Kilraven during the holidays. But if his cold case was heating up, she could understand that he'd want to be in the middle of it.

She should have realized how single-minded he was about the past. She didn't.

KILRAVEN HAD BARELY noticed Christmas Day. Jon came by and brought him a diamond tie tack. He returned the gift with one of his own, a rare print of running horses that Jon had been looking for. Kilraven had found it on the Internet months ago and bought it, then had it framed and kept it in a closet for the big day.

"Don't you even put up a tree in your apartment?" Jon had exclaimed, looking around at the bare apartment. There wasn't even a photograph on display, no paintings, nothing personal at all. Just gym equipment in one bedroom, job-related computers and monitors in another, gaming consoles, and the bare necessities of furniture in the living room and dining room, with a fully-equipped kitchen where Jon sometimes whipped up gourmet dishes for both men.

"It's just a place to sleep. I've been busy trying to run down leads."

Jon's eyes had narrowed. "What I hear is that you've been driving people nuts trying to get them to work your cold case above pressing new murders."

"Hey, it's the first break we've had in seven years," he said defensively, and his face hardened. "It should have been worked until it was solved when it was fresh!"

"I won't argue that, but you know what it's like, trying to give your best to two dozen cases at a time, all with grieving relatives who want blood and tears from the perps."

"I know that," Kilraven said tightly. "But this is personal."

Jon moved closer. "Don't start obsessing again," he said quietly. "It took over your life for three years after it happened. I don't want to see you falling back into that abyss."

"I'm going to solve it," he told his brother. "No matter what the cost. Whoever killed my little girl is going to pay for it with his blood!"

Jon understood how he felt. He didn't know what to say. It was such a personal matter.

"They've had weeks!" he burst out. "They know the guy's name, where he lived, that he was involved with a woman who worked for Senator Fowler, that he went to a church nearby. . .for God's sake, there are church members, other employees who worked for the senator, people who lived at the motel he stayed at. . .!"

"I heard about the resident who was, shall we say, compensated for information," Jon said curtly. "That's not good police work."

"Hey, whatever works," he shot back. "He was the only man my detective could find who was willing to say anything at all and he was scared to death even to whisper certain names."

"Like the name of the junior senator's brother?" Jon queried.

"Exactly."

Jon stuck his hands in his pockets. "Mac, I'm not saying it's a bad lead, but if the case ever comes to trial, that paid informer is going to come back to haunt you. One broken link in a chain of evidence can let a murderer walk."

Kilraven's silver eyes were lawless. "Who says he'll ever get to trial?" he asked in a tone so soft with menace that it made the hair on the back of Jon's neck stand up.

"If you act outside the law, you'll go to prison," Jon said quietly. "Don't do it. Don't even think about it. We have the rule of law, and it works."

"Not all the time."

"Vigilante law has been known to kill innocents," Jon reminded him. "You don't want to run off half-cocked and finger the wrong person. Do you?"

Kilraven's face was like stone. "I want justice."

"Good. So do I. Stop talking like some Old West desperado."

Kilraven lifted an eyebrow.

"Have you ever read a real history of the old Texas lawmen on the border in the early 1800s?" Jon asked.

"Who hasn't?"

"One Texan with a badge could walk into a town across the border and residents would run away screaming when they saw just the badge," he replied.

"Those old-timers had to be tough to stay alive," Kilraven defended them.

"You're missing the point."

"Which is?"

"You can carry a threat so far that instead of respect for the law, you create panic and fear."

"Whatever works," the older man repeated.

Jon sighed irritably. "I can talk to you about a dozen other subjects and you're the soul of rationality. On this one, you aren't even coherent."

"Look at the autopsy photos. I'll give you coherent."

Jon had moved closer and laid a big hand on his brother's shoulder. "Nobody knows better what you went through than I do," he said quietly. "I'll help you, any way I can. But if you step outside the law, nobody will be able to. You understand?"

Kilraven softened, just for a minute. Jon was a hard case, but he really cared about his sibling, and Kilraven knew it. He managed a smile. "I could have done worse for a brother than you," he said.

Jon chuckled. "Yes. Me, too."

It was the closest they came to expressing the real affection they had for each other. Neither man was known for public displays of private emotions.

Now it was January, cold and barren and dry. Kilraven glared at the flat horizon with its gray skies and stark trees lifting bare limbs over frosty ground. It felt dead, as Kilraven felt dead inside. He was sorry he hadn't at least phoned Winnie over the holidays, but every new lead in the case kept him pacing the floor and waiting for phone calls. Not that he waited long. Every homicide detective in San Antonio recognized his cell phone number by now and they hung up the minute it flashed on their screens.

"Damn it!" he muttered, throwing the phone at his leather sofa after his latest attempt at communication got him a quick click followed by a busy signal.

No sooner had it hit than it started ringing.

He grabbed it up. Maybe one of the detectives was psychic.

"Hello?" he said.

"I have news," Jon said smugly. "Remember I told you that I had Ms. Perry researching Dan Jones's known associates?"

"Yes. You found something!"

"I did, indeed. The junior senator's brother engaged Mr. Jones as a gofer," he replied.

"The connection. Finally!"

"Okay, hold it right there," Jon said firmly. "You can't jump in and blow the whole investigation. We have to go slow, to gather evidence, to—"

"Damn!"

"I know how impatient you are," Jon told him quietly. "But you don't want us to blow a murder case by intimidation and threats, do you?"

Kilraven was silent.

"Do you?"

"Of course not," he said on a heavy sigh.

"Good. Now take a deep breath and promise me you won't go rushing over to the evil brother's lair and start knocking him through walls trying to pin the murders on him."

Kilraven let out the breath. "I promise."

"We have to go at him sideways. First we pin down exactly what tasks Dan Jones was known to do for him, whether any of them involved intimidation or worse. Then we have to find witnesses who saw it and are willing to talk."

"The informant at the motel might know more."

"Anything you get with bribes will be a banquet for the perp's defense team," Jon said sternly.

Kilraven quieted down. "I guess so," he said irritably.

"You know so. What you can do is find a way to talk to the senator's wife," Jon added. "We know that she's afraid of her husband's brother. We don't know why. We need some way to dig information out of her without making her suspicious."

"They have vacation property in the Bahamas," Kilraven said. His eyes narrowed. "I could fly down there . . ."

"She won't talk to you," Jon said. "I know, because I've tried. It's going to take a woman."

Kilraven's heart jumped. "The Sinclairs own property in Nassau."

"Yes, they do," Jon said. "In fact, their property sits just down the beach from the senator's. I had Ms. Perry dig that out for me."

"And we have a ranch in Lawton, near the senator's homeplace, where his grandfather was born. They vacation there sometimes, as well. Winnie Sinclair might be willing to help. We could go down there together."

Jon's voice chilled. "If you take her down to Nassau and share her beach house, gossip would get back to Jacobsville. Her reputation is spotless. It would be a shame to put a blemish on it."

Kilraven was thinking, not quite rationally. "We could get a nice ceremony at city hall the day before we left for the Bahamas, followed by a nice annulment the day we came home."

Jon glared at him. "The woman's crazy about you from what I hear. Even you couldn't be that cold-hearted, to think of marrying her temporarily just to help in a murder investigation!"

"I was kidding," Kilraven lied. "Look, I might ask her to fly down there and accidentally run into the senator's wife and have lunch or something. She might be able to find out something we can't."

"It might put her in the line of fire, too," Jon argued.

Kilraven pursed his lips. "More reason that I should be on hand, just in case."

Jon threw up his hands. "I can't talk to you!"

"Sure you can. It's a great idea. I'll go work on it."

"I didn't mean it that way," Jon said. "Mac, you can't use people who care about you."

"Why not? Everybody else does." His face hardened. "My daughter is dead. Somebody killed her and walked away, like it never happened. I want somebody to pay for it. Somebody is going to pay for it, no matter what I have to do to get an arrest in the case!"

"No matter who you have to sacrifice to do it?" Jon asked softly.

"You're twisting what I said."

"Not really."

Kilraven squared his shoulders. "Winnie's got a crush on me. She's too young to feel anything stronger than that," he said, dismissing her feelings. "She'd be thrilled to have a marriage license in her hands, even if it was for only a couple of weeks. We'd solve the case, get an annulment and go back to our own lives."

"Mac. . .!"

"Like a date, only we'd live together, briefly."

"She has a brother who eats live snakes," Jon shot back. "I know Boone Sinclair. You do not want him on your neck. He was spec ops in Iraq, and he has skills that could match yours. He's very protective of his sister."

"I'm not going to hurt Winnie," Kilraven raged. "For God's sake, we'll have a vacation together. What's sinister about that?"

"A vacation where you'll troll her as bait to catch the senator's wife."

"You said we can't get her to talk because we're men. Okay. Winnie's a female."

"You don't even know if she'll do it," Jon said. "But if you ask her, for God's sake, tell her the truth. And tell her it's risky. Because it is. You could be putting her life on the line."

"Just for talking to a senator's wife?" he scoffed. "Don't be so alarmist."

"I have to be. You're not thinking straight. You're too bull-headed about this case to be logical."

"And you're too logical to feel revenge."

Jon shook his head. "No, I'm not. I saw them, too," he added quietly. "Melly was a very special child. I may not have liked her mother, but I loved her. Just as you did. I don't want somebody to get away with killing her, either."

Kilraven relaxed, but only a little. "I'll talk to Winnie."

"Do that. But be honest. Okay?"

"Okay."

ALL THE WAY TO JACOBSVILLE, he was thinking of ways to sell Winnie on the idea without telling her too much. Jon was all business, but Kilraven's heart was bleeding all over again from the memory of what he'd seen that long-ago rainy night when he intercepted a homicide call and found his family dead. He'd had nightmares for years. He heard Melly call for him, scream for him to save her, and he tried to get up, but he was held down by ropes and he couldn't get loose. The same dream, night after night, with her screams in his ears.

He'd dived headfirst into a whiskey bottle for several weeks afterward. Jon had saved him from going even further downhill by getting him into a treatment facility. Fortunately, his bosses had understood his behavior. Counseling and time off had given him the opportunity to pretend to the world that he was over the deaths, well-adjusted and ready to go back to work. Nothing was further from the truth, but he learned to hide his feelings. He was good at it by now.

He'd taken some of the most dangerous jobs he could find in a futile effort to get the horrible pictures out of his mind. The CIA had taken him on with reservations, but discovered that he was an asset with his knowledge of foreign languages. Like his brother, Jon, he spoke Farsi and several Arabic dialects, in addition to Spanish, French, Russian, German and even Lakota

Sioux. If he wore colored contacts, he was olive-skinned and dark-eyed enough to pass for someone Middle Eastern, and he had, working covertly and sometimes with foreign governments to ferret out information vital to national security.

His specialty had become kidnapping cases, which was why he'd gone undercover in Jacobsville about the time General Emilio Machado went missing and showed up in Mexico. The general had nabbed first Gracie Marsh and then Jason Pendleton in an effort to regain his government in South America. He was friendly to the U.S. and not the same sort of tyrant who held power there, now. Kilraven had been looking for him, but hadn't realized where he was until he got involved with Rodrigo Ramirez and the DEA on a drug case. And voilà, there was Machado. He'd solved that case.

Now he had something much more personal to pursue during his leave of absence. All he needed were the tools to solve it. One of them was Winnie Sinclair. And he was going to get her to help him. No matter what he had to do—even if it meant using her own feelings for him in the process. The only thing that mattered was bringing his daughter's killer to justice any way he could.

He could still see her, the last day of her little life. She'd started toward the car where her mother was waiting impatiently to take her to day care. But she'd turned suddenly. She ran back to Kilraven with her black hair flying, laughing, her arms outstretched. He'd picked her up, swung her around and kissed her.

"I love you, Daddy," she'd whispered, and kissed him back. "Always remember."

He could barely see the road for the film in his eyes. "Always remember." They were the most painful words of all now because he remembered what had happened just a few hours later. He would never see those black eyes sparkle, or hear that musical little laugh, or open his arms for Melly to run into. He drew in a harsh breath and swallowed down the hard lump in his throat. His hands went white where they gripped the steering wheel. Three years old, and some heartless intruder had killed her. Somehow, he swore, someday, someone was going to pay the price for that murder. And he was going to make it happen. He didn't care if it cost him his job, or even his life. The killer was going to be brought to justice.

6

Winnie was having a quick lunch at Barbara's Café on her way home from work. She'd been on a split shift, working five hours of her ten-hour shift before midnight and going back in at 3:00 a.m. to pick up the rest of it. The EOC was organized so that each operator worked a ten-hour shift, and because someone was arriving as someone else was leaving, there was overlap. It allowed the incoming operators to know what was going on and saved long explanations of existing or developing situations.

She loved her job. There were times

when she was so stressed that she had to take breaks in the EOC "quiet room," a place set aside for people who needed a brief moment of solitude after hectic periods of time to come down off the ceiling. It was a high-pressure job, with lives in the balance. The training had been intensive, but after her internship she felt capable of handling most any situation that arose. And if she needed help, it was all around her. These dedicated, good-hearted people made her proud to be a part of their group.

"You look worn out," Barbara mentioned as she put a plate of salad and a grilled cheese sandwich in front of Winnie, along with a cup of hot coffee. Winnie put cream and sugar in the coffee, something she only did when she had grilled cheese.

"Bad night," she replied with a wan smile. "I worked a split shift to accommodate one of our other operators who had a death in the family. It was hectic. Much more than usual."

Barbara sat down with her for a minute. "The Tate boy?" she asked gently.

Winnie hesitated, and then nodded. It was useless to deny her involvement. In

Jacobsville, everybody knew what was going on. Besides, it would be in the newspaper the next day. Operators never talked about incidents at work otherwise. "Tragic," she said heavily. "His poor mother."

"She has friends. She'll cope."

"Yes, but it was so senseless," Winnie said.

Barbara put a gentle hand on hers. "Nothing is really senseless. Sometimes we just don't understand the reasons things happen. Like Rick getting beat up." She shook her head. "Thank God he has such a hard head."

Winnie nodded. "He was lucky. But this boy was only fifteen years old," Winnie said. "He thought it would be funny to steal a car and go for a joyride. He allegedly ran over a ten-year-old child and crippled her for life, and then couldn't avoid a power pole and killed himself." She shook her head. "I don't understand anything."

"That's what I mean," Barbara said. "I don't think we're meant to understand, sometimes." She looked up. "You need cheering up."

"That would take more than a salad and coffee, I'm afraid."

"How about something six feet tall and very good-looking?"

"Hmm?"

"How about bringing me what she's having?" Kilraven asked as he pulled up a chair and sat down beside Winnie, whose heart leaped up into her throat even as tired as she was. "Except I want my coffee black."

Barbara smiled. "Coming up."

She left and Kilraven gave Winnie a bold appraisal. She was wearing a pair of dark slacks with a blue polo shirt, her blond hair in a neat braid. She looked very young, tired and disillusioned.

"I heard," Kilraven said.

She met his silver eyes. He was wearing slacks and a black polo shirt with a wool jacket. He looked expensive and worldly out of uniform. She managed a smile. "We're all still reeling. Up until the ambulances got there, we had hope."

"You did everything possible. It was a good effort."

"We did everything possible and he still died."

"That's not your call," he replied quietly. "People die. We all do, eventually."

She managed a weary smile. "So they say."

Barbara came back with his salad and sandwich and coffee. "You have to learn not to take things so much to heart, baby," she told Winnie gently.

The endearment was comforting. Winnie sighed. "I do try."

"It's no bad thing to have a heart," Kilraven interjected.

"Yes, it is," Winnie murmured. She drew in a long breath and pushed back her plate. "It's very good, Barbara, I'm just sleepy and worn out. I almost went straight home, but I haven't had anything since supper early yesterday evening."

"You have a canteen at the EOC," Kilraven pointed out.

"Yes, but in order to eat, you have to have time to eat," she reminded him. "That wasn't the only emergency we had. It was the busiest night we've had this month."

"It was a full moon," Kilraven said as he dug into his salad.

"It was," Barbara exclaimed. "But what does that have to do with it?"

"Beats me," he said. "But it really does bring out the worst in some people."

Barbara just shook her head. "If you need anything else, let me know."

IT WAS AN INDICATION of how depressed Winnie was that she wasn't dropping utensils or spilling coffee from nervousness at Kilraven's unexpected company. She sipped coffee and stared at her discarded salad blankly.

After a minute, she glanced at him and frowned. "What are you doing down here?" she asked suddenly. "We heard you were in San Antonio, working with detectives to find connections to our DB in the Little Carmichael River."

"I was, and I have," he said. "I need a favor."

Her heard did jump, then. "What?"

"Not now. Finish your coffee and we'll take a ride."

She glanced around at the lunch crowd. They were eating and shooting covert glances at Winnie and Kilraven.

"If I go for a ride with you, we'll be the talk of the town all weekend," she said.

He chuckled. "I don't care." He looked into her dark eyes. "Do you?"

She shrugged. "I guess not."

"While they're talking about us, they're leaving somebody else alone," he pointed out.

"I suppose." She finished her coffee. "Do you think it's going to tie into your own cold case?" she asked abruptly.

His face tautened. "I think it may. We've got a lead. It's a small one, but it may pay dividends down the road. Before this is over, some big-time feathers are going to get ruffled."

She cocked her head. "Now, I'm curious."

"Good. Let's go." He swallowed the rest of his coffee and picked up her lunch tab, despite her protests, as well as his own. Then he shepherded her out the door and toward a black late-model Jaguar sports car.

She was taken aback. Used to seeing him in a prowler, this was new.

"Don't tell me you haven't ever seen one." He chuckled.

"Of course I have. I just never pictured you driving one."

"Out of curiosity, what did you picture me driving?" he queried at the passenger door.

"A squad car," she said with a smile.

He chuckled. "Point to you, Miss Sinclair." He started to open the door and then hesitated, frowning. "Sinclair. Do you know your family history?"

"Sort of," she said, disconcerted. "My people came from Scotland."

His silver eyes twinkled.

"Why does that amuse you?"

"Lord Bothwell married Mary Queen of Scots after the suspicious death of her husband, Lord Darnley. Bothwell's mother was a Sinclair."

"Why are you so interested in Bothwell?" she asked.

He pursed his lips. "My ancestors were Hepburns."

"Well, isn't it a small world?" she exclaimed.

"Getting smaller by the day. Climb in."

He went around and got in beside her, approving the fact that she fastened her seat belt at once. So did he.

"Where are we going?" she asked.

"Someplace without video cameras and an audience," he said with a grim nod toward the faces peering out of the café.

"We could go to my house," she said.

"Keely may be at work, but I expect your brothers are around the house somewhere."

"Boone is. Clark's up in Iowa, looking at cattle for Boone."

"My point, exactly. I want to talk to you without an audience."

She turned her purse over in her hands. "Okay. I'll try to stay awake."

"Poor kid," he said sympathetically. "You work hard for minimum wage. You don't have to work at all, do you?"

She shook her head. "It's just that we were all raised with a strong work ethic. We're not the sort of people to sit around and play cards or go to parties."

"Your father has been dead for some time, hasn't he?"

She nodded. "He was a good man, in a lot of ways. But he had some terrible flaws. I suppose they were because our mother ran off with his brother. He never got over it."

"That would shatter a man's pride," he had to agree. He glanced at her set features. "No curiosity about where she lives, or with whom . . . ?"

"No," she blurted out. She flushed at his sudden scrutiny.

"People make mistakes, Winnie," he said gently.

The visit from her mother still stung. "Yes, they do, and we're supposed to forgive them. I know that. But I could have happily gone my whole life without seeing her again."

"Has she remarried?"

She glanced at him, frowning. "Remarried?"

"You said she was married to your uncle. Your uncle died."

"Wait a minute," she said. "How do you know that?"

"It's one of the reasons I came down here to talk to you. Your uncle may have been on the periphery of this case."

"Boone said something about that, but not that he was actually involved. Our uncle was a murderer?" she exclaimed, horrified.

"We don't think he killed the DB," he said at once. "But they found a thermos bottle at the site where the car went into the Little Carmichael River. It was a match for one that your uncle was said to have in his house. A San Antonio detective who's working with us on this case went to his house to check it out. She spoke with his roommate."

Winnie was stunned. It had never occurred to her that her uncle might be involved in murder.

"His roommate." She blinked. She looked at him. "Our mother said that his roommate was strung out on drugs."

He looked surprised. "That's right. Well, I guess she had to go over there if she recovered your heirloom jewelry, right? Anyway, our detective also paid the roommate a visit and checked out the thermos. She was barely lucid—the roommate I mean—but she did identify a photograph of the thermos."

"My uncle's thermos was on the bank of the river next to the car of a murder victim, and you don't think he was involved?" she asked, blank from lack of sleep and shock.

He drew in a breath. "That's why I said I think he was on the periphery. I think he might have known the murderer."

She sat back in her seat, wondering at the connection and interconnection of lives. She frowned. "Do you think my uncle was murdered?" she asked.

He didn't speak for a minute. "Now, isn't

that an interesting question. I don't think we considered that his death might not have been natural. He was a heavy drug user."

"Sheriff Hayes's brother was killed by an overdose that he didn't know he was taking," she said. "So was Stuart York's wife's sister. They were given a pure form of the drug instead of a diluted one and didn't realize it."

"We'll look into that," he said at once.

Winnie looked down at the purse in her lap. "So many dead people. What did they all know that got them killed?"

"I don't know, Winnie," he said quietly. "But I'm going to find out."

He pulled into a small roadside park. It was deserted at this time of year. It was a pretty place in the other seasons, beside a tributary of the Little Carmichael River, where kids played in warm weather. The trees were bare and stark against a gray sky. The whole world looked dead. Even the grass.

"It will be cold, but I don't think we'll be a tourist attraction here," he chuckled as they got out.

Winnie pulled her gray Berber coat closer

because the wind was sharp and cold. She walked beside Kilraven, in his dark wool jacket, to the stream. She noted as she looked down that he was wearing black boots, so highly polished that they reflected the sky. She smiled. It was like him to be fastidious.

"What are you smiling at?" he asked.

"Your boots," she said. "Not a speck on them. You're elegant for a cattleman turned law enforcement officer."

He chuckled. "I guess so."

She wondered why. She was too polite to ask.

He stared at her with a faint smile. "You're curious, but you won't ask. I like that about you."

"Thanks."

He put his hands in his pockets and looked at the bubbling stream in between the shallow banks. "My mother was white," he said shortly. "She left my father when I was about two years old. She took me with her, but she liked to party. She couldn't afford a housekeeper, but she didn't con-sider that it was dangerous to leave a child alone. In fact, she seemed to forget that she had me, from time to time. My father came looking for me after he got a call from the police in a little town outside Dallas. A neighbor had heard screaming from inside a deserted house that my mother had rented. The police broke in and found a card with his name and telephone number on it, and they called him."

She waited. She didn't insist.

He drew in a breath. "My mother had been partying with a man, apparently one who liked alcohol and didn't especially like women. He beat her to death. I guess I was lucky that he didn't kill me, but he probably assumed that I was too young to identify him. He locked the door and left us both inside. It was two days before I got hungry enough to scream."

"Dear God," she whispered.

He glanced at her with hollow eyes. "My father carried me home and cleaned me up. He was going with a younger woman who loved kids. She latched on to me as if I were the only child on earth." He chuckled. "He married her, and they had Jon. But I never felt as if I were his half brother. My earliest memories are of Cammy. My stepmother."

"Cammy?"

"Her name is Camelia, but nobody calls her that." He drew in a long breath. "She's very conservative and deeply religious, so Jon and I had a strict upbringing. Our father was out of town, sometimes out of the country working for the FBI, so Cammy basically raised us both." He glanced at her with some amusement. "She'd probably make mincemeat out of you, little canary bird. She's hard-going, as at least one of our former girlfriends could attest."

"Your, plural?" she queried.

"Jon and I once had an attachment to the same girl. It ended in a rather enthusiastic altercation, from which we both emerged with dental bills. The girl, predictably, discovered that she was really in love with her former boyfriend. Too late to do us any good." He laughed.

"Your stepmother must be one nice lady," she commented.

"She is. Difficult to live with, but nice."

"I'm sorry about your mother."

"I'm sorry about yours," he replied. He turned to her and moved closer. "I've never told anyone about my mother."

She was flattered. She smiled. "I've never told anybody about mine, either. Just family."

"Does she look like you?" he asked, curious.

"Pretty much. She's older."

"She must live somewhere nearby."

"I wouldn't know." She closed up.

"Now, don't do that," he teased gently. He drew her against him. "We were making progress and then you turned into a sensitive plant and closed your leaves up."

She smiled. "Sorry." She flattened her hands against his broad chest, under the jacket. She could feel the warmth of his body through the soft fabric of his shirt.

The touch, light as it was, built fires deep inside him. His breathing changed. The scent of her body was in his nostrils, seducing him. It had been years since he'd felt a woman's body against him in the darkness, since he'd known what it was to be a man. And here he was with a woman who didn't even know what happened when the lights went out, except for what she'd heard or read.

She looked up. "What's wrong?"

His eyebrows lifted. "Well, I was just

considering how nice it would be to lay you down on the grass and. . ." He cleared his throat. "Sorry."

She laughed, delighted. "Were you really?"

He cocked his head. "Not offended?"

"Oh, no. I have all these deep questions about how it feels and what happens," she confided. "I did almost find out, once, but my brother Boone walked in and knocked the boy down the front steps into a mud puddle." She sighed. "I was fifteen. Boone felt I was too young to be the target of a twentysomething cowboy. So the cowboy went to work for somebody else and I went back into cold storage, and so did my physical education."

He burst out laughing. "Good for Boone."

"He's always looked out for me. So has Clark, in his way." She sighed. "Neither of them knew what it was like at home when they were gone, and I couldn't tell. My father hated my mother, hated her more than ever after they met and talked a few weeks after she left. He came home cursing her. We weren't told what happened."

"Sad that they couldn't work it out."

"I would have liked having a mother,"

she agreed. She looked up at him. "I was horrible to her when she showed up at the house. I guess I could have been more forgiving."

"It's hard to forgive people who sell us out," he said.

She nodded. She drew in a long breath. "All of this is very interesting, but it doesn't have much to do with why you came looking for me. Does it?"

He framed her face in his hands and lifted it. "Maybe it does." He looked at her mouth for a long time, so long that her heart raced. "Sorry," he murmured as he bent his head, "but I'm having withdrawal symptoms. . ."

His mouth hit hers like a wall, opening and twisting, hungry and insistent, warm against the cold that whirled around them on the bank of the stream. She melted into him, sliding her arms around his broad chest. Her fingers dug into his back, feeling the solid muscle there, drowning in the hunger he raised in her so effortlessly.

He liked her response. It was immediate, unaffected, totally yielding. He loved the way she felt in his arms. He drew her closer, feeling the sudden, familiar surge of desire that corded his powerful body, no longer hidden from her.

She gasped as she felt it. She tried to draw back, but his hands went lower and pressed her hips into his.

He lifted his head and stared into her wide, shocked eyes. He didn't say a word. But he wouldn't let her step back, either.

"You mustn't. . .!" she whispered.

"What happened to all that talk about wanting to know how it felt?" he asked, pursing his lips. He wasn't smiling, but his eyes were.

"Well, I do," she stammered. "But not right now."

"Not right now."

She nodded. She flushed.

He chuckled wickedly and let her move away a discreet distance. He liked her high color. He liked a lot of things about her. "Chicken," he teased.

"Chook, chook, chook." She imitated a hen and grinned up at him.

"Actually," he said, looping his arms around her waist, "I was thinking of a way for you to indulge some of that curiosity."

"You were?"

"Not to excess," he said then, feeling

cautious. It would be too easy to go in head-first, and have to repair the damage later. "You have a summer house in Nassau."

The sudden shift in subject matter hit her like a brick in the head. "Uh, yes."

"It borders on property owned by the junior senator from Texas."

"Yes, it does."

"His wife doesn't like him. He plays around with very young girls and it hurts her pride, so she goes to the summer home to escape the media spotlight. And the senator."

"That's what I've heard."

"Have you ever met her?" he asked suddenly, hopefully.

"Actually, I have," she replied. "We were at a party once, thrown by the American embassy, and I've gone to parties at her house, before her husband was a senator. She's very nice."

He smiled. "How would you like to go down to Nassau with me and stay in the summer home while we see if she might be even more talkative about her brother-in-law?"

She cooled down at once and pulled away. "I'm not like that."

"Excuse me?" he asked, disconcerted.

"I mean, I flirt a little too hard with you, and maybe it looks like I'm worldly and I'm leading you on. But I'm not. I can't, I mean, I won't. . . My brother would kill you," she added, blushing.

He understood at once and burst out laughing.

"It's not funny," she muttered, glowering at him.

"That's not why I'm laughing. I don't have an illicit weekend in mind," he assured her. His eyes smiled, too. "I'm pretty conservative myself, in case you haven't noticed. I don't have women. In fact," he said with a sigh, "I've only ever had one woman and I was married to her."

She really blushed then. "Oh."

"So I think as much of my reputation as I think of yours," he added. "I was considering that we might get married in the probate judge's office. Just for the trip," he said emphatically. "I'm not in the market for a long-term wife or a new family. I can't. . . I won't risk that again. But we can be married long enough to do some investigating."

She was gaping at him. "We'd get married so that you could ask a senator's wife a few questions in the Bahamas?" she asked blankly.

He laughed. "It sounds bad, when you put it that way."

"But it's what you want to do."

"No, it isn't." He gave her a considering look. "I won't mention what I'd like to do. But it's why I think we should get married. Just in case."

Her eyebrows arched. Her eyes began to twinkle. "Just in case what?"

"In case I can't resist the temptation to do what I'd like to do," he said wryly. "In which case, it wouldn't be an annulment, it would be a divorce."

She cocked her head up at him. "You might like me."

"I'm sure I would. But I'm not getting married again."

"You just said you wanted to," she pointed out.

"Temporarily," he emphasized.

"You're afraid I'd get temporarily pregnant if we went down there as an unmarried couple," she mused.

He glared at her. "I don't get women temporarily pregnant."

"You sure wouldn't get me that way,

because I believe very strongly that if babies get made, they should get born," she said firmly.

He sighed. "Winnie, I've had a traumatic seven years," he said. "Right now, the only thing I want to do is find out who killed my wife and child. I'm not emotionally sound enough for a new relationship of any kind."

She felt doors closing. He was brutal. But perhaps he felt he needed to be. He didn't want to give her any false hope.

His silver eyes narrowed. "This is how you looked that morning when you found me and Sheriff Hayes in bed with your brother and Keely," he said.

"Excuse me?"

"You stopped playing with me," he said somberly. "You stopped looking at me with those big, soft brown eyes as if you'd die to have me."

"I never looked at you that way," she defended herself. "I thought you were dishy. So have a lot of other women, I'll bet."

"I minded when other women did it," he said surprisingly.

"You did?"

"You're just a little violet, blooming under a stair," he said softly, touching her face with the tips of his fingers as he looked down at her intently. "Twenty-two to my thirty-two, Winnie. That's almost a generation."

"It's ten years and I'm old for my age."

He pursed his lips. "Not old in the right way, kid," he insinuated.

She glared at him. "Nobody learns things without somebody teaching them," she said flatly. "My father and my big brother made sure nobody got close enough."

"Good for them," he repeated.

"Listen, I have the makings of a femme fatale if I could just learn the basics," she told him. "Books don't tell you anything. They assume you already know."

"What sort of books have you been reading?" he asked in mock surprise.

"The same sort boys hide under their mattresses, I imagine, but I need more than just pictures! You're changing the subject." She pushed against his chest. "I'm not marrying you temporarily. You can find some other woman to go with you to the Bahamas and I'll loan you our vacation home."

"I'm not shacking up with a total stranger," he said curtly.

"Well, you're not shacking up with me, either, Kilraven," she told him.

"That's why I'm trying to get you to marry me!"

She pulled away and walked closer to the stream. She felt sick to her stomach. He wanted a no-strings marriage so that he could help solve the case. She was a means to an end for him. He didn't feel anything for her, really. He never would. He lived with ghosts. She felt more chilled by that realization than from the cold weather. She wrapped her arms around her chest.

He watched her with growing irritation. It was just like a woman to start fishing for emotional involvement. All he needed was her company so that he could get to the senator's wife. Why was she making it so hard? It was because she had feelings for him, he thought irritably. As if he could see a future with a woman only a few years out of high school. He didn't want children, so there was no point in staying married.

"You're making this complicated," he said shortly, ramming his hands into his pockets. "Why can't we just look on it as a lark? We get married, have a holiday on the beach, and build some memories that don't require anything heavy."

She turned and looked at him, horrified.

"We could enjoy each other," he said, losing ground.

"We can have separate bedrooms and behave like unmarried people," she said. "Or I'm not going."

"What the hell sort of vacation is that?"

"The only sort you're getting with me," she returned, coloring. "You think you can have fun with me and just walk away. I'm not built like that. I can't. . .damn it, I won't!" She turned away. "You can take me back to the café, right now!" She started walking toward the car.

He just stared after her. "What the hell did I say?" he asked the tree beside him.

"That's it, talk to the trees," she muttered when she was out of earshot of him. "Look out. They may start answering you!"

7

Kilraven thought about her reactions. Maybe she was right. If they could go together to Nassau and just have a few days of sun and sand and ocean, and he didn't pressure her into something she didn't want, it might pay off in a better working relationship. Working, as in courting the senator's wife. Because whatever he said, his only intent was to find out if there was a skeleton in the closet of the senator's brother. He wanted the people who killed his family. That was more important than the future, or Winnie's feelings or any other consideration. Maybe he was using her, but he didn't care. It was an obsession, just as his brother had said. He was going to catch the killer, no matter who he had to hurt to do it.

He walked behind her to the car. "Okay," he said as he unlocked the car and helped her inside. "We'll do it your way. But if I jump off the roof of your summer home in frustration and die, it will be on your conscience."

"It won't," she returned.

"Heartless girl."

She glanced at him. "And I'm not wearing anything provocative the whole time."

"Amazing willpower," he murmured. "Good for you."

She sighed. "And I'm not telling Boone. You'll have to."

His face froze. That was not a prospect he was looking forward to. He knew Boone, and that Boone had been in the military. It was going to be tricky telling him why he was marrying his baby sister. He didn't need to be told that Boone was going to be angry.

"Surely, you're not afraid of him," she said with faint malice.

He drew in a breath. "No, not afraid," he replied.

"You can tell him how you want to marry me so that we can frolic from bedroom to bedroom in the Bahamas and you can use me to dig information out of the senator's wife," she continued.

He glared at her. "You're twisting it," he muttered.

"I'm twisting it?" she exclaimed. "You want me to marry you for a few days so that you can get information that will lead you to whoever killed your family." She sobered. "I don't blame you. If it were me, I'd do anything to find out, too. But I'm the one being used. It feels dirty."

He really glared now. "Dirty."

She grimaced. "That was a poor choice of words," she said slowly.

He closed the passenger door without another word. He went around, got in under the wheel and shot the car out onto the highway. His face might have been carved from stone.

Winnie felt tears threatening. She wasn't used to confrontations since the death of her father. She didn't fight with her brothers. She was a little afraid of Boone, but she didn't advertise it. Men were frightening in a temper. She glanced at Kilraven and thought of glaciers. She knew so little about him. Most of what she'd learned was from other people, although he'd been forthcoming with her on some level. But he kept his true feelings to himself. He seemed happy to be a loner.

She looked out the window uncomfortably as he sped down the road toward Barbara's Café, where her car was parked. She was already regretting her hasty words. What would it hurt to marry him, even if it was temporary? She was crazy about him. Maybe she could store up enough memories to get her through the rest of her life, because she knew she'd never love another man like this.

But he didn't look like he was contemplating a second proposal. In fact, he looked as if he wished he'd never met her.

She wanted to apologize. She knew it was useless. She'd offended him. Not that he hadn't offended her first. What sort of woman did he think she was?

Her lips made a thin line. She knew that he'd never have mentioned a holiday with her if it hadn't been for the senator's wife living near the Sinclair beach house. She was a means to an end, and it was impersonal. He liked her. Maybe he liked kissing her. But there was no feeling behind it, except maybe a physical one. The chemistry was definitely there. He felt it, as surely as she did. But he didn't love her. Perhaps he couldn't love anyone again. The trauma of his loss had turned him cold, made him afraid to try again. He didn't want another child. He didn't want another wife, either. Winnie was a tool. He'd use her to get the information he needed, then he'd put her back on the shelf and forget her very existence. It hurt, knowing that.

He pulled up in front of Barbara's Café where she'd left her car and sat with the engine idling.

She wanted to say something. She couldn't think of anything that would express her confused emotions.

He wanted to say something, too, but he was angry. Anything he said would be too much.

Her hand went to the car door. "Thanks for the ride," she said tautly.

"Sure."

She waited for a minute, but he didn't

say another word. He didn't even look at her. She opened the door, got out and closed it behind her. She walked to her own car without looking back. She could barely see it through her tears when she heard him drive away.

"YOU LOOK LIKE DEATH warmed over," Keely said gently later, when they were fixing supper.

Winnie managed a smile as she made a pasta salad. "That's how I feel."

"Want to talk about it?"

Winnie put the finishing touches on the salad and covered the bowl before she put it in the refrigerator to chill. "It wouldn't help," she said finally.

"Well, if you do want to talk, you know where I am," Keely said.

"You're the best friend I've ever had," Winnie told her. "It was the best day of my life when Boone married you." She hugged her warmly.

"I could return the compliment. You saved my life when the rattler bit me. I thought I was a goner."

Winnie laughed. "Poor old snake," she

said, fighting back the tears that the hug had provoked.

"He never should have bitten me in the first place."

"He wouldn't have, if you hadn't sat on him," Winnie said.

"I guess so."

"You won't tell Boone, if I tell you?" she asked.

Keely's green eyes twinkled. She crossed her heart.

"Kilraven wants me to marry him."

"Winnie! That's great news. . .!" Keely began.

She held up a hand. "It's not. He wants me to marry him and spend a few days at our summer house in Nassau so that he can have me pump Senator Sanders's wife for information about her crooked brother-in-law. Then he wants an annulment when we get back. Unless I'm willing to, how did he put it, enjoy our time together, in which case we can get a divorce when we come home."

Keely just stared at her. "That silver-eyed devil," she exclaimed. "I hope you told him where to go!"

"Not in so many words, no," Winnie replied quietly. "But I did tell him no."

"Good for you. I can't believe he asked you to do such a thing!"

"Neither can I."

"You poor thing," Keely said. "I know how you feel about him."

"So does he." She sighed. "That's part of the problem. I shouldn't have been so obvious."

"It's not as if you could help it."

"Well, that's true."

"Men are a lot of trouble. Even the best of them."

Winnie leaned back against the counter with her arms folded over her chest. "I really thought he was beginning to like me. He seemed to. Then he came up with this cockeyed plan." She glanced at her friend. "I do understand how he feels. He loved his little girl . . ."

"Little girl?" Keely exclaimed. "He's already married?"

Winnie's eyes were sad. "He was. Someone killed his daughter and his wife. The little girl was just three years old. She drew him a picture. It looked just like the painting I did for him, as a Christmas gift."

Keely went quiet. "You really do have something extra in your brain, Winnie."

"I must." She laughed softly. "It made him furious. That's why he took me to his house that time, to find out why I painted a raven. I didn't even know myself. When he showed me the finger painting, I almost passed out."

"It wasn't the first time you've had odd connections. You knew Kilraven was in danger and sent backup long before he asked for it."

"Eerie, isn't it?"

"Not eerie," Keely said gently. "It's a gift. You probably saved Kilraven's life when you sent another squad car to assist him."

"He gave me strange looks after that."

"I think he's conflicted about how he feels," Keely said. "A man who's gone through a trauma like that has to work through it."

"He's had seven years."

"Yes, but he hasn't really faced it, has he?" Keely asked. "He wants revenge. It's all he lives for. But revenge is a hollow thing."

"He'll find that out."

"Yes, he will." Keely hugged her. "But it doesn't help you, does it?"

Winnie hugged her back. "Not a lot."

"Give him time," Keely advised. "Just be there when he needs someone to talk to. He seems to have told you things that he hasn't shared with anyone else. He really is a loner."

"Yes."

"Why did he want to marry you to go to the Bahamas?" Keely wondered.

"We'd have to stay in the house together. He was worried about his reputation," she added facetiously.

"His?"

Winnie flushed, when she recalled what he'd told her. "Well, his and mine," she amended without elaborating. "He said it wouldn't look right for us to be staying together, alone, when we're not married."

"Talk about a throwback to an earlier generation," Keely exclaimed.

"So says the woman who offered to send my brother packing because she thought he was looking for a good time," Winnie said and grinned.

Keely grimaced. "Touché. I guess Kilraven's like us. He doesn't move with the times. That's not a bad thing. I don't like promiscuous men any more than I like promiscuous women, and I don't care if it's supposed to be acceptable behavior to the whole world."

"Want me to get you a soapbox and a placard?" Winnie mused.

Keely laughed. "I sound like a crusader, don't I? I don't preach to people about my personal beliefs, I don't tell people what I think they should do. But I never was one to go with the crowd. Neither are you."

"We live in a whole community of dinosaurs," Winnie pointed out. "Including Kilraven."

Keely smiled. "He'll come around."

"Do you think so?" she asked miserably. "He didn't even look at me when he let me out at Barbara's. He just drove away."

"He'll think about it and then he'll call you."

"Not a chance in the world."

Keely pursed her lips. "I'll bet you some homemade rolls."

"You can't make homemade bread," Winnie pointed out.

"That's how sure I am that Kilraven will be back," she returned. "Wait and see."

Winnie only smiled. But she didn't believe it.

KILRAVEN WENT TO SEE JON. He was fuming about Winnie's refusal and at a loss as to how to change her mind. Maybe Jon had some ideas.

But Jon didn't. Worse, he kept grinning, as if the whole thing was a joke.

"It's not funny!" Kilraven growled.

Jon glanced at him from his lounging position on his sofa. "Yes, it is."

Kilraven sat down in the easy chair. There was a soccer game on, two European teams slugging it out with feet, heads and shoulders on the huge green field.

"You have to see it from her point of view," Jon said gently. "She's lived a sheltered life. She doesn't really know much about men. If you know her brother, Boone, you've already figured that out. I imagine that protective attitude of his kept a lot of men away from Winnie when she first started dating. Most grown men are afraid to stand up to him. From what you've told me about her, I can guarantee you that Winnie won't even try."

Kilraven sat back in the chair and crossed his long legs. He let out a frustrated sigh. "This is the best chance I'm going to get to see if the senator's wife knows something," he said. "All I want Winnie to do is go down to Nassau with me for a few days."

"No, you want her to move in with you and do what comes naturally for a few days. She isn't buying it. She's the sort of woman who won't settle for anything less than marriage, but a permanent marriage, not a pretend one. She sees right through you. That's what you can't take."

He shrugged. "It's damned inconvenient."

"What is?"

Kilraven looked at the television screen. "She's attractive."

"But you don't want anything permanent."

"That's part of it."

"Is there another part?"

He nodded. "She's twenty-two, Jon."

"Oh. Now I begin to see the light."

"Twenty-two to my thirty-two," he continued. "She's already learned about the generation gap from her parents. Her mother was twelve years younger than her father. She ran off with his younger brother. Winnie saw the dangers."

"Then why is she still interested in you?"

"God knows. I'm an old, worn-out, used-up lobo wolf," he said heavily, staring at his shoes. "She's innocent and unsophisticated." He laughed. "Funny. When I first met her, I had this idea that she was a bored debutante playing a game, pretending to be naive. But it was a far cry from the truth. She's very naive, but she doesn't play games and she's greener than grass. I don't know how she's managed to stay so innocent for so long in the circles she and her family travel in."

"Which brings us back to big brother Boone, who would knock your teeth in for playing around with his baby sister."

Kilraven smiled. "I guess I wouldn't blame him. It was a stupid thing I suggested to her. Still, I'm not taking her to Nassau and staying in the house with her without some legal ceremony. She's a fine young woman. I don't want to mess up her reputation."

"Or your own," Jon mused.

Kilraven shot him a glance. "At least I don't have the police lead women out of my office handcuffed."

He shrugged. "What can I say? She tried to bend me back over my own desk."

He shook his head. "My mother needs therapy."

"I would never have said that," Kilraven replied. He grinned. "But I'm glad you did."

"We should have taught Cammy how to recognize a call girl."

"Too late now." He pursed his lips. "Ms. Perry still giving you hell at the office?"

"Come to think of it, no." Jon frowned. "I can't figure out why. I did praise her for doing such a good job of digging up info on our murder victim. She's been different since then."

"Different, how?"

"You know, I haven't really thought about it," Jon said. "She's stopped sniping at me. She smiles once in a while. Things like that."

"Look out."

He chuckled. "No need. She's not interested in me. She doesn't like men."

"She has a child."

"Strange thing about that. She seems afraid of men, if they come too close physically."

"Where's her husband?"

"He wasn't her husband," Jon replied

somberly. "He went overseas and got killed. Maybe there was some violence in the relationship. But before she got involved with him she didn't date much, either."

"She might have other preferences."

"She might, but she doesn't. She keeps to herself."

"What's the little boy like?"

"Don't know," Jon said. "I've never seen him."

"Don't you have those Bring Your Child to Work days?"

Jon glared at him. "We have an FBI office—we don't encourage employees to use it as a day-care center."

Kilraven held up both hands.

"I don't like children."

Kilraven was giving him an odd look. "Why?"

"I just don't."

"Oh. I remember. The soap thing."

"It was not a soap thing," Jon corrected him. "The kid wrote obscene words all over the passenger side of my car, and I didn't notice until one of my coworkers was rolling in the aisles laughing about it."

"I thought you had to be observant to work for the FBI," Kilraven said innocently.

"Observant? Who looks at the passenger side of his car every morning?" Jon asked belligerently.

"CIA personnel, checking for bombs," Kilraven replied.

"In your case, I'd even be checking the paint for C-4," his brother pointed out. "But nobody ever tried to blow me up."

Kilraven chuckled. "It wasn't much of a bomb." He recalled the incident his brother was alluding to. "The brown envelope he'd shoved it into was torn and you could see the wires sticking out."

"Lucky for you."

"Lucky for him, too. He's only doing five to ten for attempted murder. He could be facing the needle for a capital crime."

"I believe the defense attorney was insinuating that we need a better educated class of criminal and looking straight at you when he said it?"

"So I cost him a couple of gold stars on his defense record as a public defender," Kilraven scoffed. "One of the lowlifes he got off raped a girl one day after he was acquitted. The pissant knew he was guilty—he defended him anyway and got him off. I just made sure the prosecutors knew that the public defender had 'encouraged' a witness not to testify at the first trial. He got a reprimand from the bar association." He glanced at Jon. "Pity we don't still have the rack and public stocks."

"You need to lay off that sixteenth-century Scottish history," Jon advised. "Why don't you read something modern?"

"I do. Combat manuals and books on antiterrorism."

Jon threw up his hands.

BUT JON HAD, AT LEAST, convinced Kilraven that he wasn't going to get anywhere with Winnie if he continued with his present plan. He went back home to his apartment downtown to think about his next move.

It was a nice apartment, roomy and open. He had three bedrooms, one of which he used as an office. It contained all his high-tech equipment, weight-lifting bars and traveling accessories, including a bag that remained packed year-round in case he was sent overseas on a mission with a few minutes' notice. That had happened in the past. It wouldn't anytime soon because he was officially on a leave of absence.

There was a bed in the room, also a

desk where his laptop stayed connected to the Internet—hard-wired and monitored, to make sure he had no hackers on board.

There was a guest bedroom next to his own, with the minimum of amenities. It was just a place to stay, in case some out-of-town agent needed a secure place to bunk down.

His own bedroom was Spartan, just a double bed, because he liked room to turn over, and a chest of drawers and bookcase. The bookcase was almost the size of the bed, and chock-full of historical tomes. In a corner was a big Schmidt-Casssegrain telescope, which he rarely had time to use.

In the living room was a spacious white-leather-covered sofa and matching chair. In front was a fifty-inch TV with the latest technology, a satellite receiver and three complete gaming systems, his favorite of which was the Xbox 360, which he accessed with Xbox Live. He had most of the newer games, but his favorite was *Call of Duty,* followed by the *Halo* series. He had one sword and sorcery game—*Elder Scrolls IV: Oblivion*—and played it for variety.

He plopped down on the sofa and activated the television. He had access, through the Xbox, to all the latest movies on download. He'd just put on the latest *Star Trek* film before he went to see Jon. Now he keyed it up, popped the lid on a wine cooler he'd brought from the fridge, and settled down to watch Kirk, Spock and McCoy begin all over again for a new generation. He grinned as he watched. The original *Star Trek* was his favorite retro TV series.

THE NEXT DAY, HE GOT into his car and drove down to Jacobsville again. He wasn't sure how he was going to convince Winnie to go to Nassau, but he was going to try one last time. He couldn't afford to give up now, when he was so close to finding that one vital clue that would finally solve the tragic murder of his family.

He drove up to her front door. He'd already checked with the EOC center to make sure she wasn't working this morning. Sure enough, when he rang the doorbell, she came herself to answer it.

She looked at him warily. She was dressed in jeans and a red T-shirt that said President of the Jacobsville Dog Chasing and Cursing Society.

He read the T-shirt and burst out laughing.

She hadn't realized what she was wearing because she was still drinking her first cup of coffee of the day, so the laughter surprised her. Then she looked down and recalled the legend on the shirt, and she laughed, too, breaking the ice.

"Where the hell did you get a shirt like that?" he asked.

"Had it made," she said simply. "It was after one really bad day, when I got yelled at by three different callers for not sending an officer to deal with a stray dog." She smiled. "It was the day the branch bank was robbed and we had every officer dealing with it. Not a lot of time to go looking for a stray dog."

"Especially a giant German Shepherd Chihuahua that was gray, black, off-white and had three legs, they thought," Kilraven quoted the report.

"That's the one." She shook her head. "You wonder why eyewitness testimony is supposed to be so valuable when you get calls like that."

"Exactly."

She opened the door. "Come on in. But

if you came to try and convince me to go with you on a trip, Boone's in the living room." It was a threat.

"I didn't. I need to talk to him, though."

Surprised, she waved him through to the next room.

Boone was watching the news. He looked up when Kilraven walked in. He pursed his lips and turned off the television. "I know why you're here," he told him. "And the answer's no."

Kilraven dropped into an armchair across from him. "She's over twenty-one," he pointed out. "Old enough to decide for herself."

Boone leaned forward. He looked formidable. "You want someone to help you open a can of worms. This is a big can, and it might contain pit vipers instead of worms. Just by asking her to go with you, you could be putting her life in danger."

Kilraven's face was impassive. "I know your background. I think you should know mine. I've spent the past few years as a special operative. They send me in when the situation is considered too dangerous for unskilled personnel. I'm trained in every method of combat known to man, and a few I made up as I went along. I've had four partners, one of whom I saved three times from certain death. I can defuse a bomb, build one, disarm an armed man, blow up a bridge and recruit men to work for me in some countries that are barely on the map. I'm also a skilled negotiator. I'm trained in weaponry, martial arts and my specialty is innovation. There isn't a man alive your sister would be safer with. Possibly, not even you. And if you think I'd permit anyone to harm her, despite my own interest in solving this case, you are grossly mistaken."

He sat back and waited for Boone to take that in and reply.

Boone was surprised at the admissions. He knew very little about Kilraven, except that he worked undercover for some federal agency. Now he knew more. He respected the man for laying it on the line. But he was still uneasy about letting Winnie become involved in this.

While he was debating his next sentence, Winnie came walking in with two mugs of coffee. She handed one to Kilraven and sat down beside her brother.

"You can decide whatever you like," she

told her brother without actually meeting his eyes, and her hands shook. "But I'm going with him."

Kilraven and her brother wore the same perplexed expression.

"It's dangerous," Boone said gently.

Her hands became steadier. She'd been bluffing, but it seemed to have worked. Boone wasn't trying to dominate her, as he had most of her life. She was scared to death of him, but she kept seeing Kilraven's eyes when he spoke of his little girl who had been killed. That look, more than any of his words, had changed her mind. She'd been waiting, hoping, that he'd ask her again. Keely had been right. Kilraven had come back.

"Life is dangerous," Winnie said. "I do know Senator Sanders's wife, and she won't think it strange if I show up in our beach house. Even with a husband." The word made her color slightly. She'd dreamed, hoped, wished that someday Kilraven might want to marry her. She'd never expected that it would be a sham marriage. But even a few days was more than she might have expected in the normal run of things. She had to take the chance that he might like her enough to keep her.

Boone glanced at Kilraven, who was watching her with an impassive face. His silver eyes, however, were glittery with feeling. He could feel the man's anguish. Cash Grier had told him quite a bit more about the case than Winnie knew. He didn't have the heart to interfere, even if his gut instinct was to do just that. Anyway, if there was a threat, he knew how to deal with it. So did Kilraven. It wasn't right to let the men who'd killed a child walk.

"Keely and I can stand up with you, if you need witnesses," he said finally.

Winnie smiled at him. "Thanks. But first, he and I need to discuss the parameters of our new relationship," she told Kilraven bluntly.

He grinned. "Okay. We'll drive up to San Antonio and I'll show you how to get past the Hunters in *Halo: ODST.*"

"Nobody can get past those damned Hunters," Boone scoffed.

"I can," Kilraven said, grinning.

"You'd better teach me," Boone told Winnie, smiling.

She laughed. "That's a deal. I'll just get my coat." She couldn't believe it. For the first time in her adult life, she'd told Boone what she was going to do. She'd actually gotten away with it. Maybe all it took was enough courage to say no. Even if your knees knocked together and your teeth chattered while you said it!

8

Winnie and Kilraven were almost to San Antonio when he got a call on his cell phone. He activated the phone from the steering wheel, putting it on the speakerphone.

"Kilraven," he said.

"Marquez," came the reply. "Thought you might like to know that it's open season on detectives investigating your case."

"Somebody else got mugged?" Kilraven asked.

"Shot," Marquez said flatly. "My partner. They just took her to the Marshall Medical Center. I'm on my way there right now."

"I'll be right behind you." He shut off the

phone and glanced at Winnie. "Sorry, but this concerns me. She's a friend of mine."

"Let's go!" she said, waving him on.

He floor-boarded the gas pedal.

FORTUNATELY, HE DIDN'T have to stop and explain why he was breaking speed limits. He arrived at the hospital and parked as close to the emergency room as he could get. He and Winnie ran for the entrance.

Marquez was waiting in the hall, looking morose. He looked up when they entered.

"Any news?" Kilraven asked.

Marquez shook his head. "All they could tell me was that it didn't look lethal," he said. He shrugged. "Like you can tell. I've seen so-called flesh wounds take a man out."

"So have I," Kilraven said quietly.

Marquez glanced at Winnie. "Hi."

"Hi," she returned.

"Do you know her?" Kilraven asked. When Marquez frowned, he said, "This is Winnie Sinclair."

"Oh!" Marquez exclaimed. "You work at the EOC center," he added, just when she thought he was going to come out with something about her family and its wealth.

Pleasantly surprised, she grinned. "That's me. I work with Shirley. And I have lunch at your mother's café most days. She's a great cook."

"She is." He started to add something, but the doctor came toward him, still in his surgical greens.

Marquez stepped forward. "Well?"

The doctor grinned. "She's a tough one," he said. "We got the bullet out. She came to and looked at me and said, 'You get me patched up quick, I'm going after the blankety-blank fool who did this to me!'"

Marquez chuckled. "That sounds just like her. She'll be okay?"

He nodded. "A few days in the hospital— she won't like that, either—and she'll be on sick leave for another couple of weeks." He cocked his head at Marquez. "Any chance the two of you could give up ticking off criminals in my city? I could use some rest!"

"Complaints, complaints, when we give you the opportunity to practice your craft and perfect it," Marquez taunted.

The physician chuckled. "So you do."

"When can I see her?"

"In about an hour. They'll wheel her down

to a room. She breezed through the surgery." He shook his head. "Wish all my patients did half that well."

He walked away.

"We'll wait with you," Kilraven told him, glancing at Winnie to make sure she agreed, which she did. "I feel responsible."

"What for? It was my idea, and hers, to reopen the case. You were the holdout," Marquez reminded him.

Kilraven still felt guilty. She was a good woman. A good investigator. She'd been helping him. He hadn't realized what she was risking until now. And he wanted to put Winnie in the line of fire. What if she got shot? What if the perp had a better aim next time? He felt sick to his stomach.

A noise behind them heralded the entrance of two uniformed officers and another plainclothes detective, who went straight to Marquez to find out the patient's condition. They relaxed when told that she was out of surgery and had a good prognosis.

"That's like Rogers," one of the policemen chuckled. "She's tough as army leather!"

"You ought to know," Marquez joked back, "she was your training officer before she was bumped up to homicide."

"Bumped up, the devil," the plainclothes detective muttered. "You patrol guys get to take coffee breaks and sleep all night. We get dragged out of bed every time they find a body, even if we're not on duty."

"Always on call, that's us." Marquez chuckled.

The detective glanced at Kilraven and frowned. "Don't I know you?"

"Ought to," Kilraven said, stepping forward with his hand out. "You trained me back when I worked for SAPD."

"Kilraven? Damn, you've got old!" the man joked.

"Fine wine ages," Kilraven said haughtily, "it doesn't get old."

"What are you doing up here? You know Rogers?"

Winnie listened idly, not participating in the conversation. Her mother's maiden name was Rogers. What a strange coincidence. But it was a common enough name. Anyway, she was sure it wouldn't be a relation of hers. Her mother had no relatives in Texas. They were all in Montana, and only cousins.

"Marquez called me on his way to the hospital. Rogers has been working my cold case with him," Kilraven said. "Stubborn woman. Knowing what happened to Marquez here just made her dig her heels in harder. She's a good detective."

The detective sobered at once. "Damned shame about that case. I wasn't on homicide then, I was just a patrol officer, like you. But at least one detective quit the force because he couldn't continue on the case. He said it broke his heart."

"It broke mine, too," Kilraven said heavily.

The detective clapped him on the shoulder. "Even the coldest cases get solved. You wait. When Rogers gets out of here, she'll turn San Antonio red looking for clues. They'll wish they'd sent a better shot."

"They won't get a second chance at her, or me," Marquez said solemnly. "I promise you."

"He's good at his job," the suited man told Kilraven, "but he chases crooks in the nude." He shook his head as Marquez started to protest. "Brings down the tone of the whole department."

"The perp stole my laptop right out of my own apartment!" Marquez protested. "What was I supposed to do, get dressed before I started chasing him?"

"You could have called for backup, Marquez," came the droll reply.

"I could have, if I hadn't left my cell phone in my car!"

"See?" the detective told Kilraven. "Back in our day, we'd have called on a landline. I don't guess you've got one of those, do you, boy?" he asked Marquez blithely.

Marquez glared at him. "Who needs a landline? It's like carrying a telephone booth around!"

"You need a landline to save L.E.O.'s butts," Winnie piped in when the local law looked her way, surprised. She was using the term for law enforcement officers. "I work at our county's emergency operations center. I'm a 911 dispatcher."

"Nice work, Kilraven," the plainclothes detective said admiringly as he grinned at Winnie. "If you need saving, here she is."

Kilraven chuckled. "She did save me," he said. "Sent backup before I asked for it, and spared me a face full of buckshot from a drunken perp."

"Good woman," the detective said, nodding.

"Oh, he's worth the effort," Winnie joked,

smiling at Kilraven. "We hate losing him down in Jacobsville."

"Losing him?" the detective asked, surprised. "You working small towns these days?"

Kilraven shook his head. "I was involved in some undercover work, breaking up a kidnapping ring."

"I heard about that. General Machado was up to his ears in it, wasn't he?" Marquez asked.

Kilraven chuckled. "He was. Last we heard he took the ransom he got for Jason Pendleton and went back to South America to retake his country."

"More power to him," the detective said somberly. "There are some barbarians heading up the junta who ousted him. My niece married a professor from over there. He's one of the people Machado's opposition put in prison. She's hoping she can generate enough publicity to make them turn him loose, but no luck so far."

"How about some coffee?" Marquez asked. "I had to get out at 4:00 a.m. to investigate an attempted murder in the south side apartments. I'm about to go to sleep standing here."

"What's unusual about that?" the detective asked with a grin. He held up both hands. "Okay, I'll stop. In fact, I'll buy you a coffee, Marquez."

"No, Hicks, I'll buy you one," Marquez said, moving toward the canteen. "That way, it goes on my expense account!"

Kilraven led Winnie along, her small hand tucked into his big one, down the hall to the canteen. She was in her element among uniforms. The feel of his fingers linking into hers made her heart race. She looked up into warm silver eyes that smiled at her. She felt closer to him than she ever had.

IT WAS ALMOST TWO hours later when Marquez went to check on Detective Rogers and came back to announce that she was in a room and complaining about the doctor's assessment of her condition.

"We'd better get up there before she breaks out a window and tries to leave." Marquez chuckled.

"Will they let us all in?" Kilraven asked.

"Sure they will," Hicks drawled. "One of us can divert the nurses at the duty station while the rest of us sneak into Rogers's room."

"I have a better idea," Kilraven mused. "I'll flash my badge and tell them it's federal business."

"Just like a Fed, isn't it?" Hicks asked. "They always want to steal the show."

"Okay, flash your badge and tell them it's police business and see how far you get," Kilraven dared.

Hicks chuckled as they filed into the elevator. "The way my luck's been running, I'd get arrested for impersonating a detective. We'll do it your way."

Kilraven could lie with a straight face and sound very sincere, Winnie thought with admiration. He got them past the nurses, although Winnie got odd looks from the staff as she followed behind the men.

She was curious about this detective, who was so brave and dogged about Kilraven's case that she was willing to risk her life to solve it. Her own life hadn't been overfull of women as role models, but this one sounded interesting. She was keen to meet her.

"There you are, all dolled up and looking pretty," Hicks told the woman in the bed.

"There you are, looking like a vulture dressed up in a suit," came the sarcastic reply. "Will you get me the hell out of here? I want to find the SOB who shot me!"

Winnie was behind the tall men and couldn't see the woman, but she was surprised at how familiar her voice sounded.

Then she moved around Kilraven and got the shock of her life. There, in the bed, bandaged and bruised and indignant, was her mother!

Detective Rogers didn't see Winnie, and she was furious that a little flesh wound was keeping her off the job.

"He says I can't come back to work until he certifies me fit for duty!" she raged, alluding to the doctor. "Meanwhile, that slimy lowlife who shot me is all over San Antonio bragging about it to his lowlife friends!"

"I was in the same boat and you weren't overflowing with sympathy for me," Marquez pointed out.

"You got manhandled, Marquez. I got shot!" she flung back. She took a deep breath and ran a hand through her unkempt hair. "I can't stay in here! I have to get home . . ."

"You get right back in that bed," Marquez said with authority, and moved closer to force her if he had to. "You're probably still in shock. You're certainly foggy from the anesthetic."

"He's home by himself," she said miserably. "The sitter will have to go to work. Good Lord, what time is it?"

"Eight," Marquez said.

"She'll leave in half an hour. He can't stay by himself!"

"Who can't?" Kilraven asked, moving forward, curious. "Your boyfriend?"

"My son," she said heavily. "Matt."

Her son? Winnie felt her head spinning. Her mother was a police detective and she had a son. Her uncle's son. None of the family had known. She recalled the passenger in her mother's car at the house, a short man. It had been the boy!

She moved into view. Her mother glanced at her and glowered. "Great. Just what I need to make this day perfect."

Winnie didn't know what to say. She was shocked speechless.

Kilraven didn't connect the odd phrase with Winnie, so he ignored it. "I'll go by your apartment and arrange for someone to stay with him," Kilraven said, still unaware who Rogers was or Winnie's connection to her. "You just get well."

Rogers studied Winnie's pale face. "Why are you here?"

"I'm with him," Winnie said in a small voice, indicating Kilraven.

"Yes. We're getting married," Kilraven told her, curious at Rogers's response to his blond companion.

Rogers's eyes widened. "You're marrying him?" she exclaimed. "Are you out of your mind?"

"Thanks a hell of a lot," Kilraven growled.

"You're not in any shape to be marrying anybody, least of all my daughter!" Rogers muttered.

Kilraven went very still. "Your daughter?" He glanced at Winnie. Slowly, he added up the similarity and odd bits of information. "Your daughter."

"Yes. I left her father twelve years ago."

"And married my uncle," Winnie said coldly.

"Briefly," Rogers replied with faint humor. "I divorced him six days later."

Winnie gaped at her.

Rogers shrugged. "He was so strung out on coke, he didn't know his name."

"Right up until the end," Kilraven agreed. "But I'm still not sure he wasn't helped into

the next world. He might have known something, too."

"Indeed. But that has to be looked into
before we'll know for sure." Rogers regained
her composure. "There's a Hispanic woman,
Señora Del Rio, who lives two doors down
from my apartment. She's Juana's grandmother. Juana's sitting with Matt today." She
gave him the address. "Ask her if she'll keep
Matt until I get out of here, and I'll make it
right with her. Juana's got six kids," she
added with a wan smile, "and they love Matt.
He lets them play games on his old Nin-
tendo. But she can't keep him at night. She
works. The kids stay with her aunt."

Games. Kilraven's eyes lit up. "I'll find
her. You stop worrying."

Rogers lay back on the pillows and grimaced. "I hate bullets."

"So do I," Kilraven said heavily. "I remember how much they hurt. Don't you do
something stupid, like trying to escape from
here. We'll just hunt you down and bring
you back."

She made a face at him. "Okay."

"Can I talk to you for a minute?" Marquez asked Kilraven.

"Sure."

The uniformed officers said their good-byes and filed out while Marquez and Kilraven were in the hall. Winnie moved closer to the bed to stare at her mother.

"You didn't say what you did for a living," she told her mother.

Rogers stared at her without smiling. She looked terrible, washed-out and pale and in pain. "You didn't need to know."

"You have a son," she began hesitantly. "Dad never told us . . ."

Rogers stared at her with icy brown eyes, the same shade as Winnie's. "My life is none of your business. I made a mistake and paid for it. I'm still paying for it. You don't need to stick around to rub it in. You made your opinion perfectly clear the last time I saw you."

Winnie hesitated. She'd been so sure of herself, of her righteous indignation. Now she felt oddly in the wrong.

"Do you need anything from your apartment?" Winnie asked politely.

"If I do, I'll ask one of the officers to get it for me."

It was a cold rebuff, but Winnie was too

shocked to take offense. She was reeling from the revelations of the night.

Kilraven walked back in. "We'll get on the road. Need anything?"

Rogers shook her head. "Just to get out of here. I guess you don't take bribes?"

He raised an eyebrow. "What would you bribe me with?"

"I'm broke until payday, so you'll have to do it for affection," Rogers laughed. "Tell Matt to get me a couple pairs of pajamas, my robe and my slippers. I'll ask one of the boys to pick them up tomorrow."

"I'll bring them back tonight," Kilraven told her firmly. "But you owe me."

She made another face.

Kilraven caught Winnie's hand. "I'll be back later," he told the detective.

"They won't let you in," Rogers told him.

"I'm a Fed. They'll let me in."

"Snob," Rogers murmured, but the aftereffects of the anesthetic were catching up with her. She closed her eyes and nodded off. Winnie was still reeling from the news that she had a half brother that neither she nor her brothers knew about, and that her mother was in law enforcement. It was a shock.

THEY WERE HALFWAY TO the apartment before Kilraven spoke. "You never told me she was your mother."

"I didn't make the connection," she said. "The last we heard, she was living with my uncle in Montana. Then she showed up at the house with the jewelry. I was horrible to her," she said quietly. "I didn't mean to be. I thought she came to see us to get money." She shook her head. "And she's a cop. I can't believe it."

"She's a detective," he corrected. "A damned good one, too."

She wasn't handling this well. She wasn't ready to have a new member of her family, and she hated being put in the position of having to deal with a child.

"I wonder how old he is?" she said aloud.

"Who?"

"My mother's son."

He glanced at her with narrow silver eyes. "Your brother," he corrected. "Jon and I don't share a mother, but that doesn't make us less related."

Her jaw tautened. "Yes, well, you've had your whole life to get used to having him around. I only found out about mine a few minutes ago."

He sighed. "Point taken. I guess it was a shock."

She shook her head. "Dad never said a word! He must have known, especially if she's been living in San Antonio all this time!"

"Maybe it was too much for his pride to admit that his brother had a child with his ex-wife," Kilraven ventured.

"Her son was with her at the house," she said dully. "We saw someone in the car with her, but he didn't come in."

"She came to see me later that same day, I guess. I saw him, too, but I didn't make the connection that he was her child. I knew she'd been married and that she'd had some personal problems. Marquez didn't elaborate." He glanced at her. "I don't suppose he connected her with your family, either. Certainly, she never told us that she was related to anyone in Jacobsville."

Almost, she thought, as if her mother was ashamed to admit it. Perhaps she was. She'd said that she made a mistake that she was still paying for. Winnie had only thought of her own ordeal because of her mother's desertion, and Boone's and Clark's. It had never occurred to her that her mother wasn't happy, or that she might have divorced her new husband so quickly.

"How strongly was my uncle connected to your case?" she wondered aloud, remembering their talk about her uncle.

"I don't know. The thermos is a strong indication that he might be," Kilraven told her. "I just can't be certain how he would have fit into this, unless he had some connection with Hank Sanders, the senator's criminal brother." He glanced her way. "Given your uncle's apparent drug use, Hank might have been his supplier. Or he might have done odd jobs for Sanders. I don't know yet."

"It's a sick feeling, to think that a member of my family might be responsible for someone's death."

"Winnie, it doesn't mean that you're in any way responsible for it," he said gently. "Don't think like that."

She bit her lower lip. "Sorry. I'm just nervous." She watched cars whiz by in the other lane. Neon signs flashed past as they drove. "Her son is going to be scared to death when he finds out what happened to his mother."

"Obviously."

"But she'll have to stay in the hospital for several days, won't she? What if the woman can't take care of him?"

"Let's cross bridges when we get to them, okay?" He turned a corner. "If she's not available, I'll find someone who is. He can't be left alone."

"No. Of course he can't."

KILRAVEN DROVE SLOWLY down the street, looking for the apartment number Rogers had given him. He stopped in front of a unit and cut off the engine.

It wasn't a good neighborhood. The apartments needed a paint job. The number signs on them were faded. It looked as if the shingles hadn't been replaced in recent memory. The street sign nearby had gang graffiti.

Winnie was taking all that in, thinking what a comedown it must have been for a woman who lived with a millionaire to find herself here, in this type of neighborhood.

"Let's go in," Kilraven said, opening his door.

They walked up on the concrete front porch, what little there was of it, and knocked on the door.

"¿Quién es?"

"Somos amigos de la señora que vive aquí," Kilraven replied in his elegant Spanish.

The door was opened, just a crack, by a dark-haired young Hispanic woman. Her black eyes surveyed the two people outside. She must have decided that they looked trustworthy, because she undid the chain latch and opened the door.

There were three children gathered around a small color television set, playing an old Xbox game. Two were Hispanic. The third had thick, dark brown hair and brown eyes, and an olive complexion. He was wearing jeans and a faded black T-shirt. He looked up.

"Hello," he greeted them, curious. "Did you come to see my mom? She's not home yet. Juana and her kids were staying with me, but she has to go to work soon."

Winnie was shocked at the boy's appearance. Her uncle had been almost blond, like her mother. The boy was the spitting image of Boone and Clark.

"Are you Matt?" Kilraven asked.

The boy seemed to sense something. He put the controller down and lifted his chin. "It's my mother, isn't it? Something's happened to her." He waited, stiff-lipped, for the reply.

"She's been shot, but she's all right," Kilraven said quickly.

"Shot?" The boy seemed to crumple for a minute, but then he rallied. He took a deep breath, as if to steady himself. "Shot. But she won't die?" he added quickly, hopefully.

Kilraven smiled. "Not a chance. She's one tough bird."

Matt caught his breath. He smiled back, hesitantly. He had perfect white teeth. That smile changed his whole look. "Okay." He glanced at the little woman next to him. "Juana has to go. She's already late for work and she has to take her kids to her aunt's house. It's all right," he told the little woman. "I can stay by myself. I'm twelve."

"You cannot," Juana argued.

"His mother said that a Señora del Rio who lives a couple of doors down might be able to stay with Matt," Kilraven began.

"But, no," Juana said at once. "That is

my *abuela,* my grandmother. She went to see her sister this morning! Her sister is in Juarez!"

"I told you, I don't need babysitting," Matt argued. "I've stayed by myself after school, until Mom got home. I know not to answer the door unless I know who it is."

"You cannot be alone," Juana argued. "You are not able . . ."

"I am so!" Matt flashed back. "I'm perfectly all right!"

Juana looked at the newcomers with anguish.

"Everybody makes such a fuss," Matt muttered. He shifted on the sofa, dragging himself toward the arm.

That was when Winnie noticed the wheelchair. Matt pulled it toward him, placed it within reach and propelled his small body into it with efficiency. "I can do everything except walk," he muttered. "I can even cook. And there's a phone. I can call for help if I need to."

Winnie felt her pride drop to her ankles. The boy was proud, and he didn't like being thought of as handicapped. But he certainly couldn't stay by himself.

"I must go," Juana said. "I'm so sorry."

"We'll take care of Matt," Kilraven said easily. He smiled. "I'm sure his mother is grateful that you stayed so long."

"It was nothing. She sat with me when my husband was in the hospital. Here, in this neighborhood, we look out for each other. Tell her I pray for her, okay?"

"I'll do that," Kilraven said.

She and her children left, but not before Juana bent to hug Matt and assure him that his mother would be all right.

The door closed behind her.

"Who are you?" Matt asked his guests. "Law enforcement?"

"I am," Kilraven said. "She's a 911 dispatcher." He indicated Winnie.

"I'm going to be a detective when I grow up," Matt assured the tall man. "There's nothing I can't do, if I want to. Mom taught me that. She's really going to be all right?"

"Honest," Kilraven said. He glanced at the game console. "That's an old one."

"Yeah," Matt said, grinning, "but it still works pretty good. Mostly I play the original *Halo* and it's great for that one."

"You play online?"

Matt shook his head. "Can't afford that," he said easily. "Do you play?"

Kilraven grinned. "Everything," he said. "I've got three game systems and about three dozen gaming discs."

"Wow," Matt said. "It must be nice," he added with a wistful smile. He moved the wheelchair away from the sofa. "I had a nice motorized one that Mom bought for me last Christmas," he said, "but Dad came by and said he needed to borrow it for a friend of his. He just sold it to buy drugs," he added. "Was Mom furious! But she couldn't get him to replace it, so she borrowed this one from a neighbor whose father had used it before he died."

Winnie felt sicker by the minute. "Your father took the wheelchair away?" she asked, shocked.

"Yeah. He was always coming by and taking things, usually he didn't even ask. He sold anything he could get to buy drugs with." He shook his head. "I'm never using drugs. I don't ever want to end up like him."

"How did that happen?" Kilraven asked the boy, indicating his legs.

"Dad had this idea that he'd wreck the car so he could get insurance money," he replied. "He ran out in front of a semi and it hit on my side of the car. Mom said he had a big insurance policy on me and he meant to kill me." He avoided looking at them. "He didn't get a dime. Mom tried to have him arrested, but they wouldn't take my word for what he did."

Winnie was hearing her mother talk about paying for her past and now it made terrible sense. She couldn't believe her uncle would treat a child like that. But people on drugs weren't especially reasonable.

"You look like my mom," Matt said suddenly, staring at Winnie.

"I guess I should," Winnie said, smiling despite the lump in her throat. "I'm your sister."

9

Matt studied her with open curiosity. "We went to see you down in Jacobsville," he recalled. "Mom said I might get to meet you, but when she came back out, she was all quiet. She said it wasn't a good time."

Winnie could have gone through the floor. While she'd been shouting at her mother and cursing her for the past, this young, disabled boy had been hoping to meet his family. Nobody knew anything about him. She and her brothers hadn't even known that he existed. She felt her sins line up and laugh at her. She'd never felt quite so low.

"It wasn't a good time," Winnie said, swallowing her regret.

He cocked his head as he looked up at her. "Mom said I had brothers."

"You do.Two of them." Winnie pulled out her cell phone. "I think it's time you met them, too." She started punching in numbers.

WHILE THEY WAITED FOR BOONE, Keely and Clark to show up, Kilraven sat down with Matt and played one of the games with him. Matt had a spare controller, a present from one of his mother's coworkers.

"Hey, you're pretty good." Matt laughed when Kilraven fought him to a draw.

"Sometimes my job takes me to places where there isn't much in the way of entertainment."

"What do you do?"

Kilraven grinned. "Sorry. Classified."

Matt was impressed. "Can you tell me who you work for?"

"Sure. CIA."

"Wow! You're a spy!"

"Not really," Kilraven said easily. "I do all sorts of covert jobs. Last one was trying to break a kidnapping ring."

"Did you have to shoot anybody?"

"I don't shoot people," Kilraven assured him.

"Then why do you carry a gun?" came the wry reply, because the holster of a small automatic handgun was visible under Kilraven's jacket when he used the controller.

"So people won't shoot me," the tall man replied with a grin.

Matt laughed and they went back to another round of the game.

Winnie watched, sitting on the wreck of a sofa. The whole place was no-frills. The pictures on the walls were cheap, like all the furnishings. The only expensive thing in the room was that used game console and games for it. Her mother's priorities were obvious—Matt came first. It touched her and made her feel very guilty that she had anything she wanted while her half brother and her mother were living almost at subsistence level on a police detective's salary. It was a good-paying job, she knew from talking to Marquez; but anyone with a handicapped child had more expenses than parents of healthy kids.

The knock at the door was surprising. Boone must have flown up from Jacobsville.

She went to open the door. She grinned at Boone. "What did you do, put a jet under that Jaguar?" she asked.

He chuckled. "Just about. I noticed Kilraven's car out front, too." He paused. "Where is the boy?"

She opened the door. Matt stopped playing in midjump and turned to look at his visitors with wide, surprised eyes.

"You look like me," he said when Boone moved into the room, dark haired and dark eyed, very imposing in his boots and white Stetson.

"I do," Boone said, surprised. He moved closer, his eyes on the wheelchair.

"Don't let the wheels fool you," Matt said easily, when he perceived the big man's reaction to the wheelchair. "I'm faster than you are."

"You like video games, huh?" Clark asked, moving forward. He smiled at Matt. "We haven't introduced ourselves. I'm Clark. That's Boone," he indicated the tall man. "That's Boone's wife, Keely." He introduced the smaller woman who was hugging Winnie. "We're Sinclairs."

"I guess I'm your brother," Matt said hesitantly.

"I guess you are," Boone replied. His glance around the room took in everything Winnie had already learned about their half brother.

"Why didn't you know about me?" Matt asked reasonably.

"Because we weren't on speaking terms with your mother," Winnie said for all of them. "Something I'm really sorry about now, Matt. We made assumptions."

"Yeah, because she ran off with your uncle," Matt replied, grimacing. "She said it was the stupidest thing she ever did. She knew what he was the day they got married, when he started shooting up on their honeymoon. She left him. Then your father came to see her, later, but I was on the way and he thought I was Dad's child."

The three older Sinclairs went very still.

"What do you mean?" Winnie asked for them.

"Well, see, she never slept with Dad," Matt said in a very grown-up way. "She said he was so repulsive to her that she couldn't let him touch her."

Which meant, obviously, that Matt was their father's child. Their true brother.

"Oh, boy," Clark said heavily. He was

thinking, they all were, that their mother had gone through years of hell with a child alone, trying to support them, because of a mistaken belief.

"Here it comes," Matt told Kilraven with some sarcasm. "Now we'll get the hugs and the gushing about how I look like my real father and everybody will feel guilty. Give me a break!"

Boone burst out laughing. "Okay. Now I know he's a Sinclair."

Matt lifted an eyebrow. "Well, you don't look like the gushing type," he told Boone.

"He's not," Clark assured him. "He was in Special Forces in the army."

"Wow," Matt said admiringly. He glanced at Kilraven. "Does that mean he's better at hand-to-hand than you are?"

Kilraven gave Boone an apologetic grin. "No. I was part of a SWAT team at SAPD before I became a Fed. I'm also a master trainer in hand-to-hand combat."

"SWAT? Really? I watch these shows on TV about SWAT teams all over the country. They're real brave," Matt said. He sighed. "I wish I could do stuff like that when I grow up, but I guess I'll be a desk guy. Anyway, I'm going to be in law enforcement, like my mom. Except I hope I don't get shot, like she did."

"Your mom got shot?" Boone asked, shocked.

Then Winnie realized that she hadn't said much when she told them about Matt and that they should come up to San Antonio on the double.

"Yes, but not lethally," she said quickly. "His mother—our mother," she corrected, "is a sergeant of detectives with SAPD," she said. "She works homicide. She was shot in the line of duty. She's in the hospital, but she's going to be okay."

Boone was surprised, as were the others.

"She's good, too," Matt said. "Sometimes she gets these hunches, feelings, about cases, and she can solve them when other detectives can't. They say she's spooky."

Winnie flushed because she had the same kind of hunches, and now she knew where the gift came from.

"Do you get them. . .feelings?" Boone asked him.

"Sometimes," Matt said. "I knew something was wrong tonight, but I didn't know what."

"He's going to be here alone," Winnie

said. "Someone who doesn't want that cold case reopened—" she didn't name it in front of Matt "—is assaulting people on the case. Marquez got beaten up, our mother got shot. She'll be okay, but she's going to be in the hospital for a few days. Matt needs someplace to stay."

"He can come to the ranch," Boone said, glancing at Matt. "We've got plenty of horses. You can go riding with me."

"I can't ride," Matt exclaimed. "I mean, look at me!"

Boone smiled. "We have handicapped kids out riding one day a week. It's therapy for them. We have the means to put you on and keep you on, safely, and the horses are very tame. Not that you'd go out unsupervised."

Matt rolled his wheelchair closer to Boone. "I would really like that," he said quietly. "I've never even seen a horse close up. Do you have cattle, too?"

"Sure do."

"I wouldn't be in the way?"

"Not at all," Keely assured him with a smile.

"You can play video games with me,"

Clark said. "I've got all the *Halo* series, including *Halo: ODST* . . ."

"The new *Halo?*" Matt exclaimed, all eyes. "Oh, I read about it in some of the gaming magazines Mom brought from the office after the guys finished with them. I'd love to play the new ones, but this won't play anything much except the old games. I don't mind," he said quickly, defending his mother. "Mom does her best for us."

The Sinclairs exchanged guilty glances.

"Yes, she does," Winnie said. "She's very brave, Matt. They had to force her back into the bed." She chuckled. "She was trying to climb out and go after whoever shot her."

Matt laughed. "Yeah. She's like that. Some guy down the street tried to take our new push lawnmower off the front porch last summer and Mom saw him. She chased him down, jumped a hedge to get to him quicker, threw him down, cuffed him and called for backup to take him down to booking." He laughed. "She's my role model. Not that I want to be a woman when I grow up," he was quick to add, and they all laughed.

"Let's get you packed, if you're coming with us," Keely said.

"Okay!" Matt said with enthusiasm. He wheeled into his bedroom, leaving her to follow.

The Sinclairs moved into a group, all morose-looking. "I wish I'd known any of this twelve years ago," Winnie said heavily.

"You aren't the only one," Boone agreed.

"We've been willfully blind." Clark sighed.

Kilraven joined them. "He's a great kid," he said. "I wish I'd realized the connection before this, but Rogers never spoke about her family. We only knew that she'd had a lot of personal problems. Her ex-husband hounded her, you see," he added, "always trying to get things from her to buy drugs with. He carried off Matt's new motorized wheelchair and sold it."

"What a bum," Winnie said angrily.

"We'll get Matt a new one," Boone said. "No problem."

"We can get him an Xbox 360, too, and some games for it," Kilraven said. He glanced at the tiny television. "And a bigger TV to play them on."

"Maybe an Xbox Live gold card, too," Clark suggested.

Kilraven was thoughtful. "He can stay with Winnie and me for a few days, after we're married," he said. "I have a three-bedroom apartment. We won't be able to go down to Nassau for a couple of weeks. The senator's wife had a change of heart and went to visit her sister in New York, but she's supposed to be going to the Bahamas week after next."

"You spies know everything," Clark said.

Kilraven grinned. "Of course we do."

Winnie moved closer to him. "We could wait to get married. . . ."

"No, we couldn't," Kilraven said firmly, looking down at her.

She averted her eyes, but the reply pleased her. Maybe he was getting used to the idea, and just maybe he wouldn't want a divorce at the end of the pretense.

MATT WAS BUNDLED INTO Boone's big Jaguar, along with a ratty suitcase full of things he thought he'd need, and the apartment door was locked.

"We'll bring you up to the hospital tomorrow to see your mother," Boone assured Matt. "I want to see her, too."

The others voiced their assent.

"I'll bring Winnie home in a little while," Kilraven told them. "We still have things to talk about."

"We'll leave a light on," Keely said with a smile.

They waved the Sinclairs off and got back into Kilraven's own Jaguar.

"This has been a very strange night," Winnie said heavily. "I have a brother I didn't know about, and a mother who's a well-known police detective. I feel as if my life just turned on its axis."

"I can understand that." He moved out into traffic. "He's quite a boy," he said, smiling.

"Yes, he is. It's amazing, how easily he speaks of his handicap."

"It's only a handicap if he makes one of it. I had a friend in Iraq who had lost both his legs to a rocket attack. He was fitted with artificial ones and he wins races now. He said that as long as he still had his life, he wasn't bothered by trifles. Trifles!" He laughed. "Can you imagine?"

"Soldiers are tough," Winnie said. "Boone came out of the service with wounds much worse than he ever told us about. Keely said some of them were bone deep. He never said anything, and we never knew."

"We all have scars of one sort or another."

She glanced at him. "You said you'd had bullets dug out of you."

"I have." His tone was grim. "One out of my lung, another out of my hip and one out of my arm. When I'm older, I'll probably have some arthritis because of the way the bullet went in. They did repairs, but no repair is as good as the original part."

"Battle scars," she said quietly.

"Yes."

Her eyes narrowed. She looked at him evenly. "You wanted the most dangerous assignments you could find," she said aloud, speaking as if she were accessing information from some intangible source. "You asked for them. One took you right into an enemy encampment and you walked straight at a man firing a machine gun. . .!" She broke off because he slammed on the brakes. Thank goodness they weren't in traffic.

"Who told you?" he asked curtly. "Who?"

She was disconcerted. "Nobody," she said at once.

His eyes narrowed. He wasn't buying it.

"I don't know anyone who was with you overseas, Kilraven," she said reasonably.

"Then how did you know that?"

She grimaced and looked away. "I don't know."

He was remembering what they said about her mother's intuition, and then came the memory of Winnie painting the raven and sending backup when he was in great danger in Jacobsville.

"You have the same ability your mother does," he said aloud.

She grimaced. "I guess so. I didn't know where it came from. Not until tonight." She glanced at him apologetically. "It's freaky, huh?"

He sighed and started the Jaguar forward again. "Not so much. It just takes a little getting used to."

"And you don't like talking about personal things."

"No," he replied at once. "I don't." He glanced at her. "But I've told you more than I've ever told anyone else, except Jon, about my private life. So I guess I trust you."

She smiled. "Thanks."

He pulled into the parking lot at his

apartment building and led her inside, where a security guard kept watch from a desk.

He walked to the desk. "Kilraven," he said, "Apartment 5A. I brought a woman here for illicit purposes. . . ." He indicated Winnie, who gasped and flushed and started protesting.

"It's okay, ma'am," the security guy chuckled. "He says the same thing when he brings other male agents home with him. We're used to it."

Winnie burst out laughing and slapped Kilraven on a big, muscular arm. "You beast," she muttered.

"Actually, we're getting engaged," Kilraven told the security guy with a grin. "You can see why. She's a trouper. She's a 911 operator in Jacobsville."

"I'm impressed," the security guy said. "My sister is one for San Antonio EOC. Tough job. You have to love it to do it."

"Isn't that the truth," Winnie agreed.

"We won't be here long," Kilraven said. "I just need enough time to convince her that I'm a good prospect. She's reluctant."

"Well, if you didn't go off on secretive missions, shooting people and coming home with wounds, I might try to help you convince her. She probably thinks she'll be a widow in a few months," the guy replied.

"You shut up, or I'll tell everybody who comes in here that you wear women's lingerie under your uniform."

"You wouldn't dare," the security guy said indignantly.

"Just try me."

The security guard gave him an international signal with one hand.

"Yeah, and the horse you rode in on." Kilraven chuckled.

They went into the elevator and up, silently. Kilraven opened his apartment with two keys and invited her inside.

It was amazingly elegant and neat for a man's living space. There were original paintings on the wall and the furniture was good quality leather, white and spotless. The television was state-of-the-art. Several gaming consoles were connected to it. The carpet was beige, and the curtains were earth-toned.

"You said you didn't watch television," she accused.

He chuckled. "I don't. But I have two,

one here and one at the rental house in Jacobsville, to play games on." He looked around. "How do you like the apartment?"

"It's very nice," she said, surprised.

"Did you think I lived in a cave?" he asked.

She grinned. "It wouldn't have shocked me."

"Well, this is my cave, and you'll notice that I can pick up after myself."

"I did notice that. Good job."

"Don't be condescending or I won't marry you," he assured her. "Coffee?"

"I'd love some."

"Come on."

He led her into a spacious kitchen with built-in appliances. There was a micro-wave, and sitting next to it, a huge coffee-pot.

"I drink a lot of it," he explained as he made coffee. "Most nights, I don't sleep."

She could see why, but she wasn't keen to bring up his past. "It's a nice kitchen."

"Spacious," he agreed. "And bright. I don't use half the gourmet appliances I've got, but my brother comes over once in a while and cooks something for us. He's a gourmet chef, very accomplished."

"I heard that."

He put out mugs and sat down at the kitchen table with her. "You've got a brother you didn't even know about."

"It came as a shock. Like my mother's profession. I've spent years hating her for what Dad did to me," she said heavily. "He hated her. I guess he thought the child was my uncle's and he couldn't forgive her for it. I'm sure she tried to tell him that Matt was his. Obviously, he didn't believe her. My father was a proud man, but inflexible. He didn't forgive people. Boone's a lot like him, but less judgmental."

"I like your brothers."

"Me, too."

The coffee was ready. He poured it, black, into two mugs and handed her one as he sat back down. "Down to business. We can get married by a probate judge here or in Jacobsville. Where do you want to do it?"

"Jacobsville," she said without thinking about it.

"No frills," he added firmly. "It's a temporary marriage."

She nodded. "Got you."

"And no roomful of witnesses. Just

Boone and Keely. I might have asked Jon, but he's going to be out of town."

"Okay."

He scowled. "You're taking this very calmly for a woman who wanted to beat me up a few days ago when I suggested it."

"I changed my mind," she replied.

He sipped coffee. "I won't change mine, Winnie," he said suddenly. "If you're thinking I'll be reluctant to end the marriage when this case is closed, don't. I meant it when I said I didn't want to remarry or have a child."

"I know all that."

He drew in a long breath, and suddenly he looked older, worn. "Rogers got shot working this case. Marquez got assaulted. A man who wanted to tell me about it was murdered and left unrecognizable." He glanced at her worriedly. "I'm not sure it's a good idea to involve you at all. Maybe Boone was right. I could be putting you in the line of fire."

That was flattering, that he was worried for her. "You also told Boone that there was no man around who could protect me better than you could."

"Well, that's true."

"Of course it is. And it's not like I'm going to be walking into a machine gun," she added wryly. "I'm just going to help you get in touch with the senator's wife."

He sipped coffee again, thinking. "She's the only hope we have of getting any inside information. The junior senator has already tried to stop the investigation. If it wasn't for Senator Fowler's help, we'd already have been forced to give it up. But I'm still not sure we won't face more roadblocks. If the junior senator's brother is involved in these murders, he'll probably go the limit to try and save him. It's just human nature," he added solemnly. "I'd do anything to protect Jon, although he'll never need it. He's as honest as any man I know."

"So are you," Winnie said.

He smiled. "Thanks."

"Why did you offer to let Matt stay with us?" she wondered.

He gave her a sardonic look. "Birth control."

She flushed.

He chuckled. "Nothing gets by that young man. He'll keep us honest. Besides," he added, "he's great at video games."

"So am I," she pointed out.

"Suppose you prove it?" he challenged with a grin.

He turned on the television and his game console and loaded the newest *Halo* game. They sat down and took up twin wireless controllers, and the game began.

But, as always, the dire Hunters started taking Winnie out the minute she encountered them. Kilraven gave her a sympathetic look and proceeded to take down the Hunters as if they were the humorous little grunts in the game instead of the sturdiest villains.

"How do you do that?" she exclaimed, breathless.

"It's not that hard. Watch." And he proceeded to show her his tricks.

Two hours later, they were still playing, except now Winnie wasn't getting blown away by the Hunters every few steps.

She glanced at the clock and gasped. "It's two o'clock!"

"Awww, and the coach turned back into a pumpkin, didn't it?" he sympathized, blasting his way through a barricade.

"You don't understand, I have to be at work at eight!"

He blinked. He looked at her. "Eight?"

She nodded.

He sighed and turned off the console. "Bummer."

She chuckled. "It is, but I have to go."

He put the controller down. Then he turned her into his arms and looked down at her with quiet, piercing silver eyes while her heart hammered up into her throat.

"Pretty and brave and plays video games," he murmured. His eyes dropped to her mouth. "And tastes delicious . . ."

He bent and kissed her. It wasn't like any way he'd kissed her before. It was soft, tender, teasing. And then, quite suddenly, it was fierce and hungry and demanding. He wrapped her up in his big arms, riveted her to his hard body that grew harder by the instant. He groaned, his mouth insistent as it pressed her lips apart.

Seconds later, she was stretched out on the leather couch with Kilraven's body over hers. One long leg was in between both of hers and his hands were all the way under her blouse and bra, bent on exploration.

She would have protested. She just couldn't get her mouth away from his long enough. Then he had her bare to the waist and he was poised over her, looking down at small, firm, pretty pink breasts with hard little dusky tips, and the expression on his face stopped the words in her throat.

He touched her as carefully as he'd have touched a butterfly's wings. "My God," he whispered, and the words sounded reverent.

She was breathless. She watched him, watching her, and her eyes were dark and soft.

He traced around a hard nipple, propped on one elbow, fighting for control. "I wondered what you'd look like," he whispered deeply. His silver eyes glittered as he studied her with soft appreciation.

"I'm. . .small," she managed.

He laughed. It had a predatory sound. "I like small." He bent and brushed his lips very softly over the warm flesh, drawing a shocked gasp from her. He lifted his head and searched her eyes. "You haven't done this before," he said, surprised.

"I told you I didn't believe in that sort of thing," she managed.

"Yes, but most women indulge in petting at some point."

She swallowed. "I've been rushed, grabbed, lunged at. . ." She searched his eyes. "You make it feel. . ."

"Dirty?" he asked shortly.

She remembered what she'd said to him, at the roadside park, and she winced. "I didn't mean that," she said. "I was scared."

"Of me?" he asked, shocked.

"You're a steamroller, Kilraven," she told him. "You walk right over people. I was afraid you'd rush me into something I wasn't ready for, and I fought the only way I knew how. It's not dirty when you touch me," she whispered. She managed a self-conscious smile. "I like it."

He raised an eyebrow. "You do?"

She nodded. "I might point out that I am lying here naked," she began.

"No, no," he said, "naked is when you have all your clothes off." He grinned. "Shall I demonstrate that?" he asked with gleaming eyes.

She slapped his hands when they went to her slacks, but she was laughing. "Don't you do it!"

"Spoilsport." He sighed. "Okay, I'll do

my best to exercise some restraint." While he was saying that, he was stripping off his shirt.

Winnie's breath caught at the wide, thick wedge of curling black hair that covered him to his belt buckle, and probably beyond.

He pursed his lips. "Impressed?"

"Oh, yes," she said, far and away gone from hope of subterfuge.

"And I will tell you, it feels as good as it looks," he murmured, easing down over her, so that she got the full impact of the soft, curling hair as it tickled her breasts before it settled down on them. He nudged her legs apart. "No, no, you mustn't discourage me, you'll hurt my feelings," he chided as he bent to her mouth. "You wouldn't want to make a grown man cry. . .?"

She couldn't have answered him if she'd wanted to. He was immediately passionate. He never seemed to lead up to it. He didn't need to. The impact of his sexuality was so intense that it just blew away all her defenses at once. She arched up into his hard body and slid her arms around him, her nails digging into his muscular back as he kissed her, as if he never meant to stop.

At the same time, she felt his hips shift. There was a threatening hardness where their bodies met, and she started to protest just as he moved in. The feverish motion of his hips brought a surge of pleasure so unexpected and intense that she cried out, gasping.

He felt that explosion of breath against his mouth and lifted it. She was shivering. Her eyes were wide. He looked into them, seeing her innocence, her shock, her enjoyment as he moved sensually against her.

"Feel it?" he whispered.

She gasped. Of all the outrageous things to ask. . .!

"Now, think how it would feel, pushing slowly down into your body," he whispered at her lips, "into that warm, moist darkness, hard and deep!"

"Kilraven!" she gasped at the outrageous comment.

He laughed. But the need was growing by the second. His hips curled down into hers, hard, emphasizing how capable he was. He groaned softly and shivered.

"There's a big soft bed just a few feet down the hall."

She groaned, too, but her hands were pushing, not pulling. "No," she managed in a husky little voice. Her face was flaming, and not only from the intimate position. She hadn't dreamed that men would say such blatant things to women! "I'm not on the pill!"

That stopped him dead. His mind wasn't working. It was enslaved to the throbbing hunger in his lower extremities. He dragged in a harsh breath, and then another. He didn't have anything, either. He didn't carry around prophylactics because he never slept with women. She could get pregnant. Just for an instant, he thought about a baby in her arms and his whole soul felt grief like a lance. No! Never again!

He dragged himself up into a sitting position, his head in his hands as he fought down the nausea and pain. He'd almost let it go too far. He didn't dare look at her. She was even more perfect than he'd imagined, under her clothes.

She hurried back into her things, swallowing down her embarrassment. But she realized, belatedly, that he was still struggling to regain his composure. It made her feel better about the loss of her own. She sat back down beside him, a little uneasy.

He lifted his head and met her wide, worried eyes.

"I know. I'm a bad man. Luring you in here with video games, seducing you with promises of cheats and victory codes. . ." He chuckled when she hit him playfully.

"Seducing women with video game cheats," she accused, relieved that he wasn't mad. "You villain."

"Hey, whatever works," he teased.

"Take me home, so I can get enough sleep to do my job." She chuckled, getting up.

She got her purse and waited until he turned off the television and the lights and opened the door.

"It amazes me," he said.

"What?" she asked.

"How very innocent you are," he remarked quietly, staring straight into her dark eyes.

She colored prettily. "I'm getting less innocent by the day," she said tautly.

He grinned. "Didn't know men said such blatant things to women?"

She colored even more. "Kilraven!"

He laughed. "I shouldn't tease you. I can't help it. You fascinate me," he said involuntarily. He caught her hair at her nape and drew her face up to his. "Pretty little breasts," he whispered, and brought his mouth down on hers, hard, before she could protest. "We'd better go."

THEY WERE ON THE WAY to the car. He studied her admiringly. "You're richer than sin, your whole family is, but you work at a minimum-wage job."

"The work ethic was pounded into us at an early age," she said simply. "Boone works on the ranch with his men."

"I know. I read the magazine article in *Modern Ranching World.*" He chuckled. "In fact, there's a copy of it on my coffee table. Your brother is unique. So is Clark, in his way."

"Clark is always trying to be Boone, and knowing that he never will be," she said sadly. "I think it must be terrible, to be the younger sibling of an overachiever."

"Don't tell my brother that. He'd never understand."

She laughed. "Your brother is like you, an overachiever with an abundance of intelligence and courage. He could never feel like a second son."

"No, he doesn't," Kilraven agreed, warmed by her opinion of him. "He's excelled in his chosen profession."

"So have you."

He shrugged. "I had reasons for overachieving, though."

"Yes, I know you did," she said with sympathy. She stopped at the Jaguar and turned to face him. "You'll break the case," she said. "I'm sure of it."

He touched her cheek gently. "Blind trust or some secret knowledge of the future?" he teased.

"I don't know. Both, maybe."

He sighed. "Maybe. We'd better go."

He drove her down to the big Sinclair mansion in Comanche Wells and let her out at the front door.

"I won't come in," he said from behind the wheel. "It's too late."

She noted the lights still on in Clark's room. "I guess they'll be up all night playing video games," she said enviously. "Clark has the new *Halo,* too. So does Boone."

"You can tell Boone how to get past the Hunters," he chuckled.

"And I will. See you."

"Tomorrow," he said. "I'll drive you and Matt up to see your mother. What time do you get off?"

"Four, tomorrow," she said. "It's usually a longer shift, but one of the girls wanted to be home when school's out for a teacher workday, so she's doing the night shift for me."

"Nice."

She grinned. "Very."

"I'll see you at four. We never did set a date for the wedding," he added. "How about Friday?"

Her heart jumped. She was thinking of all the arrangements and invitations and a gown and flowers. Just as quickly, she remembered that she wasn't going to have any of those traditional things. Not for a sham wedding. A temporary affair.

She managed a smile anyway. "Okay. Friday it is."

"See you tomorrow."

"See you."

He didn't move. He waited. She realized that he wasn't leaving until she was inside. It was flattering. She went into the house and closed the door. Only then did she hear the car drive away.

On her way to bed, she went through a dark house. The only room alive in it was Clark's. She poked her head in the door. Matt was sitting in front of the game console, in his chair, while Clark perched on a beanbag chair beside him. They were whacking grunts in *Halo.*

"Having fun?" she asked.

The two males grinned at her, looking so much alike they could have been twins.

"Never mind. Watch out for sticky grenades," she advised.

"We've been sticking them on Hunters," Matt told her.

"Does it work?" she asked, never having tried it.

"Watch," Matt said. His avatar tossed one at the huge Hunter. The next minute, the fearsome creature was on the ground.

"Excellent," Winnie said, giving him a thumbs-up. "I'll have to try that. Kilraven's coming up to take us to see Mom tomorrow just after I get off work at four," she told him.

"Your brother. . .I mean, Boone, called

to check on her. They said she's sleeping and doing well," Matt replied.

"Good. Sleep well."

"Eventually," Clark promised.

She shook her head and went to bed.

10

Winnie had a boring day at work. It was the norm to have a few days of routine calls and then one that taxed personnel to their very limits. On a difficult shift, there could be terrible wrecks, attempted robberies, suicides and futile foot chases after suspects that ended in frustration. There could be officers injured. There could be suspects who resisted arrest. There could be drunks with guns daring police to evict them from an abused wife's house. There could even be dog attacks or wild animal attacks. But this day was uneventful, except for a chase after a stolen car that finally resulted in an arrest.

"Guess who made the collar?" Winnie asked Kilraven when she and Matt were in the Jaguar with him, headed for the hospital in San Antonio.

"I'll bite," Kilraven said.

"Macreedy," she replied.

He gaped at her. "Him?"

"Him," she said. She glanced at Matt in the backseat, who was frowning, curious. "He's a deputy with the sheriff's department. He's famous for losing funeral processions in inaccessible places. He has no sense of direction. So when he does something like this, we're all surprised."

Matt grinned. "I get it."

"Maybe Carson Hayes was right, and all he needed was a little self-confidence," Kilraven said.

"Maybe so." Winnie laughed.

THE HOSPITAL WAS CROWDED. Kilraven maneuvered Matt's wheelchair through the crowds with Winnie following close behind as they made their way to Detective Gail Rogers's room.

"Mom!" Matt exclaimed, reaching up.

She laughed and leaned over, grimacing at the painful effort to hug him. "You're okay, then?" she asked, fighting tears.

"Of course I'm okay," he scoffed. He sat back down and grinned at her. "You look pretty good," he said. He was fighting tears, too, although he tried to hide it.

"I just got shot," she said. "No big deal."

"Right," Matt drawled.

Rogers looked past him at Winnie and Kilraven. "I think I may have missed something. The nurses said he went home with the Sinclairs. How did he end up at the ranch?"

"We knew who his father was the minute we saw him," Winnie said quietly. "I would try to apologize, but I don't know where to start. Boone and Clark feel the same way."

Gail lay back on her pillows and looked at her daughter with quiet pride. "I never tried to explain," she said after a minute. "Your father was furious when he knew I was pregnant. I tried to tell him the child was his, but I couldn't get him to listen. Finally, I just quit trying. I knew it was no use to try and contact any of you kids. He would have stopped any attempt and he'd have made you pay for it. I had Matt and got on with my life. He's been a joy," she said, glancing at her youngest child with a smile.

"That's in between being a holy terror." Matt laughed. "That's what she calls me."

"He likes to take the chair for rides down hills," she said, making a face at him. "See these gray hairs," she asked him, pointing at the top of her head. "You gave them all to me."

"I like going fast," Matt protested. "Not that I get much speed in this old thing," he muttered. " I'm not complaining," he added quickly. "It helps build up my arm strength."

"We've got a motorized one ordered," Winnie said, surprising everyone in the room. She smiled. "Boone had them do a one-day ship. We'll have it tomorrow."

"Well!" Gail exclaimed.

"You can't argue," Winnie added firmly. "You know how the Sinclairs are when they get the bit between their teeth. Boone and Clark want to see you," she said then. "But they won't come until you say it's okay."

She bit her lower lip. She was hesitant, and Winnie understood why. She moved closer to the bed. "We've all had a rough time," she said slowly. "It isn't going to be easy, trying to put our family back together. But we all want to. Especially me."

Gail took in a long breath. "We can try."

Winnie smiled. It was a genuine smile. "Yes. We can."

"When do I get to come and stay with you?" Matt asked Kilraven. "Not that I don't like the ranch, I like it a lot," Matt said. "But he works for the CIA," he said in a loud whisper. "Maybe he can use his influence to get them to hire me when I get out of college."

Kilraven laughed. "Maybe I can. If I still have any by then."

"I'll bet you've got all sorts of top secret gadgets, too, don't you?" he persisted.

"A few," Kilraven admitted. "But some of them are classified."

"Darn."

"You can see the ones that aren't."

"When?"

Kilraven glanced at Winnie. "We're getting married Friday."

"Wow! Will it be in a church with a minister and everything? Can I come?"

"It will be in a judge's office," Winnie

said calmly. She smiled. "Of course you can come."

"Oh." Matt seemed very disappointed.

Kilraven felt uncomfortable. "I want coffee."

"I want hot chocolate," Matt said. "Can we go get some and bring it back here?"

"I guess so. You want something?" he asked the women.

"Coffee would be nice," Winnie said.

Gail shook her head. "They'll never let you give me caffeine. I know. I tried to bribe one of the nurses to bring the pot in here. Vicious girl," she muttered. "Made all sorts of threats. If I just had my service weapon. . .!"

"Now, now, no shooting up hospitals," Kilraven chided. "What would people think of the department if Marquez had to bail you out of jail, and you in a hospital gown?"

Gail glowered at him. "I hate hospitals."

"Yes, well, they save a lot of lives," Kilraven reminded her.

"So they do."

"We won't be long," Kilraven said. He pushed Matt ahead of him out of the room.

Winnie stared at her mother with wide, soft eyes. She was trying to reconcile the memories of twelve years ago with the woman in the hospital bed.

"You've changed," Winnie said finally.

"Yeah," her mother said with a chuckle. "I've gotten older and meaner."

"I meant, you. . ." She bit her lip. "It's hard to put into words. I remember you always waiting on Daddy, bringing him things that he could have gotten for himself. He wouldn't even make himself a sandwich. You were always jumping up, every time he called. You aren't docile like that anymore. You're like, well, you're like the people I work with in Jacobs County," she said with a faint smile. "They're hard people, because they do a hard job. But they're always there when you need them. They never let you down. That's what I mean."

"I let you down, though, didn't I, baby?" she asked sadly. "I was such a wimp, Winnie. I let your father walk all over me, from the day I was sixteen and we got married. I was raised thinking that's what women are supposed to do." She smiled. "Your uncle Bruce was a high roller. He was flamboyant and full of dreams, funny and fun to be with. I'd never met anybody like him. He came to see your father twelve years ago and made a dead set at me. I'd been dominated and ignored and taken for granted for so many years. . ." She broke off. "I didn't know he hated your father and wanted to score off him. I didn't know that's why he'd kept his distance from us, except for Christmas cards once a year. I fell, and fell hard. So we ran away together." She shook her head. "We went to Vegas and I got a divorce, then we got a quickie wedding and went to the Bahamas. That was when I knew why he was always so hyper. He was a drug user. He shot up in the room, and wanted me to join him." She lay back on the pillows, agonizing over the memories. "I used my ticket and came back to the States. I wouldn't sleep with him. He came to see me and confessed that he'd only wanted me because he hated your father for, as he said, cheating him out of the ranch. It didn't happen that way, but that's another story."

"You never slept with him?" Matt had told her as much, but she needed to hear it from her.

She shook her head. "I found him repulsive when I saw him using drugs. I could never do that. You know, I never even had a parking ticket my whole life. My grandfather was a U.S. Marshal."

"Wow," Winnie said, impressed. "That would be my great-grandfather."

Gail nodded. "He was quite a guy. I used to have clippings of some of his exploits, but I wouldn't know where to look for them, after all this time. I imagine your father threw all my things out."

"Actually, he didn't get the chance to," Winnie told her. "You remember old George, who drives the cattle trucks for us?"

"Yes."

"Daddy put the stuff out and told him to carry it off, but George hid it in the attic while Daddy was gone hunting."

Gail was surprised. "And you didn't throw it out, Winnie? You had good reason to."

"I didn't think about it," Winnie confessed. "I was just ten years old. George said we had to keep it, and he was a grown-up, so I kept the secret." She smiled. "I hadn't thought about it in years! All those things, even your trunk, they're still up in the attic." She hesitated. "You might like to come down and look at them sometime."

Gail smiled hesitantly. "I might."

"What happened after you got home from the Bahamas?" Winnie asked.

"I had no money, your father had cut off my credit card and emptied our joint bank account," she said with a sigh. "I had a little savings account that he couldn't touch, just a few thousand dollars, but it was enough to get me an apartment and a few clothes to wear. I didn't know how I was going to make a living, but I thought about Granddaddy, and I knew I might have a future in law enforcement. I was athletic and healthy and strong for my height, and I looked younger than I really was. So I applied, and they accepted me. I did the police academy thing, graduated with honors, and got a job with the San Antonio Police Department. Last year, I got promoted to homicide detective sergeant. It's the best job I've ever had. I love it."

"I worked as a clerk for the Jacobsville Police Department for a while, before I got the job as a 911 operator," Winnie told her. "I figured I was too soft to be a cop."

Gail laughed. "So did I. But I seemed to fit right in."

"Our uncle . . . He lived in San Antonio, didn't he?"

"Oh, yes, he did," she said heavily. "He was a pest, always needing money, wanting loans, wanting me to go back to your father and make it all up to him so that he could get forgiven and back in your father's good graces." She shook her head. "All those dreams he had, but the drugs got in the way of anything he tried to do. In the end, they killed him. But not before he'd done permanent damage to Matt."

"Matt told us about that," Winnie said coldly. "I couldn't believe a man would be so coldhearted as to do that to his own nephew."

"He could do that, and more," she said. "He got mixed up with Senator Sanders's hoodlum brother," she added. "I thought he was just a 'gofer,' just an extra hand for the local bad guys. But he might have had his hand in more than that. I didn't want anything to do with him, but especially after he crippled Matt and almost killed him. I swear to God, if I could have proved it, I'd have had him sent to prison for life for attempted murder. But it was only Matt's word against his." She shook her head. "He always could talk his way out of anything."

She lay back on the pillows with a grimace. "Then he had the gall to come to the apartment when I was working and tell Matt that he needed to borrow the motorized wheelchair. Matt's so good-hearted, he said sure." She winced. "He sold it to buy drugs. I saved every extra dime I had for almost a year and a half just to afford it, and then my coworkers put in the last couple of hundred dollars I was short. . ." Her voice trailed off.

"Matt will have a new one tomorrow," she said gently. "It's all right."

Gail looked at the ceiling, fighting tears. "One stupid mistake. I made one stupid mistake, and I've paid for it, over and over again. If I could only go back and change it." She shook her head. "But there's no way. You kids paid a higher price than I did for that one mistake I made. I'm so sorry, Winnie. So sorry. . .!"

She was sobbing. Winnie ran to her, pulled the blond head into her arms and rocked it, crying, too.

"It's okay, Mama," she whispered. "It's okay."

The sobs grew louder. Gail had gone so

long without hope, missing her children, wanting to see them. It had been impossible. Now here was her daughter, forgiving her, comforting her. It was like a new start. It was even worth getting shot.

Winnie laughed, because she'd said that last bit aloud. "Please don't get shot again," she said gently.

"I'll do my best, baby," Gail promised. She drew back, dabbing at her eyes with the sheet.

Winnie pulled out a paper towel and dabbed at her own eyes.

Kilraven appeared in the doorway and hesitated.

"Women's Terrorist and Sobbing Society?" Kilraven quipped.

"What a great legend for a T-shirt," Winnie exclaimed. "I'll have some made up right away." She glanced at her mother and laughed. "You can have one, too."

"I'll wear it to work and drive my lieutenant bonkers," Gail promised, laughing.

Kilraven handed Winnie a cup of coffee in a plastic cup. "It looks weak."

"I don't care. It's still coffee," she said.

Gail shook her head. "What I wouldn't give for a cup of that."

"I'd let you share it, but the nurses would probably smell it on your breath and have us thrown out," Winnie reasoned.

"Evil girls," Gail muttered.

"I understand from the night nurse that you've been an interesting patient," Kilraven said with pursed lips and twinkling eyes. "Sneaking out the door and down to the street in your gown and a robe to have a cigarette?"

She glared at him. "You can't smoke in here, they won't let you."

"You could quit," he pointed out.

"You know what you could do, too," Gail shot right back.

He chuckled as he glanced at Winnie. "See? That's you in twenty years."

"God forbid!" Gail said.

"Stop that," Winnie told her. "You're not bad."

"I guess I ought to quit smoking, sure enough. But it won't help my other short-comings. I yell at people, I do terrible things to uniformed officers," Gail began.

"What do you do to uniformed officers?" Kilraven wondered.

"Only if they threaten to mess up my crime scene," Gail said defensively.

"What?"

"I send them to other precincts to question people I think might be involved in my cases."

"Oh? That doesn't sound too bad," Winnie commented.

"I give them false names of people in lockup," she confessed.

"And you're calling the nurses evil?" Kilraven asked.

She glowered at him. "They won't let me smoke and drink coffee."

"You should quit smoking," Kilraven pointed out.

"Oh, sure, it's easy, I'll start right now," Gail said sarcastically. "Have you ever tried to quit?"

"Sure. I quit two years ago." He frowned. "And I quit five years before that. And I quit seven years ago." He smiled.

"Have you ever stayed quit?" she persisted.

"I've been clean for two years," he pointed out. "And as long as I don't have anything traumatic to upset me, I probably can stay quit for the rest of my life."

Gail was looking at him curiously. "That's a big if."

He shrugged. "I like cigars." He glared at Winnie when she made a face. "I'm not the only person around who likes a good cigar. They say the governor of California likes them, too."

"Smelly, stinky things," Winnie scoffed.

He lifted his eyebrows. "Yes? Well, if you marry me, you'll just have to get used to them, won't you?"

"Not for long," she said under her breath.

He leaned back in his chair. "Yes. Not for long."

"I wish I could come to the wedding," Gail said heavily. "But they won't let me out for another few days. I don't even know how many. The doctor won't come in here anymore so I can ask him."

"I saw him in the hall," Kilraven told her. "He says he's never coming back in here, because you grill him like a murder suspect."

"I do not," she said haughtily. "I only wanted to know when I could go home."

"It's the way you asked him," Kilraven said. "Need to work on your people skills, Rogers," he pointed out.

"Blow my people skills," she returned hotly. "I can't sit around here in my underwear while whoever shot me goes from bar to lowlife bar, bragging about it! I want to lock him up and throw away the key, as soon as I find out who the hell he is!"

"He may not be bragging about it."

"Of course he's bragging about it, he shot a cop and got away with it," she said, smoldering. Her dark eyes narrowed. "But not for long. I'll track him down if it takes me five years!"

"See?" Kilraven said, nodding toward Winnie's mother, "that's why she makes a good detective."

"Speaking of detectives, are they any closer to finding out who blindsided Marquez?" Gail asked, diverted.

"No," Kilraven told her. "They're still working the case. They'll add yours to it. I'd bet half my pension that they're connected, somehow."

"It's all connected," Gail said. "The murder of your family, the DB in the Little Carmichael River in Jacobsville, the death of Senator Fowler's employee, Marquez's mugging and my wounds. All tied together. Something else, Kilraven— I seriously think we should reopen the case of that young girl who was found murdered just before your family was killed."

Kilraven's silver eyes glittered. "You still think there's a connection. Why?"

"Look at the cases," she said intently. "Both victims were found in such a condition that only DNA could identify them. The killers have never been found. I heard that the killer left a thermos near the submerged car that the perp was driving. Left it out in the open, wiped clean of prints." Her eyes narrowed. "Bruce Sinclair, my ex-husband, had one just like it. My question is, how did it wind up in Jacobsville?"

"Did your ex give it to someone?" Kilraven asked.

"I don't know. But we need to find out. You might go to see that hophead girlfriend of his, the one who was living with him," Gail suggested. "I don't know if she's sober enough to remember anything, but it's worth a try. Just be careful," she added. "Somebody's targeting people connected with this case."

"This isn't the time to be careful," he replied. "It's time to put the heat on the perps, take the fight into their own territory. I have a hunch that Senator Will Sanders's brother is up to his neck in these cases."

Gail nodded. "So do I. How do we prove it?"

Kilraven leaned back in his chair. "I'm going to put the word out on the street that Hank Sanders is being looked at as a potential suspect in two assaults on law enforcement officers. Let's see what happens."

Gail's dark eyes sparkled. "What original thinking."

"Thank you," he replied with a chuckle. "It just might flush somebody out."

"Or he might sacrifice somebody to get the heat off himself," she replied.

"Or he might tell his brother the senator, and the two of you might be out of a job," Winnie said solemnly.

"In which case," Kilraven told her, "we'll go to Senator Fowler and plead our cases. He had Sanders back off before when he took your mother off the case and busted her back to traffic duty."

"Senator Sanders had you demoted?" she asked Gail, shocked.

Gail nodded. "I didn't know it at the time, not until Alice Jones let something slip about her fiancé's father. That's Senator Fowler," she added.

"Yes, Harley's father." Winnie nodded.

"Who?" Gail wanted to know.

"Harley Fowler. He works for Cy Parks on his ranch."

Gail shook her head. "That's after my time, I'm afraid. I don't know Mr. Parks."

"He's very nice."

"Nice." Kilraven chuckled. He glanced at her. "Listen, that old lobo wolf may be married and have kids, but don't think he's tame."

"I forgot," she told Gail with a smile. "Mr. Parks was a professional soldier, a mercenary, for many years before he settled in Jacobsville. We all thought he was just another rancher until drug lords started setting up camp nearby. He and Dr. Micah Steele and Eb Scott went after the drug lords with Harley, and shut down the whole operation."

"I did hear about that," Gail replied, smiling. "It was in all the papers, even on the television news. No interviews, though."

"That would take magic," Kilraven commented. "None of those dudes likes publicity, even now that they've retired.

Well, maybe Eb Scott wouldn't mind. He runs a state-of-the-art training camp for counterterrorism in Jacobsville. We use his firing range for practice. It's formidable."

"So is Mr. Scott, from what we hear." Winnie laughed. "He got married, too, a few years back. He and his wife have a son, I believe."

Kilraven had that faraway look in his eyes. He thought of his little girl, the last time he'd seen her. His face hardened. Too many people were getting away with murder. That teenage girl—he and Jon had commented on it.

He looked at Gail and frowned. "You were talking about reopening that case, the one with the teenage girl. That was just before you got shot. Did you mention it to anyone downtown?"

She blinked. "Well, to a couple of people, I guess," she said.

"The senator's little brother probably has an ear in your department, otherwise how would the senator have known that you were reopening my cold case?" he asked.

"Good point, Kilraven."

"So what if this dead teenager is the

case they don't want anyone looking at? What if there's a connection?"

"I was thinking that, too," Gail replied.

"You may be onto something. There's another thing—there was a statutory rape case against Senator Sanders some years ago, remember it?"

Gail frowned. "Yes. A teenage girl, fourteen, I believe. Her father and mother refused to let her testify against him. The charges were dropped."

"Yes, and the next day, Daddy was driving a new convertible Jaguar. How ironic," Kilraven said sarcastically.

"That was a case I wanted to reopen," Gail muttered, "just so I could tell her father what I thought of him."

Kilraven was adding up clues in his head. "That might be the way to break the case wide-open," he said, thinking aloud. "Maybe you could talk to the girl."

Gail nodded slowly. "She might be able to tell me something about how the senator handled her. Or rather how his brother handled her. That might give us a lead into how he operates when he wants something hushed up."

"We're getting close, but in a way we

didn't even realize," Kilraven said. "When you get out of here, that has to be your priority." His eyes narrowed. "There's one living witness who could testify to Senator Sanders's tactics with teenage girls. The teenager would be a woman now. She might talk to you."

"It's been some time since the case was dropped," she mused. "Anything could have happened in the meantime. The girl is grown, and living on her own, I'd imagine. Away from her father's influence, she really might be willing to talk to me. It's worth a try."

"Yes," Kilraven said. "Well worth it. But first you have to get well."

She grimaced. "I can't believe I was stupid enough to let myself get shot."

"That's what Marquez keeps saying, although he got beaten up instead of shot," Kilraven commented.

"Either way, we're sidelined," she said heavily. She shifted and groaned. The pain medicine was wearing off. She reached beside her and jiggled the drip catheter. She sighed. "That's better. Damned thing gets sluggish from time to time. They put the painkiller right in it," she added. "Beats having to call them in here four times a day to put it in me manually." She sighed. "I really hate drugs, you know. But right now, I can't say much against them. It really helps with the pain."

"I know," Kilraven said solemnly. "But it gets better. It just takes time."

"Time." She nodded. Her eyes closed. "I'm so tired."

"You should get some rest," Winnie said. She stood up and moved to the bed, bending to kiss her mother's forehead and smooth back the blond hair. "I'll come back to see you tomorrow. We'll bring Matt. . ." She stopped, looking around. "Where is Matt?" she asked, realizing that he hadn't come in with Kilraven.

"He met a girl about his age in a wheelchair down at the drink machines. They both love video games." He chuckled. "He was going to have his hot chocolate with her."

They heard wheels rolling about that time and turned to see Matt coming in the door.

"Sorry," he told them. "I forgot the time. There was this girl, nice girl. I got her e-mail address," he added. He grimaced. "If I ever get e-mail, I can send her one," he corrected.

"I have e-mail," Kilraven said easily and smiled. "You can use mine."

"Thanks!" He moved the chair beside Gail's bed. "Sorry I wasn't in here. I was supposed to be visiting you. But that girl has an incredible score at Super Mario Brothers," he exclaimed. "She got busted up in a car wreck, too, but it was really an accident, not deliberate like mine. Are we leaving already?" he added when Winnie slipped into her coat.

"Your mother's tired," Kilraven said gently. "She needs rest, so she can get well quicker."

"Yes, I do," Gail agreed. She smiled and held out her arms to hug Matt. "You be good for your brothers and sister," she said.

"I'm being very good, aren't I, sis?"

It took Winnie a minute to realize it was her he was addressing. She flushed a little and laughed. "Yes, you are, little brother," she replied, and felt warm inside with the words.

He grinned. "Trying to be, anyway," he amended. "We'll see you again tomorrow. Won't we?" he asked the other adults.

"You bet," Kilraven promised.

"See you tomorrow, Mom," he told Gail. He hesitated. "You know, they're right about the smoking," he said unexpectedly serious. "I know you do it outside, so it won't affect me. But it's affecting you. I don't want to lose you. See?"

She held out her arm, fighting tears, and hugged him close. She drew in a long breath. "Okay, kid. If that's what you want, I'll do it."

"Really?"

"Really." She looked past him at the two adults. "Just don't be surprised when you all have to come and bail me out of jail for climbing walls and threatening other police officers."

Kilraven pursed his lips. "There are new products that deal with the side effects."

"I could buy a yacht for what they cost," Gail muttered.

"That isn't a problem, and don't argue," Winnie said at once. She gave her mother a firm look.

"Well!" Gail exclaimed. She glanced at Kilraven. "She's me in twenty years, huh?"

Kilraven nodded.

"No wonder he's planning on a short marriage," she told Winnie.

Winnie laughed. It was easier to joke about it than face it. "You get well. We'll see you again, soon."

"Take care."

The others said their goodbyes, too, and left.

Winnie ruffled Matt's hair. "You'd better be good, or I'll tell Boone," she threatened.

"Horrors!" he said, but he laughed.

Winnie looked up at Kilraven and smiled. "Thanks for driving us."

He slid his hands into his pockets and shrugged. "I'm not overburdened with work right now. I enjoyed it. Your mother's in a class of her own."

"Yes," Winnie said proudly. "She is."

THE WEDDING WAS A quiet affair. Boone and Keely stood up with Winnie and Kilraven, while Matt and Clark and a few local citizens who'd heard about the wedding filled the benches near the doors outside the probate judge's office.

The judge, a woman, looked from one of them to the other. "You ready?" she asked.

They nodded.

"Please join hands." She looked at her book. "Do you, Winona Sinclair, take McKuen Kilraven for your husband. . ."

"McKuen." Winnie said it softly, surprised.

"I was named for a famous poet," he said, glowering at her.

She smiled. "I noticed. It suits you. I like it."

He smiled back. "Thanks."

"Ahem."

They glanced at the probate judge.

"Sorry," Winnie said.

She laughed, shaking her head, then she continued.

And they were married. Kilraven bent to brush his mouth gently over Winnie's, but not with any great enthusiasm. He looked uncomfortable in his dark suit, distinguished and almost untouchable. Winnie was certain he was remembering his first wedding, and she was positive it wasn't in some probate judge's office. Probably his first wife had had all the trimmings, including a beautiful gown and flowers and. . .

"Congratulations, Mrs. Kilraven!" Keely laughed, and hugged her.

"Mrs. Kilraven," Winnie said, shocked at the sound of the name that was now hers.

"Hey, that's you," Keely teased.

"Sorry. I was just thinking," she replied, and then flushed. She couldn't admit she'd been regretting her wedding.

"Don't," Keely advised. "Just be happy."

"It's only temporary," Winnie whispered.

"Is it?" Keely replied in a whisper, and winked.

Boone bent to kiss his sister's cheek. "You made a pretty bride," he said, admiring her neat figure in the white suit she was wearing with a pillbox hat and a tiny veil.

She was clutching a small bouquet that she'd had made up, of white roses and baby's breath. Kilraven hadn't even noticed her suit or the bouquet. She was certain he hadn't thought of offering her one. He was somber and quiet and introspective. She knew it wasn't the happiest day of his life. But it was exciting to her. She was married! Even if it only lasted a few weeks, she was Kilraven's bride. She smiled so radiantly that the newspaper photographer covering the private affair was almost too stunned by her beauty to snap the picture. But he managed.

11

Kilraven pulled himself together and tried to stop thinking back to his first wedding. He should have offered Winnie a bouquet, at least, but he hadn't even done that. He'd been resentful that he had to marry her just to question a senator's wife. It was his own idea; why was he blaming her for it?

No, the pain came when he remembered Monica walking toward him down the aisle, dressed in a lavender gown with a bouquet of lilac. It wasn't traditional, but neither was she. She'd been lovely. The most beautiful woman alive, with her long wheat-colored hair and her laughing blue eyes. He'd been in love. Deeply in love. The wedding had been the happiest day of his life, at least until little Melly was born. Then his life began, even as Monica was finding other partners for her sensual adventures. Kilraven had lived for his little girl. Until that night . . .

He heard voices around him and realized that he'd been staring into space while people were trying to congratulate him. He smiled and returned handshakes. He wasn't being fair to Winnie. Whatever his own feelings, she was in love with him. It wasn't right to treat her so coolly on her wedding day.

He moved to her side and curled her fingers into his. She looked up at him, surprised.

"You really do look beautiful," he said softly, studying the way her long, thick, wavy blond hair radiated around her face, the way her dark eyes seemed to smolder in her face with its oval shape and peaches-and-cream complexion.

She flushed. "Thanks," she stammered.

He bent and brushed his mouth over her forehead, just below the tiny veil she'd pushed up when they were saying their vows. "I should have offered to buy you a bouquet," he whispered. "That's the groom's part of the deal."

She smiled. "It's okay. I had this one made up."

"I like it."

"Thanks."

"Well, where's the reception?" Cash Grier asked, moving up to the front of the office.

Kilraven blinked. "We aren't having a reception."

"I guess I can go home, then." He chuckled. "It's only at the receptions that we have to arrest people."

"What are you talking about?" Winnie asked.

"Don't you remember Blake Kemp's wedding?"

"Oh," she said, nodding. "Yes, I do. Cake and punch went flying and several of the witnesses ended up in jail."

He grinned. "Best reception I was ever at," he commented. He glanced at Kilraven. "You're sure you're not having a reception?"

"Sorry. No time."

"Oh," Cash mused. "In a hurry, are you?"

Kilraven glowered at him. "It's not that sort of marriage, and please get your mind above your belt!"

"Whatever do you think I meant?" Cash asked with an angelic expression. "I was only going to offer to give you a police escort out of town. All the way to San Antonio, if you like."

"No, thank you," Kilraven said firmly. "You'd have Hayes send Macreedy, and we'd all end up driving the back roads of Florida or some other state hoping to be rescued."

Cash shook his head. "You have a suspicious mind."

"Absolutely." Kilraven nodded.

"Well, I do wish you the best." He extended his hand. "I've enjoyed working with you, for the most part.But there were times I wanted to put you in a barrel and float you down to Mexico." He added with a grin, "I guess we can overlook those times."

Kilraven laughed as he shook hands. "I won't mention that I've had the same impulses about you."

"Have you really?" Cash asked. "Thing

is," he added in a conspiratorial tone, "we don't have any barrels in Jacobsville."

"Oh, I think we could find one if we really looked," Kilraven murmured.

"Are we ready to go?" Winnie asked her new husband. "We're on our way to the hospital to see Mom," she added with a smile. "She wanted to see me in my wedding suit."

Kilraven felt guilt stab at him. It was Winnie's first wedding, and he'd cheated her. It should have been a religious service, in a church with a pastor. The thought stung.

"Yes, we'd better go," he said, in a harder tone than he meant to.

"You okay?" Matt asked, frowning.

He patted the boy's shoulder. "Sure!"

But Winnie knew better. He was regretting the impulse that had made him ask her to marry him. It was all a sham, a pretense. They were going to interrogate a politician's wife and it had to look natural, so they were married. But it wasn't going to be happily ever after, and she wouldn't keep him for long. It was just temporary.

"Now you look all gloomy," Matt said, eyeing his sister.

Winnie perked up. "Do I?" she asked, smiling at him. "I don't feel gloomy," she lied.

He smiled. "Okay. Just checking."

HER MOTHER MADE A fuss over the pretty white suit and protested when Winnie got a vase from one of the nurses and made a bouquet for Gail out of her bridal bouquet.

"No, you'll want to save that," Gail protested.

"What for?" Winnie asked, smiling. "It's just flowers. Our marriage probably won't last much longer than they will."

Kilraven felt those words like a stab in the heart. He looked at Winnie as if he thought she was needling him, but he realized quite suddenly that she wasn't. Maybe he was taking the lack of frills at their wedding harder than she was. Winnie was a realist.

His hands were clenched in his pockets as he watched her move around the room. She had an easy grace in her walk, elegance personified. She was pretty and sweet and intelligent; she'd finished two years of college before she quit and went home to work for the Jacobsville Police Department as a clerk. He frowned. Why had she dropped out of college, he wondered. He'd never asked.

Of course, he'd never talked to her long enough to get around to personal questions. He'd tried to be remote and inaccessible, to discourage her from daydreaming about him. This marriage wasn't going to do much to cure that crush she had on him, that was for sure.

Still, if anything happened down in Nassau, he wouldn't be taking advantage of a single woman. He pursed his lips as he studied her trim figure, her slight breasts, her long, pretty legs. He loved that long, blond hair. He remembered the feel of it, clenched in his fingers while he kissed her. He remembered the taste of her bare breasts. . . His body made a sudden and visible statement about how it had enjoyed that long, sweet taste of her. It wanted more.

"Going for coffee. Want any?" he asked Winnie, as he started toward the door.

"Yes, please," she said.

He waved a hand and kept walking.

"He's acting very oddly," Winnie remarked. She grimaced. "I think he's comparing me with his first wife," she told her mother, "and I don't imagine I compare well."

"You don't know that," Gail said soothingly. "It's hard for men to get married. He's got a lot on his mind, too."

"Yes. This case." She perched on the chair by her mother's bed. "I painted a picture of a raven and gave it to him for Christmas. It was supposed to be an anonymous present, but he knew immediately that I'd done it, and he was furious. He walked out without saying a word to me." She sighed. "Then he took me to his house and showed me a picture just like it. His daughter had drawn and colored it just before she was killed. They were identical. He wanted to know how I knew to paint something like that. I don't know."

"I've had that ability all my life," Gail told her. "I can crack cold cases that other detectives can't. I get feelings, intuition. I can feel it when something's not right."

"So it runs in the family."

"I don't know. I don't recall my parents or their parents ever knowing something was going to happen before it did." She smiled. "I guess you inherited it from me. So did Matt," she added. "He knows when I'm in trouble."

"And you know about him."

Gail nodded. "He's quite a boy."

"Dad would have been proud of him," Winnie told her. "I'm so sorry he wouldn't listen to you."

"Baby, you're not half as sorry as I am," Gail said. "But the past twelve years have taught me to be self-sufficient, to take care of myself. I went from my home straight into marriage, at an age when most girls are just learning about boys and dating. I missed so much." She smiled sadly. "Your father was handsome and charming. He convinced me that marrying him was the smart thing to do, so I did it. He was twelve years older than me. That's not a lot, but it's almost a generation."

"I know," Winnie said quietly. "That's the argument Kilraven uses with me. He's ten years older than me."

"He's dangerous," Gail said, her voice quiet and intense. "I don't mean that he'd ever hurt you, I know he wouldn't. But he takes chances. He lives on the edge. He's done things you wouldn't believe in the line of duty."

"Warning me off him?" Winnie teased.

"It's far too late for that," Gail replied. "Just try not to go in headfirst, okay? You may be hoping for a long-term commitment, but that man isn't ready for one. He hasn't faced his own tragedy. Until he does, he's a walking time bomb, waiting to self-destruct."

"I couldn't say no," Winnie replied. "I love him," she confessed, averting her eyes.

"I know that. I'm sorry."

Winnie shifted in the chair. "He might discover that he can't live without me."

"That's a very long shot."

"Well, we have to have goals to aim for," Winnie said, trying to rally her sense of humor. "Some women want to go to Mars, I just want to keep Kilraven."

"The women going to Mars will get their wish long before you get yours," Gail assured her.

"You are so cynical." Winnie laughed. "Just like Kilraven."

"We're L.E.O.s," she replied with a wan smile. "The job makes us that way."

"I do understand, a little," Winnie said. "I work with people in law enforcement. I know what you go through, what you have to look at. I know how hard you work, and how unrewarding it can be. I know how critical the public is of you. The media

notices every tiny slip you make, and ig-
nores the big drug busts and the simple
acts of kindness and the danger you en-
dure just to do the job. I think it's a great
job," she added with a smile. "And I'm proud
that you're one of those people."

"Thank you," Gail said softly. "That means
a lot."

There was a metallic sound, followed by
a loud hum, and Matt came into the room.
"Finally got here!" he exclaimed. "I got
stuck on an elevator going up and I couldn't
get to the front in this to press the button
for your floor. Kilraven and I got separated
downstairs at the elevators. Where is he?"
he asked suddenly.

"Gone after coffee," Winnie said with a
grin. She looked at her mother. "How do
you like it? You should have seen Kilraven
trying to disassemble it to get it in the trunk
of the Jaguar! It's complicated."

"Yes, but he's a whiz at machinery," Matt
enthused. "I wish I had the gift."

"Don't we all." Gail sighed. She grinned
at her son. "I do like the chair."

"I hugged Boone," he said. "He's the
greatest."

"Yes, he is," Winnie agreed.

"I like Clark, too," Matt said quickly. "He's great at video games!"

"And of course, that's the best character reference he can give," Gail said drolly.

Matt made a face at her. "Video games are my life, what can I say?"

"In about five years, girls will be your life, so enjoy it while you can," his mother told him.

"Girls. Yuuck." He hesitated. "Although, that girl in the wheelchair sure was pretty. I still have her e-mail address," he added, and levered his eyebrows up and down.

"He's going to be a ladykiller." Winnie sighed.

"I am not killing women when I grow up," Matt said indignantly.

"That's not what it means," Gail told him, and explained.

He grinned. "That wouldn't be so bad. I could charm women out of their video games."

"I think you have a problem," Winnie told her mother.

"I know I do," Gail replied.

Kilraven came back with coffee and they had a short visit. Matt was keen to get to Kilraven's apartment and see those game consoles he'd heard about; not to mention the collection of first-person shooter games.

"Bloodthirsty boy," Kilraven accused when they'd said goodbye to Gail and were on their way in the car.

"I'm not bloodthirsty, I just like to kill monsters," Matt defended.

"Me, too." Kilraven chuckled. He glanced over the backseat. "There's this game, *Elder Scrolls IV: Oblivion,*" he began.

"I played that at a friend's house once. Everything in it looks so real!"

"Yes, it does. Well, every so often when I play it, I go to a tavern, get drunk, slug an Imperial Guard and steal his horse and ride it away." He sighed. "I usually get halfway down the hill before they catch up with me and shoot me full of arrows." He glanced at Matt, who was laughing. "Of course, I make a save just before I do all that, so I can go back to the save and it never happened. I do like to be law-abiding on record."

Winnie was laughing, too. "That's evil!" she charged.

"No, it's evil if I do it in real life." He leaned toward her as he stopped at a red light. "Not many Imperial Guards riding horses around San Antonio," he added.

She laughed again. "I guess not."

He pulled into his parking lot and reassembled Matt's wheelchair, grabbing his overnight bag before they went into the lobby.

"I have returned with two people," Kilraven began, addressing the security guard, "and I intend to take them upstairs for illicit purposes. . ."

"Oh, for God's sake, Kilraven, get out of here!" the guard groaned.

Kilraven glared at him. "Have you no sense of honor at all? Will you sully the name of this fine establishment by allowing me to. . ."

"Out!" the guard gestured, standing. "Or I call the cops."

"But I am the cops!" Kilraven wailed. "And I just got married!"

"A likely story!" the guard retorted.

"No, I did. Look." He tugged Winnie's hand toward the guard and displayed the pretty gold ring he'd put on her finger.

"Well!" the guard exclaimed. He smiled at Winnie. "My condolences, Mrs. Kilraven," he said formally. "You have put your neck in a guillotine that . . ."

"That's enough," Kilraven huffed. "Peasant!"

"Schwartzriter!" the guard shot back.

Kilraven grinned, took Winnie's hand, motioned to Matt and headed for the elevator.

"What's a swartz. . .whatever he said?" Matt asked.

"Black rider. It's German. They were famous in the sixteenth century," Kilraven told him as they crowded into the elevator. "They carried several braces of pistols and rode in formations of columns. The first men on the line would fire and ride to the back of the line and reload. Their comrades would follow suit. They were like light artillery. Brave, cunning and deadly. He can call me a black rider anytime he likes."

"I've got other names!" the security guard called as the door closed.

Kilraven chuckled. It was an ongoing battle of words and insults that he enjoyed. The security guard was also a history nut, and he was as deep into the sixteenth century as Kilraven was.

"You know a lot about that stuff, don't you?" Matt asked.

"I do. I was a history major in college," he confessed. "I still love it."

"I hate history. It's all dates and boring things."

"Boring!" Kilraven exclaimed, horrified. "History?"

"Well," Matt began, hesitating.

"When Lord Bothwell was falsely accused of insulting the queen of Scotland, he was sent into exile in England, where he was arrested. He wrote a note to an enemy of his, an earl who lived on the northern border of England and Scotland, asking for refuge. He was notorious for raiding the earl's lands, mind. Well, the earl was so amused by the request that he honored it and invited Bothwell to stay at his estate and agreed to be his keeper. In the process, he discovered that Bothwell was intelligent and, as the Earl of Northumberland said, 'not the man he was rumored to be.' Does that sound boring?"

Matt laughed. "Not really. But don't you have to memorize dates?"

"I do it for love of it, not because I have to," Kilraven said, smiling at the boy.

"You like that Lord Bot. . .Bottle. . .?"

"Bothwell. James Hepburn, Earl of Bothwell. He was the son of the 'Fair Earl' who was a suitor of the mother of Mary, Queen of Scots. Bothwell had no legitimate children, but his nephew—who was the son of his sister and the half brother of Mary Queen of Scots—inherited his title and estates. He was a bitter enemy and sometimes supporter of James the First of England. James was the son of Mary Queen of Scots."

"Wait, wait," Matt pleaded. "Too much information! My brain is exploding!"

Kilraven chuckled. "Sorry. I do tend to get carried away."

"I'll bet you've got every book ever written on the subject," Winnie guessed.

He winked at her, smiling when she colored prettily. "I have, including a number of out-of-print ones. We're home."

He opened the apartment door and let Matt go in first.

"Hey, this is nice!" Matt exclaimed.

"Very nice, indeed. Come here, woman," he told Winnie and abruptly bent and scooped her up in his arms. "I'm carrying you into my cave, in the best macho fashion."

She clung to his neck, laughing. He was fun to be with.

"I like your cave," she remarked.

He swung her around, making her hold on tighter. Then he bent his head and kissed her with muted hunger, mindful of small eyes watching.

"You're home, Mrs. Kilraven," he said, and he made the words sound new and bright.

She caught her breath. Her heart was racing like a wild thing. "Thanks, Mr. Kilraven," she replied, smiling.

He rubbed his nose against hers. "Can you cook?"

"Can I cook!" she exclaimed haughtily. "I can make real bread. My sister-in-law taught me how."

He was surprised. "Real bread? Honestly?"

"Honestly."

He put her down. "Prove it."

"Do you have yeast?"

He blinked. "Yeast what?"

"Yeast, like you put in bread, to make it," she exclaimed.

He frowned. "I don't know." He moved into the kitchen and began rummaging through cabinets. "Jon made some sort of sourdough starter once. I think he used yeast . . . yes! Here it is. We've got plain flour, too."

"How do you know the difference between plain and self-rising?" she asked curiously. "I don't think of you as a cook."

He grinned at her. "I'm not. I can do a few dishes, but I mostly get takeout. Jon is a gourmet chef," he reminded her. "He can make anything. Well, mostly anything. He accidentally got the self-rising flour when he was making biscuits with baking soda. It was a disaster. He used some very bad words."

"What bad words?" she teased.

"Oh, no, I'm not using them in front of a minor," he said, indicating Matt, who was listening and grinning.

"I am not a miner," Matt told him. "I don't even own a shovel or a pick."

"Smart mouth," Kilraven muttered.

"It runs in the family," Winnie told him. "Now if you have an apron, and you'll leave the kitchen and stop distracting me, I'll make yeast rolls."

"Heaven," Kilraven said, almost groaning with pleasure. "I haven't had them

since Cammy stopped making holiday din-
ners."

"Cammy?" Winnie asked, surprised.
"Who is she?" She was hoping it wasn't
some shadowy girlfriend.

"My stepmother," he said, grinning when
he realized what she was thinking, especially when she flushed. "Her name is
Camelia, but we always called her Cammy.
Remember? I told you when we were
standing in the roadside park."

She'd been thinking of other things and
had forgotten. "Oh."

"She wants to meet you," he said hesitantly.

"That would be nice," Winnie replied,
busy with her bread materials.

"Oh, I'm not sure you'll think so, after
you meet her. She's very possessive. She'll
probably give you a hard time."

She glanced at him. "I can take care of
myself."

"Okay. But I warned you." He went into
the living room and turned on the television, and then the game consoles. In minutes, he and a fascinated Matt were in the
middle of the new *Halo* game, so involved

that they didn't stir until Winnie insisted that cold bread and chicken weren't good.

"This is delicious," Kilraven said as they plowed through the homemade bread, heavily buttered, served with a simple chicken dish and asparagus tips with hollandaise sauce. "I didn't know you could cook like this!"

She smiled. "I learned from one of our housekeepers. She was a wonderful cook. That was when I was in my teens."

"You're good," he said.

"You really are," Matt seconded. "This is great chicken!"

She laughed. "Glad you like it."

MATT WAS BACK AT THE game console, and Winnie and Kilraven were having second cups of coffee when the doorbell rang.

He went to answer it. As he opened the door, he gave Winnie a concerned look. A tall, dark-haired, dark-eyed woman in a tailored suit with her long hair in a bun came into the apartment, wearing spiked high heels and an attitude. She gave Winnie a long look that didn't soften the ice in those eyes.

"This is your new wife?" the woman asked haughtily.

"Yes, Cammy," Kilraven said. "Don't I get a hug?"

She did hug him, warmly, laughing. "You look wonderful. Who's that?" she asked, frowning at the boy in the wheelchair.

"I'm Matt," he said with a grin. "I'm Winnie's brother. Don't let the wheels fool you, I'm dangerous. I shot five Hunters!"

"Halo," Cammy groaned. "Is there any male in Texas who doesn't play that game?"

"Not many, including my brother, who has his own copy," Kilraven assured her. "Come and meet Winnie Sinclair. She works for Jacobs County EOC as a 911 operator."

"Does she?" Cammy went into the kitchen, her arms folded tight across her breasts. She gave Winnie a cold appraisal.

"It's nice to meet you," Winnie began apprehensively.

Cammy made a sound in the back of her throat. "McKuen hasn't said anything about you at all. This is a very quick wedding. Are you pregnant?"

Winnie gave her an astonished stare. "Well, if I am, we'll call the local television stations and offer them interviews. It will make headlines everywhere!"

"Excuse me?"

"A woman getting pregnant without having sex," Winnie said in a low voice so that Matt wouldn't hear.

"You won't sleep with him?" Cammy asked, shocked. "Well, some wife you're going to be! Did you trick him into marrying you when you found out he had a big ranch and was rich?" she continued doggedly. "You're after his money, aren't you?"

Winnie stood up to her full height, which was almost a head shy of Cammy's. "For your information, Mrs. Kilraven. . ."

"Blackhawk," came the terse reply. "My name is Blackhawk. So is his," she indicated Kilraven, "but he won't use it."

"My choice, Cammy," came the droll reply.

"For your information, Mrs. Blackhawk," Winnie continued haughtily, "my brother is Boone Sinclair of Comanche Wells. You might have seen his photo on the cover of the national ranching magazine this month? The issue about going green on the range?"

Kilraven retrieved his copy of *Modern*

Ranching World from the coffee table and helpfully handed it to Cammy. His eyes were twinkling with amusement.

Cammy read ranching magazines. She loved the ranch. And she knew exactly who Boone Sinclair was the minute she saw his face on the cover of the magazine. "Those Sinclairs?" she asked hesitantly.

"Yes," Winnie said icily. "Those Sinclairs. My people are related to every royal house in Europe. My great-grandmother was the daughter of a titled Spanish don, and quite wealthy. Her mother was the niece of the King of Spain!"

Cammy wanted very badly to throw a loftier genealogy back at Winnie, but her ancestry had produced no person more elevated than a grain merchant in Billings, Montana. She went red in the face.

"As for marrying your stepson for his money," Winnie added cuttingly, "I could probably buy and sell you on my inherited oil and gas holdings alone!"

Cammy swallowed. Hard. She glared at Winnie furiously, looking for a comeback.

"If you'll excuse me now, I have to do the dishes," Winnie said with a huff, and turned back into the kitchen. "By the way,

I can make homemade bread, too. Can you?"

Cammy marched back into the living room, grabbed her purse and coat, and glared at her stepson, who was trying his best not to laugh. She slammed the magazine into his outstretched hand.

"I am never coming back to this apartment in my life as long as you're married to that. . .that little blond chain saw!" she exclaimed with a furious dark glare toward the kitchen. "Goodbye!"

She stormed out of the apartment and slammed the door for effect.

Kilraven burst out laughing. He kept it up until his eyes teared. "Well, that's a first," he told Winnie, hugging her affectionately. "Cammy used to send women running. Jon and I couldn't keep a girlfriend when we were in high school. I thought she'd cut you up like fish bait. And you send her running out the door." He hugged her again, rocking her in his big arms. "My little blond chain saw," he murmured at her ear, and kissed it.

"You're not. . .mad?" she faltered.

He lifted his head. He smiled at her. "I'm not mad."

"I didn't mean to be so unkind," she began.

"Cammy will conveniently forget everything you said and come back with a wedding gift in a day or two, then she'll try to make friends with you." He grinned at her dubious expression. "You'll see. She's all bluff. What she dislikes most is people she can run over."

"I used to let people do that," she confessed. "Working with you inspired me to greater heights."

He bent and nuzzled her nose with his. "I'm inspired, too. Cammy ran like a scalded cat. I've got to call Jon and tell him. He's in New York on a case," he added, reminding her why his brother had missed the wedding.

Matt winked at her. He'd heard all that, but didn't comment.

Kilraven pulled out his cell phone. Winnie, feeling elated and proud of herself, walked back to the kitchen.

"Hey, Jon," Kilraven said into his cell phone, "guess who married a little blond chain saw today!"

12

Winnie settled down with Matt and Kilraven after she'd put the dishes in the dishwasher and stored the leftovers. There were only two controllers and they were using a split screen to battle each other. But when Winnie came in, Matt relinquished his and sat coaching her. It was fun.

About midnight, Matt said good-night and wheeled himself into Kilraven's equipment room where a bed had been made up. Kilraven walked Winnie to hers, making it obvious that he had no intention of sharing it with her, wedding night or not.

"We agreed," he said gently. "Didn't we?"

She smiled. "Yes." She tried not to sound disappointed. She'd had sleepless nights since their interlude on his sofa.

He caught her waist and lifted her up so that he could put his lips to her ear and wouldn't be overheard. "But just in case, are you on the pill?"

She shivered at the deep, husky note in his voice. She cleared her throat. "Yes. The doctor started me on it two days ago."

"Good."

"We aren't going to," she began.

His lips slid from her ear down to her soft mouth and claimed it suddenly with a hunger and intensity that made her shiver from head to toe. His big hands lifted her hips up into his and ground them into the sudden hardness. A surge of heat throbbed down her stomach and made her breath catch under his mouth as he rotated her thighs against his and she moaned helplessly. She felt him smile as he suddenly lifted his head and looked straight into her shocked eyes.

"We aren't going to?" he mused. "Are you sure?"

Her face flamed. He was driving her mad, but she had to consider where this was going to end. He was going to take her to Nassau to get him a conversation with a senator's wife, and then he was going to toss her out the door. She had to keep that in mind.

"Yes," she said quietly. It didn't help when she shivered.

His eyebrow jerked. He set her back on her feet and studied her for a long, somber moment.

"Addictions are hard to cure," she said with as much dignity as she could muster. Hard, considering that her knees were shaking and her voice was unsteady. "The best way to avoid them is not to create them."

"Sensible," he agreed. A corner of his very sensuous mouth curved up. "Little blond chain saw," he added in a soft, amused tone as his silver eyes glittered possessively over her flushed face. "Sleep well."

She managed a smile. "You, too."

He turned and left her. He didn't seem particularly disappointed, because he went right back to his game as if nothing had happened.

Winnie went into the guest bedroom,

put on her pajamas and crawled under the covers. It must be the strangest wedding day any woman ever had.

SHE GOT UP EARLY THE next morning after a viciously sleepless night and cooked a nice breakfast. Matt wheeled into the kitchen a few minutes later, grinning.

"Smells good," he said. "I'm not used to anybody cooking breakfast, especially since Mom got back on homicide," he added. "She gets called out at all hours of the night. Sometimes she doesn't even get home until I'm ready to leave for school."

"What do you eat?" she wondered.

"Cereal, mostly," he said. "I like it, you know. I wasn't criticizing. Mom works hard."

She smiled at him. "Matt, you've got to be the nicest boy I ever met," she told him sincerely. "I'm glad you turned out to be my little brother."

"Thanks," he replied, surprised.

"Oh, it's not what you think," she teased. "The older ones always picked on me because I was the baby. Now you're the baby!"

He chuckled. "I get it. I'm the lowest link in the food chain."

"Or thereabouts." She laughed.

"Where's Kilraven?" he wondered.

"Probably still asleep," she said. "I'm sure I heard plasma rifles going off around daylight."

"Poor guy. I guess he doesn't get much time to play games when he's really on the job."

"I guess not," she agreed.

"It was a nice wedding," he said.

She nodded. "I thought so, too."

"You sure you're really married?" he asked in a deliberately discreet tone.

She glanced at him and smiled. "You ever hear about going undercover?"

"Sure. Mom knows a narc who does that."

"When you go undercover, sometimes you do things so they appear to be one thing, when they're really another thing," she continued.

He was quick. "So you're pretending to be married, but you have a license to prove it if anybody asks."

Her eyebrows lifted. "You're good," she said.

"My mom's a homicide detective," he reminded her. He frowned. "Our mom's a homicide detective," he corrected.

She smiled. "I forgot."

"We going to see her today?"

"You bet," she said enthusiastically. "When do you go back to school?"

"Did you have to bring that up?" he groaned.

"Sorry. I did."

"Monday." He sighed. "I've got homework for it, too, can you imagine? Over the weekend!"

"Education is not for the weakhearted," she pointed out.

"I guess so. Did you like school?"

"Not really," she confessed. "I went to college for two years, but I got sick one winter and failed a course when it was too late to do an 'incomplete.' Blew my GPA. I didn't really like my major, anyway, so I went home and got a job working as a clerk for the Jacobsville Police Department. That's where I met Kilraven."

"His first name's McKuen," he reminded her. "Why don't you call him that?"

"I'm not sure it would be safe," she said thoughtfully.

"You could always call him Mac."

"Going to loan me some body armor first?" she asked dubiously.

He laughed. "Right."

"One of us had better tell him breakfast is ready," she said when she put biscuits and eggs and bacon on the table. She started to set the table.

"One of us. He's your husband."

"Yes, but he's your brother-in-law," she replied. "I think you should call him. He might throw things."

He shot her a grin and turned the wheel-chair. "No guts, no glory," he called over his shoulder.

She sighed with relief. She hadn't wanted to mention that Kilraven might sleep raw, and she wasn't walking into that bedroom if he did. Prude, she told herself, you're married. Yes, she answered herself, but remember what you told yourself about addictions?

She turned right back to the cabinets and pulled out silverware.

KILRAVEN DRAGGED IN five minutes later, fully dressed, his hair immaculately combed. But he was red-eyed and half-asleep.

He pulled out a chair, yawning, and sat down, smiling at Winnie when she put a cup of hot coffee under his nose. "Thanks," he said. "I didn't go to bed until the early news came on."

"I heard," she said.

"Excuse me?"

"Plasma rifles, sniper rifles, grenades. . ."

"Sorry," he said as he sipped coffee.

She laughed. "Don't feel guilty. When I have days off, I do the same thing. I wasn't really sleepy, either," she confessed, avoiding his suddenly amused glance, "but I finally drifted off myself. Matt slept like a rock."

"I always sleep like a rock," Matt said with a grin.

Kilraven didn't reply. He slept fitfully, and it was rare even now that he spent an entire night asleep. The past haunted him.

Winnie saw the pain in his face that he couldn't quite hide, and she felt a stab of conscience that she couldn't be the person he wanted her to be. She couldn't spend a night in his arms and go on with her life, she thought miserably, even if he could.

He sipped coffee, ignoring the food.

"Aren't you hungry?" Matt asked. "These biscuits are really good."

Kilraven glanced at him, frowning, then at the platters of food. "Good Lord," he exclaimed, looking at Winnie. "You made biscuits?"

She nodded. "I can do all sorts of breads."

He reached for one, pulled it apart, buttered it and put on strawberry jam. He bit into it and his eyes closed. He almost groaned. "I haven't had a homemade biscuit since I was a kid," he confessed, smiling. "We had this cook, Laredo, who could do almost anything with flour, even cakes. He made the most delicious biscuits, but these are even better."

Winnie smiled. "Thanks."

He reached for the platters of bacon and eggs. "I'm not used to a hot breakfast, but I'll bet I could adapt, if I tried."

Matt chuckled as he reached for another biscuit. "Me, too. Homicide detectives don't have time to do a lot of cooking."

"Neither do Feds," he pointed out.

"Or 911 operators." Winnie raised her hand.

"This lady at dispatch saved Mom's life last year," Matt related. "She went to interview a witness in a homicide and he turned out to be the perp. Mom managed to hit 911 on her cell phone, inside her coat while the guy was threatening her with a gun."

He grinned. "She had two squad cars in less than two minutes, believe it or not, with sirens and lights going full tilt. While they were diverting the suspect, Mom disarmed the perp, knocked his legs out from under him and cuffed him, all this before the uniformed officers even got to the door!"

"Wow," Winnie said, impressed.

"The dispatcher knew Mom," Matt continued, "and she found two squad cars in the vicinity on her computer and sent them."

"Quick thinking," Kilraven said. He grinned at Winnie. "Your sister saved my butt in a similar manner."

"You did?" Matt asked, waiting to be told how.

Winnie shrugged. "I just had a hunch that he needed backup."

"Yes, and sent it before I was able to call and ask for it," he added pointedly.

"Mom knows stuff before it happens, too," Matt said. "She was at the hospital when they brought me in, after her ex-husband tried to kill me." His face was somber. "She said she knew. She saw it, in her mind. It's sort of scary, sometimes."

"Yes, it is," Winnie confessed. "I see things that I wish I couldn't see."

"Well, I'm glad you saw that I needed help," Kilraven informed her, "or we wouldn't be having this conversation."

She grinned at him. He grinned back.

HE FINISHED BREAKFAST and pulled out his cell phone. "I've got to call my brother and find out if there's any new intel on the case."

He moved into the next room. The phone rang and Joceline Perry answered it.

"Hi, Perry," he said, using her last name, as he always did. "Is the boss in?"

"I understand that he doesn't do many concerts these days," she cracked, referring to the real "Boss," Bruce Springsteen.

"Funny girl," he muttered.

"And that was a movie with Barbra Streisand," she said with mock excitement.

"Give me my brother or I'll come down there and anoint you with India ink."

"Terroristic threats and acts!" she exclaimed.

"Joceline. . .!"

"That's more like it," she told him.

There was a click. "Blackhawk," Jon's voice came over the line.

"Can you do something for me?" Kilraven asked.

"Sure. What do you want?"

"Go out into the waiting room, find something wet and dump it over Joceline's head."

"Let me check the deductible on my medical insurance first," Jon mused. "What do you want? Advice on how to manage the 'little blond chain saw' or how to calm Cammy down?" he added with a chuckle.

"Cammy's been talking to you," he replied.

"Not talking so much as shouting," Jon replied complacently. "I'd just turned my cell phone on when I got back from New York and walked into my apartment, and it was already ringing. I gather that Cammy's sense of superiority was temporarily displaced by feelings of inadequacy." He chuckled. "I have to meet Winnie. She must be a firecracker."

"Actually, she's not," Kilraven replied pensively. "She's shy and quiet around people she doesn't know. But Cammy was pretty overbearing, especially when I mentioned that Winnie was a 911 operator. I'm sure she knew that Boone Sinclair was recently on the cover of the nation's top cattle magazine because we all subscribe, but she didn't connect Winnie with him until I put the magazine in her hand." He chuckled. "She does now."

Jon chuckled, too. "I've never known my mother to be at such a disadvantage with anybody."

"Me, either," Kilraven replied. "But let me give you some advice, if you ever get engaged, make sure she wears body armor. If Cammy's that bad about me, just imagine how she'll be about you."

"No worries there. I've got too much work on my desk to be thinking about women. Plus Giles Lamont is due for parole soon," he added darkly.

Kilraven felt uncomfortable at the mention of the man's name. Jon was the arresting officer in a federal case that had put Lamont, a gambler with underworld ties, behind bars for five years. He'd sworn that he'd kill Jon if he ever got out of prison, even if it meant going back in stir forever, or getting the needle. "You could go to the parole board," Kilraven began.

"And do what?" Jon asked curtly. "Do you know how many death threats I get a week? He's just one more. Like they're going to keep a man in prison just because he threatened a federal officer!"

"Terroristic threats and acts," Kilraven began.

"Without witnesses," Jon replied.

Kilraven cursed under his breath. "Listen, you watch your back. You're the only brother I've got."

"Thanks, I'm fond of you, too," Jon quipped. "On a more cheerful note, guess who just bought a first-class plane ticket to Nassau?"

Kilraven's heart skipped. "Senator Sanders's wife?" he asked hopefully.

"The same. She's leaving tonight."

"Then we're leaving first thing tomorrow," Kilraven told him. "Keep me in the loop if you hear anything else, okay?"

"Will do. Have a nice trip, and don't seduce Winnie."

"What?"

"If she stood up to Cammy, your opinion must be important to her," came the quiet reply. "Don't break her heart trying to solve the case."

Kilraven felt his temper bristling. "My daughter was murdered," he reminded Jon. "I'll do anything, hurt anybody, whatever it takes to find her killer. I can't help it. She was my whole life," he gritted.

Jon drew in a long breath. "I know how much you loved Melly," he said gently. "I'm working as hard as I can on the case. But you just remember that several people are already dead because they knew too much, and the people responsible have assaulted two police detectives assigned to the case. Get my drift?"

"I'll watch my back," Kilraven promised. "Keep digging. If we can get anything on Hank Sanders, anything that connects him to the DB in Jacobsville or the assaults, we can hang him out to dry. Then we have a way to bargain with him."

"Bargain with a killer?"

"I'm not convinced that he is one," Kilraven said suddenly. "It doesn't sound like a decorated navy SEAL, does it? His big brother likes young girls and he has enough money to buy and sell them. I can't get that fourteen-year-old girl he drugged out of my mind. Rogers is going to try to find her and talk to her when she gets out of the hospital. If we can get her to talk to an assistant D.A., maybe she'll implicate the senator. He might plead to lesser charges and confess something."

"You're assuming that the Sanders boys were responsible for Melly," Jon said quietly. "You have no evidence, not a shred, to base that assumption on. Just because one man operates outside the law, it doesn't mean he kills people."

"I know that."

"So walk softly," Jon continued.

"I will."

"Sure you will, wearing steel-toed combat boots with spikes." Jon sighed. "Remember when we were on the FBI Hostage Rescue Team together?" he added, smiling at the memory.

"I do," Kilraven said. "Those were good days, while they lasted."

"You jumped in and got shot, thumbing your nose at proper procedure," Jon reminded him. "That's why they threw you out."

"Well, the CIA caught me when the FBI tossed me," Kilraven mused. "They like people who think outside boxes."

"Just don't do any more jumping. Okay?"

"Hey, if I lose it all, I can go back to the ranch and be a cowboy," Kilraven said. "Or move to Jacobsville and work for Cash Grier."

"You'd never fit in a small town or on a ranch," Jon said quietly. "You live for the adrenaline rush."

"It's the only thing that keeps me sane," Kilraven said heavily. "I don't need a lot of time to sit around and think."

"That's why we have video games," Jon replied. "I've got a new one for Xbox 360, *Dragon Age Origins* and I just signed up for *World of Warcraft* on the PC."

"I'm still working my way through *Halo: ODST*," came the amused reply. "In fact, I was up until daylight playing it."

"Gamers are not sane."

"Speak for yourself." Kilraven chuckled.

"You take care," Jon told him. "And if you need help, call me."

"Hey, I'm taking my own personal dispatch person along with me," Kilraven replied. "If I need help, she can get it for me immediately!"

Jon chuckled, said goodbye and hung up.

Joceline stuck her head in the door. "I'm

going to lunch," she said. "Would you like a sandwich?"

Wary of her, because she never offered to bring him food, his eyes narrowed as he stared her way. "Would I like. . .?"

She nodded. "They make great ones at Chuck's, near the airport road. But if you're going, you should go now, it gets crowded early," she told him, grinned and closed the door again.

He threw a book at the door.

"I saw that!" she called back, and kept walking.

KILRAVEN WALKED BACK into the kitchen. "I've just booked us on a flight to the Bahamas, first thing in the morning," he told Winnie, who looked stunned. He glanced at Matt. "Sorry, sport, but you'll have to go back to the ranch for a while."

"That's okay," Matt said. "Boone's going to teach me how to ride a horse!"

Winnie grinned. "You couldn't be in better hands," she assured him. "I'll miss you."

"You could take me along," Matt told her, grinning.

"Oh, sure, we're pretending to be on a honeymoon with my kid brother tagging

along. I'm sure everyone would believe
that," Winnie mused.

"Just kidding," Matt said. He shook his
head. "Life's funny, isn't it? A few days ago
it was just Mom and me. She got shot and
now I have a whole family." He looked at
Winnie affectionately. "It's nice."

She smiled. "Very nice."

Kilraven glanced at his watch. "If we're
going to see your mother, we need to leave
pretty soon. We'll have to have time to get
the future *Halo* champ moved."

"Me?" Matt asked. "I've only gotten past
the first level."

"In one day," Kilraven said with mock
disgust. "Took me three."

"Wow!" Matt enthused.

"Let's go," Kilraven told his companions.

"But the dishes," Winnie began, nodding toward them, stacked in the sink.

"The dishes can wait," he said. He wasn't
rude, but he said it with an odd note in his
voice, as if he didn't like having her work
around his apartment.

She held up both hands. "Okay. It's your
apartment," she said, and managed a
smile. "I'll just grab my purse and my coat.
Matt, can you get yours. . .?"

"Sure." He buzzed off toward the spare bedroom.

KILRAVEN WAS SOMBER all the way to the hospital. He smiled at Matt and talked video games with him, but there was a sudden coolness in his manner toward Winnie. She couldn't help but notice it. She wondered if she'd offended him by making breakfast.

They found Gail sitting up in bed, but less animated than she had been.

"Third day," Kilraven said, nodding. "It's always the worst one."

"I'm finding that out," Gail replied after she'd hugged Matt and her daughter lightly. She was favoring the arm on the side where she'd been shot. "It hurts like hell and I'm running a temp. The doctor is gloating. I tried to make him let me go home yesterday, and he wouldn't. Now I see why. It would be all right if he wasn't so damned smug about it," she muttered.

Kilraven chuckled. It was the first hint of humor in him since they'd left the apartment. "He was the same way with Marquez," he told her. "But he might have a case on you. He's divorced."

"He's years too old for me," Gail said haughtily.

Kilraven lifted both eyebrows. "He's a year older than you are."

"Exactly," Gail said.

Winnie burst out laughing.

Gail's eyes twinkled at her. But she was feverish and subdued because of the pain.

They didn't stay long. Winnie and Matt didn't want to tire their mother. Winnie made sure she had Boone's cell phone number.

"Yes," Gail said softly. "He and Clark and Keely came to see me last night. I didn't realize how much Clark and Matt favor each other."

"Boone was probably reserved, wasn't he?" Winnie asked, nodding when her mother looked surprised at the comment. "He's always like that until he gets to know you. It's been a long time."

"He's very much like your father," Gail said. "He has the same strength and he's just as reserved, but you always know you can depend on him."

"Yes," Winnie said, and she smiled.

"Clark's a great gamer," Matt told her.

"He's been showing me new ways to use grenades! It'll be great training for when I grow up and join a rolling SWAT team," he added with twinkling dark eyes.

Gail groaned. "No! You are not joining a SWAT team, and I don't care how fast you are in that thing!" she indicated the wheelchair.

"That's just jealousy," Matt told his sister. "She tried to get into SWAT, but they said she was too old."

"Too old!" Gail burst out. "Can you imagine?"

"Delicately aged wine requires careful handling," Kilraven said smoothly, repeating one of his favorite adages.

Gail looked at him. "You drunk?" she asked sharply.

He glowered. "I was trying to make you feel better."

"Good idea. Go find the so-and-so who put me in the hospital and lock him up for twenty years, that will make me feel better!"

"Sorry, we have another priority right now. Winnie and I are flying down to Nassau tomorrow."

Gail's eyes narrowed. She turned to

Matt. "How about taking a dollar and getting me a soft drink at the canteen?" she asked him.

"Sure! You want a Coke?"

She nodded. She started to reach in her drawer, but Kilraven was quicker. He handed Matt a dollar bill. "Don't use it to impress girls," he teased.

"Some impression this would make," Matt scoffed. "These days, it takes a Jaguar." He pursed his lips. "You're my brother-in-law. How about loaning me the Jag in four years when I start dating?"

"Get out of here," Kilraven said in mock anger.

Matt chuckled all the way out the door.

Kilraven moved closer to the bed, all teasing gone out of him. "The senator's wife is on her way to her beach house. It sides on property the Sinclairs own," he said. "Winnie's going with me so that we can get to know her, in hopes that she might feel confident enough to share some information about her brother-in-law."

"You got married to pump a suspect's relative?" Gail exclaimed.

Kilraven glared at her. "I'm not ruining Winnie's reputation by having her live with me for several days while we court the senator's wife."

Gail smiled. "You're not a bad guy, Kilraven."

"Yes, he is," Winnie mused, but her eyes twinkled.

Kilraven gave her a wink, laughing when she flushed.

"Well, both of you be careful," Gail cautioned. "These people play for keeps."

"You're good with hunches," Kilraven said. "What do you think? Are we following a cold trail, or could the senator's brother have a stake in this case?"

Gail was silent for a minute. "I don't really know. I think the senator's up to his ears in parts of it," she said. "I want to talk to the mother of that young girl who was found dead."

He was somber. He'd thought about questioning the teen who lived, but never about asking the mother of the girl who was found dead. "You think she might know something more than she told the police at the time it happened?"

"Could be. She supposedly went on a date and turned up dead in a condition where her own family wouldn't have recognized her, just like our DB on the Little Carmichael River. Her car was even found next to a river. It just seems too close to be a coincidence."

"I agree. But it would be a long shot."

"I'm famous for long shots."

"You won't get out of here for several days," Kilraven said.

"Not unless I can K.O. the doctor." Gail sighed.

"When we get back, maybe we'll have some new information to work with. Meanwhile, I've got a buddy watching out for you, just in case your assailant comes calling again."

"I'm a cop," she pointed out.

"Yes, and your department's budget is less than my annual video game allowance," he said sarcastically, "so I don't imagine they're lining up for overtime to trail you."

She grimaced.

"My buddy is between jobs and he loves catching crooks. You won't see him or know who he is, but he'll be around."

"Thanks, Kilraven," she said.

"You're my temporary mother-in-law." He chuckled. "It's the least I can do."

"Don't turn your back, even in Nassau," Gail cautioned them. "The senator's wife may accept you being there on face value, but I'm betting her husband wouldn't. One thing I did find out before I was shot— there's an old family retainer, Jay Copper. He's very protective of Senator Sanders. There's been gossip that he's really the senator's father. He was in prison for several years for a messy homicide, got out on a technicality. Anyway, he was charged at least once with intimidating a reporter who was digging into that statutory rape case. Threatened to have his family blown up with a shotgun."

Kilraven's intake of breath was audible.

"Yes, I thought that might sound familiar." Gail nodded, her eyes cold. "Copper doesn't like Hank Sanders or the senator's wife, Patricia. One of my contacts said that the main reason Patricia stays out of the senator's way is because she's afraid of Copper."

Kilraven's eyes narrowed. "I heard something about that old guy. They called him copperhead, back in the seventies, when he was supposedly involved in drug trafficking in Dallas."

"That's the one. He's still on the job, intimidating everybody he can to keep the senator nice and safe."

"What about Hank Sanders?"

She pursed her lips. "Now isn't that an interesting question. I went to see Garon Grier down at the Bureau a few days before I was shot, and guess who was waiting for him in the parking lot, trying not to be seen?"

Kilraven's heart jumped. "Hank Sanders."

She nodded. "Why is a notorious criminal keeping company with one of the more notorious conservative FBI agents?"

"There's another curious fact. Hank was a decorated navy SEAL."

She pursed her lips. "That turns us in a whole other direction. And I have a theory."

"So do I," Kilraven replied. "But we'll keep that between us until Winnie and I get back from the Bahamas. Maybe we can find out more."

"Even if Jay Copper didn't go with Patricia Sanders to the Bahamas, ten to one he's got one of his goons there keeping an eye on her," Gail added. "Word was that she was trying to divorce the senator, until

Copper mentioned that it would hurt the senator in the polls and he wouldn't like her to try it. She backed off at once."

His eyes narrowed. "I get the idea."

"Be careful," she told him firmly.

"I'm always careful." He smiled as he glanced at Winnie. "And don't worry. I'll take care of your daughter."

Winnie smiled, but she wished he'd said "my wife" instead of Gail's daughter. Still, it was early days yet. She had time to make an impression. He was quite obviously hungry for her. And where there was smoke, there was fire.

13

They got off the plane in Nassau with the rest of the business-class section and even though it was winter back in the United States, it was perpetual summer in the Bahamas. They looked out the window of the terminal as they came onto the concourse. People were walking around in shorts.

"Why did I wear a coat?" Winnie groaned.

"Because you were cold?" Kilraven mused. "Come on. Let's get in the line for customs."

"It will be slow. It always is."

"Are we in a race?" he asked.

She hit him.

THEY LOOKED LIKE A society couple. Winnie was wearing a trim, very expensive cream-colored couture pantsuit with designer high heels and purse. Kilraven was wearing silk slacks and shirt and an expensive jacket. He made a point of telling the customs official that he and Winnie were newlyweds on their honeymoon. They walked out of the terminal past a steel drum band, unconsciously moving to the rhythm of the music.

A limousine that Kilraven had hired when he made the reservations was waiting for them. It whisked them along the winding road that led from the airport, past Cable Beach, to the road that led to the exclusive section of New Providence where so many millionaires had summer homes.

"Isn't it beautiful?" she asked, looking out the tinted window. "The first time we came here, I must have been about four years old. I saw the white sand and all the incredible shades of aqua and turquoise of the water and asked my parents if it was a painting."

"I know what you mean," he said. "Those colors look too vivid to be real."

"Have you been here before?" she asked.

He laughed. "I've been through here," he replied. "I've seen airports and hotels all over the world, but my experience with open country has been mostly in the dark."

She understood the reference at once. "You never talk about it, do you?"

"Wouldn't dare," he replied. "Most of it is classified." He pursed his lips and smiled at her. "I trust you, but you'd need a government clearance to know particulars."

She made a face. "I tell you everything," she countered.

His eyebrows arched. "You do?"

"I told you about my mother and my father," she pointed out.

His eyes grew sad. "And I told you about my daughter. I've never spoken of her to anyone outside my family, except people directly involved in the case."

"I'm sorry you lost her in such a way."

He averted his gaze to the scenery passing the windows, tall casuarina pines and royal palms lining the narrow paved road. "So am I."

She pressed a wrinkle out of the soft fabric of her slacks. "Haven't you ever thought about having another child?"

"No," he said at once, and with ice dripping from the tones.

The violence of the reply disconcerted her. She met his eyes and almost flinched at what she saw in them.

"I won't go through it again," he assured her.

"But just because you lost one child in such a horrible way. . .!"

He held up a hand. "I won't discuss it, either," he said coldly. His silvery eyes were glittering like metal. "I appreciate your help, I really do. But if you have any illusions about why we're here, let me disenchant you. We're here to ask questions and get answers, not spend a few torrid nights in each other's arms. I could walk away after and never look back. You couldn't. You're too young and too innocent for a casual affair. So we'll do what we came here to do, go back to the States and get a quiet annulment. And there won't be any complications. Least of all a pregnancy. Period."

She felt as if he'd stuck a pin in her. He

was intimidating like that. She was used to him being amused or teasing around her. He'd never been really harsh, except that one time when she messed up at dispatch and nearly got him killed. This was the real man behind the banter, and he was scary. No wonder Gail had said he was dangerous.

He realized that he was upsetting her and he forced himself to calm down. She was a normal, loving woman who wanted a home and family. Her feelings for him were getting in the way of her common sense, and that was only infatuation. She'd get over it. She was, as he'd already said, very young. Twenty-two to his thirty-two.

"Sorry," she said, and managed a smile.

"No, I'm sorry," he replied quietly. "I forget your age sometimes." He forced a smile. "You'll find a man who wants to settle down and have a family with you, one day. But it won't be me. You know that already."

She nodded. She wasn't really agreeing, but it seemed safer to appear to acquiesce. At least he wasn't looking at her with that icy glare anymore.

"Now there's a dangerous method of

travel," she said to divert him, pointing to mopeds zipping past in the other direction.

He chuckled. "I had to appropriate one of those in another country for emergency transport once," he confessed. "Rounded a curve and went right over the handlebars." He shook his head. "That's how I ended up with a steel pin in my leg. It's a lot harder than it looks."

"And you drive a Jaguar?" she chided.

He frowned. "Jags are built to be stable on the road at extremely high speeds. Mopeds aren't."

"Well, my brother thinks Jags can fly. He's never been able to convince state troopers that he should be allowed to fly them on the interstate."

He chuckled. "Me, either."

"I wish we were going downtown. I'd love to see the old British Colonial hotel," she mused.

"The what?"

"Oh, that's not what they call it now," she said. "It's the Hilton Hotel these days. It's right downtown, next to the wharf. It was the site of old Fort Nassau and the scene of many battles in the seventeeth century. It was also the place to be seen socially at the turn of the twentieth century. The Duke and Duchess of Windsor even attended parties there when he was governor of the Bahamas during the Second World War." She smiled. "There's a statue of the pirate Woodes Rogers right out in front of the hotel. Ironically, he was the first governor of the Bahamas."

"Just as Henry Morgan, the pirate, was the first governor of Jamaica," he chuckled. "His grave was lost in the late seventeeth century during a devastating earthquake that sent most of Port Royal to the bottom of the ocean."

She shivered. "Yes, there was an earthquake in Portugal in 1755 that sent a stone quay into the sea, killing people who'd rushed there for refuge. They estimated that over 20,000 people perished in Lisbon in a matter of minutes, from the earthquake and the tsunamis that followed it."

He stared at her. "You follow earthquake history."

She laughed self-consciously. "Well, yes," she confessed. "I practically live on the United States Geological Survey site."

"So do I," he exclaimed.

"Really!"

"Really. There and the Weather Channel and at www.spaceweather.com," he added. "I follow sunspots and meteor showers and. . ."

". . .and near earth asteroids on Spaceweather," she laughed. "Yes. Me, too."

His eyes were twinkling. "You have a telescope."

"How did you know that?" she asked, startled.

"A lucky guess. I have one, too. You didn't see it because it's in my bedroom. It's a composite, a. . ."

"Schmidt-Cassegrain," she guessed, smiling sheepishly when he laughed. "How big is the aperture?"

"Eight inches."

"Mine's ten," she bragged.

"Yes, but you live out in the country." He sighed. "I'm in town, and the eight-inch lets in less light pollution."

"You'll have to come look at astronomical events with me, when we get through with our undercover stuff," she said. "Boone had a small observatory built for me in the back patio. I can leave my telescope out in all weathers, because it's waterproof."

"I'd like that," he said seriously. He was looking at her oddly. "In all the time we've known each other, you never mentioned liking natural events or astronomy."

"It never came up," she said.

"I guess not." He liked what he was learning about her. But she was still far too young, especially for what he'd been thinking about when he first proposed this trip. He was vaguely ashamed of himself, more so when he recalled her recent turmoil in finding that she had a brother she didn't even know about and that her uncle might be involved peripherally in the recent murder. Then, too, her mother had been shot. Perhaps that wouldn't have bothered her some weeks ago, but since discovering her mother's true situation, it had hit her hard. And he'd been thinking of a holiday romp with her, a sexual escapade that he could forget, but that she couldn't. She cared about him. She really did. It was disturbing, on several levels.

Monica, his late wife, had liked his family's wealth. Despite his job as a policeman at the time, she knew his family had money and she'd decided she might as well marry for money as love. Perhaps she'd been fond of him, but it had never been more than that. She'd been mostly unconcerned with Melly after her birth. Kilraven had doted on the child, taking her places with him, showing her off. He clamped down on the memory. It was painful. He recalled that Cammy, his stepmother, hadn't liked Monica at all. Not that she liked any women her son and stepson brought around. But she'd often said that there was something dark and cold lying curled up in Monica's brain.

"Deep thoughts?" Winnie asked gently.

"What?" He laughed humorlessly. "I was thinking about Monica. My wife," he added when she looked puzzled. "She lived in Neiman Marcus and Saks. She loved clothes and diamonds and parties."

"She must have loved her family, too," she said.

"She loved my money." He sighed. "But she never bought a dress or a pair of shoes or even a toy for Melly. If I gave her money to buy stuff for Melly, she bought clothes for herself with it. I finally learned to shop for my daughter myself."

Winnie was surprised. In the other woman's place, she'd have been showering her daughter with presents, cuddling her, taking her places, taking photos of her night and day. . . She averted her eyes and her hands gripped her purse hard. "That's sad," she said.

"I asked her once why she didn't ever play with the baby," he recalled solemnly. "She said it was her job to have the child, mine to raise it. She'd done her part. She didn't even like children, she just got tired of me badgering her about having kids." He dropped his eyes to the floorboard. "Cammy might not be your idea of the perfect mother," he added with a deep laugh, "but she was a hell of a stepmother. She was always taking me places, doing things with me, buying me stuff. When Jon came along, he was my brother, plain and simple—she treated us both just alike. Heaven help any teacher or bully who gave us trouble at school. Cammy would be on them like a duck on a june bug. Even Dad wasn't ever so protective of us."

"I'm sure she improves on closer acquaintance," Winnie said stiffly. "I'll see if

Boone will loan me a cattle prod to carry if I have to talk to her again. . ."

He gave her an affectionate look. "Little blond chain saw," he said with pure amusement.

He made it sound like a caress. She felt warm, safe, secure. She smiled. "I'm not like that, usually."

The smile faded. "I know. You don't assert yourself enough. People will walk all over you, if you let them."

"You'd know." She sighed.

"I'm used to walking on people," he pointed out. "You have to stand up to me."

"I'm still trying to stand up to Boone," she said, wincing. "It's not easy."

"You did very well, convincing him to let you come down here with me," he said somberly. "I was proud of you."

She lifted her eyes to his. "You were?"

He nodded. "Stick around with me for a while and I'll have you eating tigers with just a little hot sauce, raw."

Oh, give me the chance, she thought. But she only smiled. "I'll follow your sterling example."

The car was slowing. It pulled up to a wrought-iron metal gate, very ornate, and

Winnie jumped out and punched a code into the computerized access panel. She got back in. The gate opened.

"Boone had it installed," she said. "We had a break-in a few years ago. Now we're very security conscious."

He nodded. He was going to make sure the security was top-notch while they were in residence. He didn't want any surprise visits, just in case they ruffled enough feathers to invite unwanted visitors.

THE HOUSE WAS WHITE with a red ceramic tile roof. It sat well back from the beach, on a plot of land that was covered with casuarina pines and palms. Around the long front porch were hibiscus and lantana, and brilliant bougainvillea climbing the patio balcony.

"Nice," Kilraven said as they walked up onto the porch, the driver following with their luggage. He had the driver set the bags down and gave him a substantial tip, with thanks. The man saluted with a big grin, and went back to his vehicle.

Winnie was putting her key in the door. She'd already disabled the security pad.

She opened it and sighed at the beauty

of the interior. The furniture was pristine, the floors spotless and highly polished wood. There were original paintings on the walls, one of Boone and Clark and Winnie as children. The house had been in the family for two generations.

Kilraven walked to the portrait and studied it. Winnie had long, wavy hair. She was wearing a white dress and holding a red hibiscus flower, laughing. She was very pretty.

"I was five years old when that was painted," she said, looking at it from beside him. "My parents were still together. We used to come here for several weeks in the summer."

He nodded. He looked around. The furnishings were nice, but they looked new. "These aren't very old," he remarked.

"No. The last big hurricane that hit the island got the original house," she said sadly. "The painting survived because it was on loan to a local gallery, which survived. We lost everything, except the shell of the house. Boone had it rebuilt. It's a replica of the original, but without the things that gave it a history."

"The painting survived, at least," he commented.

"Yes. But we learned a hard lesson. Now we don't bring heirlooms down here anymore. Just in case." She turned. He was still looking at the painting. "I'll bet you've lived through hurricanes at least once."

He smiled faintly and dug his hands into his pockets. "Hurricanes, typhoons, tornadoes, sandstorms and enemy attacks with blazing guns."

She grimaced. "I've never even been in a tornado, although one went right by the house not too many years ago." She laughed. "And I've never had to face an attack by anybody armed."

"No reason for you to have to," he pointed out.

"Thank goodness." She went toward the kitchen. "I phoned down here before we left San Antonio and had Marco come up and turn on the electricity and stock the fridge. He acts as part-time caretaker for us. He also owns a local art store." She laughed. "He's the reason we still have that painting. He has strict instructions to rush right down here and put it in storage if there's even a gale warning."

"You could take it to Comanche Wells," he said.

"It belongs here," she replied simply. "But we did have it copied."

"Good thinking."

"Are you hungry?" she asked.

"Starved." He sighed. "Peanuts don't do a thing for me."

"In defense of the airlines," she said, "they have to feed the monkeys something."

"Why can't they feed us real meals? I was on this flight to Japan," he recalled with a smile, "and I asked for Japanese cuisine. It came in several stages, just as it does in Osaka at a good restaurant. I loved it."

They went into the kitchen and Winnie opened the refrigerator. She reached in and then turned with a ham platter in one hand and a mayonnaise jar in another. "I've never been to Asia. How do they serve food?"

"In tiny bits," he said. "On one plate, you might get a morsel of meat with a small slice of fruit. On another, a spoonful of salad. Dessert comes on a plate in the form of a walnut-sized scoop of plum ice cream with a small leaf and a drizzle of syrup for decoration. It's edible art."

"Wow."

"Like they do gifts," he said, moving to the counter to find plates and bread and in a drawer to pull out a knife for the mayonnaise. "It doesn't matter what the present is, they're concerned with the way it's wrapped. The more elegant, the better."

"You liked it there," she commented.

He nodded. "Very much." He chuckled as he watched her make ham sandwiches.

"What's funny?"

"I was thinking that I could never commit a crime on the streets of Osaka without being immediately taken into custody. I'm more than a head taller than most people I met."

She grinned. She looked down at his shoes. "And with bigger feet, I imagine."

"That's another thing, if you think you may need a second pair of shoes, you're advised to take them with you. You won't find a size to fit you unless you have feet the size of yours." He was looking at her little feet in the high heels and his expression was almost affectionate. "What do you wear, anyway, about a five?"

"Five and a half," she corrected.

"Tiny little feet," he mused. "Pretty in those strappy high heels."

She flushed. "Thanks."

He took the knife out of her hand and put it on the table. His expression was unreadable as he suddenly lifted her by the waist, right up to his eyes. "You promised not to wear anything suggestive," he said.

She gasped. "Listen, I'm covered from head to midcalf. . .!"

His mouth brushed hers, sending shivers of pleasure down her spine. "Those sexy little feet aren't covered," he whispered. He nibbled her upper lip.

"My. . .feet. . .aren't covered?" she faltered.

"Sexy feet," he whispered. His tongue slid under her top lip and explored the soft, moist flesh. His big hands tightened on her waist. He moved just a few steps to the counter and lifted her there, so that she was almost on a level with his eyes. His lips whispered over her face, from her cheek to her nose, down to the corners of her mouth.

While he was exploring her face and enjoying her helpless little gasps, his hands were busy on her jacket and the front clip of the bra under it. She didn't realize it until she felt the air on her bare skin, until she saw his eyes dropping down, until she heard his breath catch.

She would have jerked at the bra, but the way he was looking at her made her heart stop. His hand traced over the high, firm swell of her breast, his fingers smoothing down over the suddenly taut nipple. It was like the night on his sofa, all over again, and she was helpless.

"Beautiful breasts," he whispered tautly. "As pink as the inside of a conch shell. Soft. Silky. Delicious."

As he spoke, his head bent. His lips took the place of his fingers in a light, whispery caress that was so tender it made her whole body clench.

"Sweet as honey," he whispered. His other hand smoothed up her rib cage, over the breast he wasn't kissing.

Winnie was on fire. She'd never been touched like that voluntarily before Kilraven came along. Once a boy had grabbed her on a date and hurt her when she fought her way out of his arms. No other man had ever been allowed to go this far.

She arched her back in helpless response to the sensations he was arousing.

"You like this, do you?" he murmured. "I know something you'll like better."

As he spoke, his mouth opened and he took almost her whole breast inside it, teasing the nipple with his tongue as the soft suction caught her in the grip of a hunger she'd never felt before.

She moaned, a high-pitched little skirl of sound that brought Kilraven's blood up, hard. His mouth became insistent, almost violent, on her soft skin. All at once, he lifted her again, only to rivet her hips to the rising hardness of his body, to show her the desire that raged in him from the contact.

His mouth bit at hers. "I had a buddy in Iraq," he whispered roughly. "He came home on leave and his wife was walking around in a short gown with nothing under it. He dropped his pants, lifted her onto him and walked around the house, bouncing her against him. He said the climax was so violent that they fell down the steps into the sunken living room and had to go to the emergency room after." His mouth ground into hers. "He said it was worth a broken ankle."

She shivered. The mental imagery made her even hotter than she already was.

His hands ground her hips into his and he groaned.

Her hands were also busy, pulling at buttons until she reached hard muscle and thick hair. She rubbed her breasts against his chest in a fever of need, moaning again at the sensation it produced.

"I can't. . .stop," he bit off. "It's been too long!"

"I don't care," she whimpered. She wrapped her legs around him, shivering. "Please. . ."

He didn't need to be asked twice. He carried her into the first bedroom he came to, put her on the bed and stripped.

Her eyes widened as she saw him without the protection of clothing. He was incredible-looking, all muscle and tanned skin, all man. She was too aroused to feel embarrassed, even when he stripped her as efficiently and tossed her back onto the coverlet.

He covered her with his body, his face taut and grim, rigid with the desire that was consuming him. He moved her legs apart and lowered himself between them.

"Are you really a virgin?" he whispered roughly.

"Sorry. Yes," she managed as she felt him against her.

He slid a hand under her hips and lifted her. His eyes held hers as he impaled her suddenly.

She cried out, shocked and hurt.

His teeth clenched. He held her still when she tried to move back away from him. "It won't hurt for long," he promised gruffly.

But it did. She bit her lower lip until blood dropped, salty and hot, on her tongue. She closed her eyes, aware of his harsh breathing, the violent downward push of his hips as he drove for satisfaction, blind and deaf to everything except the need to overcome the anguish that consumed him. The tension snapped very quickly, in a red rush of sensation that made him cry out with its intensity. He shuddered over her, ramming his hips down against hers as he filled her body with his in one final, insistent surge of passion.

He felt her tears as his face slid against hers, felt her shivering. It had been bad, and he'd lost control. He kissed the tears away. His hand smoothed tenderly over her hair, brushing it away from her wet, pale face.

He looked down into her eyes with quiet apology. "It's been seven years," he whispered quietly. "I'm sorry. I couldn't stop."

She couldn't stop shivering. "Seven years?" she whispered, surprised.

He nodded. He bent and brushed his mouth over her closed eyelids, sipping away the wetness. "I'm a prude, just like my brother," he whispered. "I think people should be married before they have sex."

She swallowed, trying to cope with the pain. "So do I."

He propped himself on an elbow and studied her face quietly. "I've never had a virgin," he confessed.

She frowned. "Your wife. . .?"

"She was a party girl," he said heavily. "I thought all women were like you, that they waited for marriage. I had a shock on my wedding night, when she shared the benefit of her sensual education with me." He managed a brief smile. "I was shocked and mad and couldn't even express it, because she got me so hot I'd have died to have her. She kept me that way for three years."

She searched his eyes. Incredible, to be lying together with him in such intimacy and talk to each other like this. "I don't know anything about men," she confessed shyly, "except what I've read in books and seen in movies."

"And heard from girlfriends?" he prompted.

"Actually, I've only ever had one real girlfriend, my sister-in-law, Keely, and we don't ever talk about such things," she told him. "So I guess I'm a prude, too."

He moved the hair away from her ear and studied it. "You have tiny little ears."

She smiled. "They match my tiny little feet."

"Sexy feet," he said again. "Some men like breasts, others like legs. I like feet."

"My goodness!"

He lifted his head. "How bad is it, when I do this?" He moved his hips, very slowly.

She caught her breath.

He lifted up and then pushed down again.

She caught her breath again. But this time, her fingernails bit into his muscular arms and pulled.

He smiled. "I thought it was best to get the pain out of the way first," he whispered. "Because I know a few things that I can teach you."

"You. . .do?" She was shivering, but not from pain. Not this time.

"Mmm-hmm," he murmured. He slid his hand under her hips and lifted her, tenderly, into the slow thrust of his body. "Put your legs together. That's right."

She moaned harshly.

"See?" His head bent and he brushed her mouth open with his lips while he moved lazily against her, each movement more arousing, more sensual than the one before.

Her fingernails bit into him again.

"Move your hands down my back and do that," he whispered.

She slid them over his hips and onto the firm muscles, digging in.

He groaned and arched, increasing his possession of her.

She gasped.

He looked straight into her eyes and shifted. The pleasure bit into him like a sweet knife. He could see the echo of it in her own face. She started to close her eyes, faintly embarrassed at watching something so intimate.

"No, don't close your eyes, Winnie," he whispered. "Watch me. Let me watch you."

She flushed as she met his silver eyes. He shifted again, catching one of her silky thighs in his hand and positioning her again, so that she groaned and shivered.

"Now," he whispered, "I'm going to show you why the French call a climax the 'little death.'"

He slid one hand under her nape and clenched it in her hair. His silver eyes glittered as he moved in and his body thrust hard and fast down into hers, each movement deep and quick and passionate. It only took a few seconds for her to go over the edge. She gaped at him and suddenly cried out.

"That's it," he whispered huskily when she arched up. "That's it, baby, come up and get me. Come on, come on, push, push, push!"

She was screaming. The pleasure was like a vice. Her eyes were wide-open and he was watching her, seeing it, laughing as she clawed at his hips and ground hers up into his in a rhythm that was faster than her own heartbeat.

"Get it, baby," he gritted. "Get it now!"

She shuddered and shuddered, twisting up, arching up, pleading in a voice that she only vaguely recognized as her own, while the pleasure suddenly built to a crescendo and exploded in her body like a rush of molten magma. She gasped almost in shock as it overwhelmed her. She shivered and sobbed, clinging to him while she was buffeted by the most incredible pleasure she'd ever experienced in her life.

His face, above her, clenched and he bit off something explosive as satisfaction shook his powerful body like a feverish chill. He arched his hips down into hers and cried out hoarsely, his head thrown back in pure ecstasy as he shuddered with her in a climax so hot that he almost passed out.

She was aware of her own heartbeat, going like a drum, of her sobbing breaths as she tried to drag in air. She felt Kilraven still shuddering against her, his voice breaking as he felt the tension explode.

Her eyes were intent on him. She'd never seen an expression like that. His face was clenched and flushed. His eyes were closed. His whole body shuddered again and again and when his eyes opened and he saw her watching, he groaned and the shudders seemed to deepen.

"Dear. . .God!" he cried, and shuddered again.

She was fascinated. All her reading hadn't prepared her for what she was seeing. He wasn't pretending, he was really blind with pleasure that she was giving him. Impulsively, she lifted against him and moved sensually. He sobbed and the shuddering increased. She loved pleasing him. It made her own body throb, all over again. She moved feverishly, arching up to him, twisting, watching him cry out as pleasure brought him into uncharted realms of passion.

It took a long time. She shivered again with surprise as another climax tightened her muscles. Watching him, pleasing him, was giving her fulfillment again and again.

He felt her body clench over and over, felt her tighten around him, as he drowned in pleasure. He was letting her see, letting her enjoy him. He was enjoying her. He couldn't remember a time with Monica when he let himself lose control to this extent. He'd always held something back, vaguely ashamed of the way she could manipulate him with sex. This was different. Winnie loved him. It was all right if she saw him helpless, if she watched him achieve satisfaction in her soft body.

He was shuddering. He made a sound in his throat, and his body ground down into hers as the last silvery rush of pleasure began to fade away.

She felt him relax. She took his full weight, hungry for the contact to continue, so satiated that she could barely get her breath.

"The little death," she whispered, and shivered one last time.

"Yes."

She closed her eyes as she felt exhaustion leave her limp and boneless under his hard, damp body. The hair on his chest felt wet against her breasts.

His cheek slid against hers with a long,

heavy sigh. "Little blond. . .chain saw," he whispered. And, incredibly, he fell asleep.

So did she, in the aftermath of something so explosive and unexpected that she knew nothing would ever be the same again.

14

Winnie came awake slowly, aware of discomfort in an odd place. She moved and winced. Then memory came flooding back and she knew why she was uncomfortable. She was under the covers, but without a stitch of clothing on. Kilraven was nowhere in sight.

In the absence of passion, nudity was embarrassing. So were her poignant memories of what she had said and done with him. Her face flamed as she jumped out of bed, still clutching the sheet, and looked for her clothes.

She had a vague memory of feeling

them stripped off and tossed onto the floor, but now they were draped across a chair. On a table, her suitcase was open.

She dragged the sheet with her, pausing every couple of steps to listen, to make sure Kilraven wasn't coming through the door. She grabbed underwear, jeans and a T-shirt and made a rush for the bathroom, almost tripping over the sheet.

A FEW MINUTES LATER, clean but still uncomfortable, she walked out into the bedroom with damp hair. She'd forgotten to pack a hair dryer and she couldn't remember where one was to be found in the summer house.

Well, it was thin hair and the heat was enough to dry it without any help, she reasoned. She went back into the kitchen. It was deserted. Kilraven had apparently put away the ham and bread and mayonnaise, and stacked the dishes in the sink. Remarkable, she thought, how neat he was.

She looked out the window and was surprised to see the sun going down in the distance. It had been early afternoon when they'd arrived from the airport. She flushed again, recalling how that time had been spent. Kilraven was nothing if not gifted in bed. If he could make a screaming, clawing passionate woman out of someone as sedate as Winnie, he could certainly lay claim to incredible skills.

She went back into the bedroom and unpacked. She wondered where Kilraven had gone.

HE WAS WALKING ALONG the beach, barefooted, wearing tan Bermuda shorts and nothing else. He felt like the worst sort of betrayer. He'd promised himself, and Winnie, that he'd take care of her and that nothing would happen to make an annulment impossible. The minute he'd touched her, all those resolutions had gone into eclipse and he'd reacted like a sex-starved adolescent.

Still, he recalled with some pride, he hadn't made a total hash of the thing. He had the marks on his back to prove it, too. He winced a little and then laughed, recalling her nails biting into him as she moaned.

He didn't want to have to go back and face her. Was she going to think he'd changed his mind about staying with her?

He hadn't. She was sweet to teach and he'd enjoyed her. But sex was a poor foundation for a marriage. And he should know. It was the only thing he and Monica ever had in common.

At least Winnie was on the pill. But he should have had more self-control. He kicked at a shell that had washed up on the sugar-sand beach and cursed. He could have kicked himself.

"What did that poor shell ever do to you?" a female voice inquired amusedly.

He turned his head and looked into the eyes of Senator Will Sanders's wife.

She was a brunette. She had long hair down to her waist. She was wearing a neat one-piece black bathing suit with oversize sunglasses, carrying a book, a towel and some tanning lotion in a bottle.

He frowned. "Am I trespassing?" he asked curiously.

She laughed. "Afraid so. Although I don't know if we own the beach just because we own the house it's in front of."

He shrugged a broad shoulder. "Why not? We think we own our beach," he said, and smiled.

She moved forward with self-confidence

and a charming smile. "I'm Patricia Sanders," she said, extending a hand.

He shook it firmly. "Kilraven," he said.

The smile faltered. "You're the FBI agent. . ."

He gave her a horrified look. "Not me!" he exclaimed.

"But someone said," she began.

"My brother, Jon Blackhawk. He's the FBI agent," he said. "I'm a Fed. But with another bureau."

She was suspicious. "Why are you walking along my beach, federal agent?"

He smiled self-consciously. "Hiding from my wife. Hoping she won't be waiting with a baseball bat when I go back to the house. It's that one," he added, playing the role for all he was worth as he indicated the Sinclair summer house nearby.

"That's the Sinclair place," she said more suspiciously.

"Yes, and Winnie Sinclair is my wife." He sighed.

The suspicion was gone at once. "Winnie?"

He nodded. He sighed again, loudly. "At least she's my wife right now. I don't know how long that will last, however. We may have the shortest wedding in Comanche Wells history."

She began to smile. "Made her mad, did you?"

He winced. "Furious!"

"I would never have thought of her as a woman with a temper."

"That's because you've never known her since she was married to me," he said with resignation. "We've been married for two days, six hours and," he looked at his watch, "thirty minutes. As of right now."

Her dark eyes were twinkling. "I see."

"How do you know Winnie?" he asked, frowning.

She gave him an exasperated look. "I have a summer home next door to hers," she said with slow deliberation.

"Oh. Oh!" He shook his head, laughing. "Sorry. I'm a bit slow at the moment."

"Arguments will do that to people," she agreed. She looked haunted for a minute.

"I'd better go back and face the music," he said heavily. "Nice to meet you. We probably won't see each other again. I'll be dead."

She laughed, and it had a delightful

sound. "I don't think she'll really kill you. You're on your honeymoon, then?"

He nodded and smiled. "I'm taking a few weeks off. We can't stay long, though. She works as a 911 operator back home, and they'll need her. She only gets two weeks."

"A 911 operator? Winnie Sinclair?" she exclaimed, shocked.

"They all work," he said. "Rich may be nice, but the Sinclairs all have an exaggerated work ethic. Especially Winnie." He chuckled. "That's how I met her. I was working in Jacobsville and she was on dispatch. Almost got me killed one night, but I calmed down when she started crying. She's quite a woman."

"I like her," the senator's wife said. "She's very sweet."

"Yes, well, she's not mad at you, is she? My stepmother calls her a little blond chain saw."

Mrs. Sanders burst out laughing. "What a description!"

"Sometimes it's very accurate."

She hesitated. Her dark eyes gave him a curious appraisal. "I'm throwing a party for some local friends Wednesday night. If you and the chain saw aren't otherwise occupied, you might come over."

"Thanks, but I don't drink," he said.

She gaped at him. "You don't? Now you have to come. I've never met a man who didn't drink. My husband can go through a fifth of whiskey in one sitting!" She laughed.

"Well, if we're free, we might come over for a few minutes. Thanks," he said, trying to sound reluctant.

"I'll make sure you have something non-alcoholic. And I've got a world-class chef preparing the buffet. You don't want to miss that."

He smiled. "Sounds nice."

"Never turn down free food," she told him in a conspiratorial tone. "I grew up very poor in Oklahoma. I got a job as a small-town newspaper reporter because I learned that if you went to cover events where food was served, you got fed for free."

He chuckled. She looked wicked when she smiled like that. "I see your point."

She tossed the towel over her shoulder and pulled down her sunglasses. "We'll start about six," she said. "But it's not on the clock. You can show up anytime be-fore midnight."

"All right. Thanks again."

She shrugged. "I get tired of the same faces day after day." The way she said it, Kilraven wondered if she might be talking about the senator's latest flame. But he wasn't about to ask.

"See you," he said, and turned, walking slowly down the beach the way he'd come.

KILRAVEN WALKED IN the back door, hesitating. He really needed Winnie to go to that party with him. He had to convince her without letting her know how important it was. If he had to apologize for what had happened on his knees it would be worth it. He'd never felt closer to solving his daughter's murder.

Winnie was curled up in a chair with a book. She jumped when she heard him come into the room.

"Hi," she said.

"Hi. Guess who I just ran into on the beach?" he asked with pursed lips and twinkling eyes.

"I'll bite. Who?"

"Senator Will Sanders's wife," he told her.

He put his hands deep in the pockets of his Bermuda shorts, pulling them tight against the strong muscles of his thighs. "She's invited us to a party Wednesday night."

She was just looking at him, drinking in the impact of that powerful, virile body that hers knew so intimately now. It made her tingle. "I guess you want to go, huh?"

"Why did we come down here, Winnie?" he asked bluntly.

Well, that was blunt enough, she told herself. She flushed a little. "Sorry. Wasn't thinking."

He drew in an angry breath. "Look, I did a stupid thing this afternoon. I didn't mean to, and I'm sorry."

How nice, to reduce a feverish interlude of breathless passion into a traffic citation, she thought wickedly.

She shrugged. "No problem. We all get parking tickets now and again."

He blinked. "Are we having the same conversation?"

She smiled faintly. "Sorry, I don't know where my mind was. Okay, I'll go with you." She put the book down. "She didn't suspect anything?"

"She did until I mentioned that we were recently married," he replied and smiled because the subterfuge had worked as well as he'd thought it would.

"So your hunch paid off."

"You might say that."

"Good for you."

He frowned. She didn't sound pleasant at all. His eyes narrowed as he saw the disappointment in her dark eyes. "Okay, let's get it out in the open. You think because we enjoyed each other that I'm going to want to keep you. That it?"

She went scarlet.

He smiled coolly. "I'm your first man," he said bluntly. "You're wrapped up in pink daydreams because I know my way around a woman's body without a road map. It was just sex, Winnie. I've abstained for seven years and we're married. Simple as that. I went in over my head because. . ."

"No need to explain," she interrupted him, standing up, but she didn't meet his eyes. "I'll admit I got off track for a while. Don't worry about it. I may build a few daydreams, but I know exactly where reality begins. I won't try to lock you in a closet

and keep you for a sex slave. Honest."
She crossed her heart.

He looked as if someone had hit him in
the face with a pie.

She moved closer and patted him on
the chest. "Now, I know you're disappointed, but I can assure you that there
are plenty of women in the world who keep
handcuffs and own closets. So you just
keep those spirits up until you run into one
of them." She yawned deliberately. "Gosh,
I'm sleepy. I think I'll have a nap. Watch
TV if you like." She waved a hand over her
shoulder as she walked toward the bedroom where her things were. "Won't bother
me."

She went into the room and closed the
door behind her. Then she let the tears roll
down her cheeks. But not until then. She
was finally learning how to stand up to
him. Brute force didn't work, but humor
seemed to. If she could just keep her heart
from breaking, she might manage to get
through the next few days. The trick, she
considered, was not to let him see her cry.

KILRAVEN WAS STUNNED. Had he really heard
her say that? He went and sat down on

the sofa with a hard breath. That was not what he'd expected. He was sure that he had little Winnie Sinclair figured out and pigeonholed. Then she came out with the sex slave quip and he was back to first base. He turned on the news. But then he grinned.

WINNIE KEPT HIM AT A distance with airy smiles and tours of the island, and never let him close enough to touch her. It seemed to irritate him at first. Then, like the quips she came out with, it amused him into relaxing. They spent three days sunning on the beach and walking around Bay Street.

She did very well by pretending that he was her brother. From time to time, she had to hide a fit of the giggles, because he was devastating in swim trunks and when they went in the ocean together and he held her up and grinned at her, she almost lost her poise. But she kept telling herself they were related and they couldn't do more than hold hands.

Amazingly, he did hold hands with her as they walked down the rows of shops. He was more relaxed than she'd ever seen him.

"You're different, here," she said as they paused to look in a shop window at some natty tourist T-shirts.

"No real pressure right now," he said simply, smiling down at her. "I live from adrenaline rush to adrenaline rush. I have for years. It's addictive. In between, I'm just waiting for the next one to come along."

"It's so much stress," she said.

He lifted an eyebrow. "Oh, you wouldn't know about that," he said sarcastically.

She laughed. Her job was one of the most stress-filled ones around. "Yes, but I don't really like pressure. Or stress. Or dangerous things." She sighed as she looked blindly at the T-shirts and realized how dull her life was going to be when all this was over and he was gone again. "I don't think far ahead. I just go day by day."

He turned to her, really interested. "Why?"

She stared down at her sandaled feet. "When I was in my second year of college, I got pneumonia. I had a good friend, Hilda, who lived in the dorm with me." Her eyes were sad. "She was killed in a car wreck. She'd stayed up all night with me when I was running a fever. She was on her way to the pharmacy to get some cough syrup my doctor had called in. And she died. Just like that." She moved restively. "It scared me. I realized how uncertain life was, and how short it could be. I didn't really like economics. It was my major and I'd sort of eased into it without thinking. I realized I didn't like big cities like Dallas, either. So I had Boone and Clark come get me and take me home."

"Tough break," he commented.

"About Hilda, yes. But I was happy after I'd been home a while." She smiled. "My best friend Keely was around to listen to me and go places with me. I didn't have the stress of exams or studying a subject I hated, and I felt I was where I belonged. In the place I loved most." She looked up at him. "Some people go their whole lives moving from city to city, job to job, never belonging to anything or anyone," she said seriously. "And that's fine, for them. But I wasn't like that, and I didn't know it until I had a crisis in my life."

He avoided her eyes. That was how he lived. He was happy with his life. He didn't want to change it. He didn't want ties, stability, a family. . .

Her hand on his arm brought him out of his thoughts. "I didn't mean you," she said gently. "I guess it sounded that way."

He searched her dark eyes. "I have nightmares," he said softly. "I see my daughter, screaming for me to help her, and I'm tied down and I can't. I wake up in a cold sweat. It's been that way for seven years."

"And you run from the pain and the memories and the nightmares," she said gently. "But you don't escape anything by running from it." She smiled sadly. "You see, I was running from my father, from his dislike, from his constant criticism. That's why I agreed to go to college in the first place. But in the end, I was more miserable away than I was at home."

"Facing the pain."

She nodded. "He was very sick, the last few weeks of his life. I nursed him. I think we were closer then than we'd ever been. He said," she recalled, "that he'd made some stupid mistakes in his life and it was too late. He said I should never let anger decide which way I stepped in a crossroads." She blinked. "I wonder if he found out about Matt, before he died."

"It's possible." He touched her face

tenderly. "You came up on my blind side," he said enigmatically. "I never wanted to get involved with you."

"I know," she said, glowering up at him. "You're an old lobo wolf and I'm just a kid."

He pursed his lips. "I have some looooong red scratches down my back," he said under his breath.

She went scarlet, stepped too quickly and almost fell. He caught her, laughing like a devil.

"You'll never be a kid again, after that," he whispered in her ear.

She flushed, and then laughed when he tugged her close and hugged her. After a minute, he let her go, took her into the shop and bought her a T-shirt with a shark wearing a bib and holding a fork that said "Fight hunger. Send more tourists!"

THEY GOT ALONG VERY well for a day or two, but then Kilraven's long abstinence and her trim, pert figure in skimpy outfits got the best of him and pricked his hot temper.

"Why the hell can't you cover yourself up?" he asked angrily when she came into the living room in a sundress that left her back bare.

She gasped. "What?"

He got up from the sofa and glared at her. "You can prance around naked for all I care, but I'm not staying married to you when we close this case!"

She raised both eyebrows. "Well, I like that," she said haughtily. "I guess I'll just have to go out and find myself another big, dishy sex slave!"

He wasn't in the mood for humor. He let out a filthy curse, turned on his heel and stormed out the door, down the beach.

Winnie wouldn't have admitted for worlds how much he intimidated her when he had those black moods. She was a little afraid of him, like she was with Boone in the same temper. She knew neither of them would ever hurt her, but they could be scary.

At least she wasn't backing down now. That had to mean she was growing as a person. It did hurt, to hear him say things like that. It hurt so much that it provoked her own temper. When he came back in, she pleaded a headache and went to bed, leaving him to go out to supper alone. He offered to bring her something back, but she swore she couldn't eat. Next morning, she went out early and alone to breakfast, starving. She spent the day in town walking the streets, just so she wouldn't have to fight with him.

But at night it was hard to lie in bed and hear him tossing and turning in the other bedroom, to see him red-eyed from lack of sleep, and know that the memories were tormenting him.

"You don't sleep," she said.

He glared at her. "You could do something about that, if you wanted to."

Her dark eyes were sad. "We've already talked about that."

He laughed coldly. "You think I can't walk away, don't you, Winnie?" he asked in a soft, menacing tone. "You think I liked it so much that I'd even stay married to you to get it again."

"I'm not that stupid," she replied. "What was to like, anyway? I don't even know what to do with a man, I'm so green." She turned away, missing his sudden wince. "I might as well be living in the Victorian age." She ground her teeth together. "The sooner this is all over, the better! I just want to go home!"

She did. It was wearing her nerves thin

to be so close to him and not touch him. That day they'd walked around town, he'd been affectionate, relaxed, tender. But ever since, he'd been like a sunburned snake, irritable and disagreeable. It would be painful, but she could hardly wait to go back to her job. Even if it meant having to get over Kilraven all over again.

THE PARTY WEDNESDAY night was attended by a duke's mixture of people, all races and all classes. There were diplomats, a motion picture star, a country-Western singer, a musician, a chef and at least two beachboys.

Patricia Sanders noted Kilraven's surprise at her guest list and grinned. "I don't restrict my list of friends to people with money and influence," she whispered. "See the country star over there?" she indicated a handsome young blond man, and Kilraven nodded. "His mother was a maid at a motel, and his father worked for a sheet metal plant. He could buy and sell my husband with what he pulls down annually."

"Not bad," he commented.

"One of the beachboys was a billionaire import-export business executive," she added, indicating a tall, handsome man with the physique of a wrestler with wavy black hair just a little silvery over the ears. "His family died in a suicide bombing while he was working a deal in the Middle East. He tossed it all and moved down here. He's living on annuities. Not likely to starve, even in this economy."

He was frowning slightly. "You really like people," he said, surprised.

"Yes, I do," she replied. She sipped her drink, noting that Kilraven was nursing a glass of ginger ale. Winnie was talking to a socialite she knew from her childhood, next to the drinks table. "Your wife is still mad at you," she said with twinkling eyes.

He grimaced. "She's not sure she wants a live-in sex slave, but she's debating my future." He realized what he'd said and actually flushed. "Sorry!"

But she was almost bent over double laughing. "That is not the Winnie Sinclair I know," she told him. "What are you doing to her?"

"Classified. Sorry." He grinned.

Winnie, noting the camaraderie her new husband was sharing with their hostess, excused herself and went to join him.

"You're talking about me, aren't you?" she asked Kilraven. "And just what are you telling Pat?" she added. They'd hardly spoken two words to each other all day, and here he was flirting like crazy with another woman. It infuriated her.

"Nothing compromising," Pat promised her. "Just that you treat him like a live-in sex slave."

Winnie gasped out loud and hit his shoulder as hard as she could.

"Spousal abuse," Kilraven muttered, holding his arm. "Stop that or I'll find a cop."

"There's one right over there, in fact," Pat said gleefully, indicating a very dark Bahamian man in a spotless white uniform with blue-and-red trim and a cap. "I invited him in case anybody got drunk and disorderly."

"I don't drink," Kilraven reminded her.

"I do," Winnie said brightly, sipping her highball. "Let's start a fight."

He took the glass away from her, disapproving. "No more for you."

"Gads!" Winnie exclaimed. "The drinks police!"

"I am not the drinks police," he muttered. "I'm your husband."

"Not for long," she said icily, and her dark eyes punctuated the brag.

"Okay, that's enough," Kilraven said firmly. "You're over your limit."

Winnie gave him a saucy smile. "Am I? And what are you going to do about it?"

He shrugged, glancing toward Pat. "Nice party. Thanks for inviting us. Sorry, but we have to go, now."

"I'm not going anywhere, and you can't make me," Winnie said pertly.

He pursed his lips and his silver eyes twinkled. "You think so?"

He swung her up in his arms with a grin in Pat's direction and carried her right out the door.

"I will never forgive you for this!" Winnie railed at him as he walked up the steps of the beach house and onto the porch. There was thunder and lightning in the distance, and a whipping wind right off the ocean.

"I don't give a damn," he said through his teeth. He put her down and unlocked the door. "You damned near gave away everything!"

"I did not!"

He picked her up again, kicked the door

shut and carried her down the hall to her bedroom. He dumped her on the cover and stood over her, smoldering, with his hands on his hips.

She looked up at him through a mental haze. He was very attractive, but her body was telling her graphically that she wasn't ready for any more bedroom gymnastics. She was extremely sore.

His eyes narrowed. "In case you're wondering, I'm not in the mood," he said shortly.

"Good thing," she replied enthusiastically, "because I've misplaced my handcuffs and my whip!"

"You've misplaced . . ." he began, puzzled. Then he got it. His lips compressed. "You're not handcuffing me!"

"Spoilsport," she muttered. "Okay, then, you can go watch television. I'll just read a book or something."

"What the hell's gotten into you?" he burst out.

She lay back on the bedspread, stretching out her arms and legs. "I'm a sacrificial victim," she said theatrically, "waiting for the volcano to go off."

"Winnie. . ."

She turned her head and looked at him through a rosy haze. She even smiled. "You are just dynamite in bed," she murmured. Her eyes closed, missing the surprised look on his face. "If we got divorced tomorrow, I could live on that night for the rest of my life. It was. . .just. . .incredible . . ." She was asleep.

Incredible. He smiled in spite of himself. He rummaged through the chest of drawers and pulled out a silky yellow nightgown with lace for cups. He held it up and appraised it with sheer masculine appreciation. His eyes cut around to Winnie. It would serve her right if she woke up in it and didn't know how she'd managed to get it on. And he would enjoy the process.

WINNIE SAT UP IN BED with her head throbbing. She couldn't remember how much she'd had to drink, but it must have been excessive. She vaguely recalled having a very public argument with Kilraven, and then being forcibly carried back here. She looked down at herself with surprise. But she certainly didn't recall putting on this nightgown. Well, there was probably a lot she didn't remember. She had no head for alcohol. But she'd just been heartsick at the way Kilraven had been behaving the past few days. Par for the course for him, she thought coldly. Then she recalled what he'd said about abstinence. Maybe he couldn't help himself. But that didn't excuse what he'd done. Damn him, she thought furiously. He never should have touched her in the first place. Now things were complicated.

When she got up and looked for her packet of birth control pills, things got much more complicated. It seemed that in the confusion and haste of their trip, she'd left the pills behind in Kilraven's apartment. That meant that she'd missed two of them. She recalled the instructions vividly. Her hand went to her belly and she swallowed, hard. It was exactly two weeks between periods, the worst and most dangerous time to be intimate, because her periods were regular.

She had to keep her cool. It was unlikely that she'd conceive after just one time. Well, more like three times, she corrected, and blushed. Amazing, that a man could do that. She'd read that they were only good for one time. Maybe Kilraven didn't read books about sex. She recalled some of the things that he'd done to her then, and she decided that he must have read a lot.

Well, it couldn't be helped now. She'd just have to hope that there wouldn't be consequences from her negligence. Kilraven would kill her. He'd have to, at that, because if she turned up pregnant, no way was she having a termination, no matter what.

SHE HAD AN UNEXPECTED phone call later in the morning.

"Hi, it's Pat," came the cheery reply when she answered the phone. "Want to go shopping with me down on Bay Street?"

Winnie laughed self-consciously. "Are you sure you want to be seen in public with me after last night?"

"Anybody can get tipsy, dear. I do it all the time. Head hurt?"

"Not so much. I have aspirin."

She laughed. "Come on. I'll pick you up at your front door. What do you say?"

"Okay," Winnie said, trying to sound reluctant. "I guess Kilraven can live without me for a few hours."

"You still call him by his last name?" Pat asked, incredulous.

"He doesn't like people using his first name, and I've heard that he actually threw something at his own brother when he used the nickname for it," Winnie replied. "I'm covering my butt."

There was a pregnant pause. "Really?"

"Oh, stop that." Winnie laughed.

"Come shopping. Girls' morning out."

"I'll be out front in five minutes. I'm not dressing up."

"Neither am I, pet. Come as you are." She hung up.

Winnie threw on a pretty yellow-patterned white sundress and strappy white sandals, ran a comb through her long hair, grabbed her purse and started down the hall. She was wearing the skimpiest thing she'd brought with her, and she hoped it made him howling mad with desire.

Kilraven was standing at the end of the hall, his hands in the pockets of his Bermuda shorts, which he was wearing with an open white shirt that showed off his broad, muscular, hair-roughened chest.

"Where are you going?" he asked coolly.

She moved closer. "Off to meet men!"

she exclaimed with big eyes. "Since we're getting divorced soon, I'm in the market for a new sex slave! First I'm going to a bar, then I'm going to sit on the piano with my skirt hiked up . . ."

"Winnie," he growled.

She made a face. "Pat and I are going shopping."

"Nice work," he said with a lift of his eyebrow.

"Not mine," she replied coolly. "She invited me."

His eyes slid over her with a new sense of possession. He knew that slender young body as no other man ever had. She belonged to him.

She saw that look, and it irritated her. He was never getting near her again.

"Ask her about her brother-in-law, if you can do it without making her suspicious," he said. "We're too close to blow it now."

We. That was almost funny. There was no "we," there was only Kilraven's obsession with finding his family's murderer. She thought about that and calmed down. She was losing her perspective, and that would never do. They weren't a happy couple on honeymoon. They were investigators. She had to keep that in mind. The future was her job and his, not a house with a picket fence.

"I can do what I need to do," she said solemnly. "I won't blow it."

She made him feel guilty. He was throwing her in headfirst, all in an attempt to avenge two murders. He didn't think she could end up on the firing line, but he couldn't guarantee it. "If anything feels wrong, back off," he said curtly. "Don't put yourself in the middle of anything."

"Pat isn't going to get me killed," she said.

His face tautened. "Not intentionally."

"Thanks," she murmured. She started toward the door.

He caught her shoulder as she passed him and looked down into her quiet, solemn young face. He didn't like what he saw. He'd pushed her into this trip against her better judgment. Now he was trying to put the blame for that torrid interlude on her. It wasn't fair.

"No. Thank you," he said gently. "You didn't want to come down here. I browbeat you into it. Now I'm blaming you for things that aren't your fault." He sighed. "I'm sorry for what happened when we got here. I just . . . lost it."

Well, that was better than nothing, she supposed. "I lost it, too," she replied. "No problem."

"You're sure you're on the pill?"

Her face flamed. She averted her eyes. "Of course I am!"

The car pulling up out front stopped the conversation.

"I'll be back," she said, moving away.

"If you need me, I'll have my cell with me."

She shrugged. "If there's a crisis about picking out a blouse, I'll be sure to call you."

"Thank you so much," he muttered.

She turned and curtsied. "We aim to please. You can always bake some cookies or tidy up the room if you run out of things to do," she added cheekily.

"My stepmother was right. You are a little blond chain saw!" he called after her, irritated beyond discretion.

"Sticks and stones. . ." she sang back.

Muttered curses followed her down the steps.

Patricia had both car windows down and she was laughing when Winnie climbed into the passenger seat of the sleek beige Mercedes. "What was that all about?" she asked.

"He doesn't think it's safe for me to go shopping without him," Winnie muttered. "I suppose he thinks I'll trip over my high heels and fall into the bay and get eaten by seagulls!"

Patricia pursed her lips and turned her attention back to the steering wheel. "Shortest marriage in Comanche Wells history, huh? I'm just beginning to think that may be right!"

BACK AT THE BEACH HOUSE, Kilraven was brooding. There had been something in the way that Winnie averted her eyes when he'd asked her about being on the pill. He walked into her bedroom and proceeded to do what he was best at. By the time he finished, he was certain that she hadn't brought anything with her to prevent a child. Not unless she was carrying the pills on her person. And that, as soon as she came back, was his priority. He was going to find out.

15

Winnie was animated while they walked down Bay Street, through crowds of tourists carrying bags and chattering. Nearby was Prince George Wharf, with cruise ships in port. This was one of the most sophisticated cities in the hemisphere, but at the same time it was like a small fishing village. There were big splashy hotels mingled with little cottages set back off the road in groves of palm trees. Winnie loved everything about it.

"Isn't it amazing that the old British Colonial is still here?" Winnie asked. "Otherwise,

Nassau is changing so much that I can't keep up."

"It is amazing," Pat said, smiling. "The grand old lady of the Bahamas. What a history."

"I used to love staying there. Then Daddy decided that we needed our own place."

"I love your house."

"Thanks. Me, too."

Patricia was watching her curiously. She moved through an arcade to a little nook with bougainvillea climbing the walls, where an open-air shop sold conch soup and mixed drinks. "Let's have something to drink," she said.

"Fruit punch for me," Winnie said with a groan. "I'm still not over my headache."

"Poor thing. You really shouldn't drink."

"I know."

Patricia gave in the order and carried the drinks to a little stone table with benches. She handed one to Winnie. "I shouldn't drink, either," she said, and the happy persona fell away. She put her sunglasses aside with a sigh. "But it's the only thing that keeps me from becoming a suicide."

"Pat!"

"Don't worry, I'm not really the type. It's just. . ." She sipped her drink and sighed. She looked at Winnie. "I'm not an idiot, you know."

"What?"

"First a homicide detective opens that old Kilraven murder file and my husband jumps in to put pressure on the police commissioner to get it closed again. That's after a murder in Jacobsville that raised eyebrows even up in Austin at the state crime bureau. Then a young woman dies who works for Senator Fowler. That's followed by assaults on both detectives working the Kilraven case after Senator Fowler had it reopened again." She looked at Winnie evenly from black eyes. "Then you and Kilraven himself show up next door to my beach house."

Winnie was a good actress. She'd been a leading lady in her sophomore year. She gave Patricia a beaming smile. "Great deduction." She held out her left hand, to display her wedding band and its accompanying diamond. "So I got married to Kilraven just to come down here and ask you questions about a murder. . ." She frowned. "What has any of that got to do with you?"

Patricia looked stunned.

"Did you kill somebody?" Winnie asked, shocked.

Pat rolled her eyes. "Oh, for God's sake, I must be getting paranoid." She took a big sip of her drink. "My husband's gallivanting all over Texas with a high-school cheerleader, with carloads of media trying to catch him in the act for their next big political scandal. Will's moldy retainer is threatening a minister. My stepmother. . .what in the world is the matter with you?"

"Sorry. I just never heard of anybody threatening a minister," she said with a laugh. "Our minister is bald and sixty and wouldn't hurt a fly. He came and sat with my father when he was dying." She was shocked to hear Pat talking about a moldy retainer making threats.

"It does sound strange, doesn't it?" Pat wondered. She took another drink. "He said the man was drawing things he shouldn't. Now I ask you, what in the world does that mean?"

"Beats me," Winnie said carelessly. She

grinned. "What are you going to do about the cheerleader?" she asked.

Pat blinked. "Do about her?"

Winnie propped her chin in her hand. "If it were me, I'd go see her folks."

Pat cleared her throat and took another swallow. A big one. "Not if you had a husband with employees like Jay Copper, you wouldn't."

"Oh, what could he do? Threaten you?"

Pat looked down into her drink. She took another swallow. And another. She blinked. "There was a girl, once," she said dully. "Like the cheerleader. She came to one of our parties. I caught Will with her. She was drugged out of her mind. She didn't even know what was happening. I made him send her home. He told Jay to drive her." She took another drink.

"I heard about that from a police officer back home," Winnie said. She frowned. "Her dad got a new Jaguar and all the charges were dropped, right?"

Pat shook her head. "This one never made it back to her house. They found her. . ." She stopped suddenly. She looked at Winnie with a terrified expression. "You mustn't ever tell anyone I said that, especially your husband. Promise me!"

"Okay, I promise," Winnie said, mentally crossing her fingers. She was so shocked she could hardly manage to put on an act. Jay Copper! Not Hank Sanders, but the old moldy family retainer had gone with the girl who was later found dead. "I don't understand why."

"Just never mind." She put down the drink. "Me and my big mouth! I've been scared to death for years, kept secluded, watched to make sure I never said anything. . .!"

Winnie put a hand over hers. "I would never do anything to put your life in danger," she said earnestly. "I mean that."

Pat relaxed. "Thanks." She grimaced. "I can't talk to anybody. My husband has me followed everywhere I go. I'm forever looking over my shoulder." She glanced behind her and froze.

Winnie turned. There was a man in a suit wearing dark glasses, standing beside a dark sedan.

"Do you know him?" Winnie asked.

"No."

"He's probably just waiting on a client,"

Winnie said gently. "You have to loosen up! You're getting paranoid. Honestly. Your husband likes young girls. That makes him a rake, but it doesn't make him a murderer."

Pat looked into her eyes. "Do you think so?" she asked anxiously.

"Of course I do!"

Pat put her face in her hands. "I drink too much. I talk too much. I'll end up in a river somewhere myself one day."

"Now you really sound paranoid. We should get moving. If you sit here, that alcohol is going to do a number on you. Come on. Shops are waiting!"

Pat laughed. "I guess so." She stood up. "You're really nice," she said. "I've only known you from parties, and you always seemed to stand in a corner while Boone and Clark did all the socializing. How are they, by the way?"

"Boone just got married to my best friend. They're very happy."

"And Clark?"

She shook her head. "Clark is mixed up with one wild girl after another. This new one seems to be different, though. She's a librarian."

Patricia smiled. "I'd have liked to have brothers and sisters."

"You can have Clark," Winnie offered.

The other woman swiped at her. "No, thanks. I'm happy as I am."

They walked away from the shop. The man in the suit pulled out a cell phone and started punching in numbers.

WINNIE WAS FRIGHTENED about what she'd learned, but she put on a happy face and wandered all over Nassau with Pat. It was dark when they drove up in front of Winnie's beach house.

"Well, the lights are on," Winnie said. "Maybe he's still there."

"You have to stop fighting with him," Pat advised.

"No. You stop fighting a man like that, and he'll walk all over you," Winnie replied firmly. "I'm not anybody's carpet."

Pat shook her head. "I'm sorry we didn't get to know each other sooner."

Winnie looked back at her. "Me, too." She grinned. "But better late than never."

Pat looked sad. "No. It won't be like that." Suddenly she turned up the car radio and grabbed Winnie's arm, pulling her closer. Her eyes were wild. She spoke into Winnie's ear. "Listen, if I'm not here tomorrow, he'll probably send me to Oklahoma, to his family's old home place," she said quickly. "Jay Copper is there, and I'm scared of what he might do. He'll know I spoke to you. . . Your husband has a ranch near there. Find an excuse to go there with your husband. Find me. Will you do that?"

"Why. . .?"

The jangling of Pat's cell phone made her start and cry out. She grabbed it up and opened it, turning down the radio at the same time. "Yes?" Her face paled. She gnawed her lower lip. "Yes. Yes, I will. Right now? Very. . .very well." She hung up. Her face was tragic. "I have to go." She leaned closer. "Remember what I said!"

Winnie jumped out of the car. Pat drove off without another word.

WHEN SHE WALKED in the door, Kilraven was waiting. He was standing in the hall, all business.

"Pack," he said quickly. "I've got a Learjet on the way to pick us up. We're going to Oklahoma."

"You heard us!" she exclaimed.

"Yes, and so did someone else." He turned away. "We'll be lucky if she lives long enough to get there."

"What do you mean?"

He turned. "The car was bugged."

"By you?" she asked hopefully.

"Yes. And probably by her husband's old family retainer. Give me your purse."

She handed it over without a thought. He opened it and turned the contents out onto the coffee table.

"Is it bugged?" she asked, worried.

He stood erect and his eyes were blazing. "Where are your birth control pills?" he asked coldly.

Her heart jumped up into her throat. She'd fallen right into the trap. It didn't take ESP to know that he'd already tossed her room. She sat down with a hard sigh. "They're still in the drawer next to the bed in your guest room. In the rush to the airport, I forgot them."

He didn't say a word.

She looked up at him. "Yes, I know the risk is exponential if you miss one." She glared at him. "But I didn't expect to be tossed onto a bed and ravished after you promised me nothing would happen!"

He stuck his hands in his pockets. "I'm a man," he bit off.

She sighed. "Oh, yes, you are!" she said with such feeling that his pose of indignation was threatened. He turned away.

"We have to beat her to Oklahoma," he said.

"Will they try to kill her, you think?"

He nodded. "Too many people have already died trying to cover up what happened."

"Do you know what happened?"

"I think so," he said. "A lot of it is theory, but I've been adding up what I know. And I spoke with your mother on the phone a few minutes ago. She filled in a few more blank spaces. Pack, and I'll lay it out for you on the way to the airport."

HE DID, SUCCINCTLY. "The senator had a party and invited one of his conquests, a little girl barely in her teens who'd put on plenty of makeup and stuffed her sweater and pretended to be in college. He drugged her and had fun with her, up until his wife caught him. He protested, but by then the girl came to and realized what he'd done, and started yelling about prosecution and told him her true age. He told Jay Copper to take her home. So he did, but with a detour so that he could enjoy her himself. The senator wasn't the only man who liked young girls in the house. She fought, he subdued her, and somewhere in the struggle she died."

"Oh, brother," she said heavily.

"So then Copper had to cover it up. He faked an automobile accident, destroyed her body so that she wouldn't be recognized and went about his business. The senator was probably horrified when he knew what his right-hand man had done, but he couldn't afford a scandal—he'd just been elected state senator and he had a much higher office in his sights. He saw a whole new world of financial stability opening up for him. The girl would have cost him his career. He wasn't having it ruined by some teen who threatened to go to the news media."

"But, your little girl," she began.

His jaw clenched. "Monica used to go

with a boy who worked for Senator Sanders. He and Hank were friends. Hank told him what happened, and he told Monica. I didn't know it at the time, not until today, when your mother dug it out of a closed file and called me on my cell phone to tell me about it. Monica's ex-boyfriend was killed, but before he died, he spoke with a detective and said he had information about the death of a teenager who'd been disfigured to cover up her identity."

"Oh, no," she said, because she realized where this was going.

"That's right. Hank figured that if Monica knew the truth, she might talk. So he sent a couple of men over, maybe Jay Copper included, to make sure she didn't. My daughter was there with her. She wasn't a target, she was just in the way." He bit his lower lip. "They didn't count on the Jacobsville victim falling in love, getting religion and talking to a minister."

"If Marquez hadn't gone to the media about the minister, he'd be dead, too."

"No doubt about it."

"Pat told me that a moldy old family retainer was threatening a minister who was drawing pictures he shouldn't. Not much guesswork involved in figuring out who, or why," she said.

"Yes. I phoned Jon and told him to get a tail on the minister, just in case."

"Good for you." She shook her head. "All those people, all dead, because of a teenager who woke up too soon and had to be silenced."

"Yes. The worst of it was they didn't find out who the girl really was until three years after she was killed. Her parents were dead by then. They'd thought their daughter was kidnapped. They joined support groups and pestered the police to find her. Then, they died in a horrendous automobile accident in a snowstorm in Colorado, before they could learn the truth."

She closed her eyes. "Dear God. And he got away with it."

"No, he didn't," Kilraven said in the coldest voice she'd ever heard.

"But there are no witnesses left," she argued. "If they can silence the senator's wife. . ."

"That's why we're going to Oklahoma," he said. "They aren't silencing her."

Her dark eyes glittered with feeling.

"They should put the senator and his brother away for a hundred years!"

"I'm all for that. But there's a very real possibility that the senator had no idea what his brother planned to do."

"That's chilling. But he tried to stop the investigation."

"He was protecting his brother," he said. He sighed. "I'd do the same for Jon." He glanced at her. "You'd do it for Boone, or Clark or Matt."

She nodded. "What about my uncle? How is he tied into this, do you know?"

He shook his head. "He probably knew someone in the chain, but he didn't know anything specific enough to make him a target. The only connection we have is the thermos. And that could turn out to be a blind alley. He might have loaned it to the murder victim."

"I like Pat," she said. "I hope we can save her." She glanced at him. "Couldn't you call the FBI?"

"And tell them what? That we have a possible murder? I didn't get tape, Winnie. It's your word against the senator's best attorneys. He'd sue the hell out of the Bureau if I brought Jon in on it." He didn't add that he knew Garon Grier had been seen with Hank Sanders just recently. That was still a puzzle to him.

She ground her teeth together. "You're a spy! Don't you know other spies who could help?"

He chuckled. "I'm not a spy. I'm an intelligence operative."

"Semantics!" she argued.

He pursed his lips. "I don't think anyone inside the law could do us much good. However, I do know a few people outside it."

"Maybe the senator's evil brother does, too."

"No. These are good guys. I ought to know," he added as he started punching numbers into his cell phone. "I trained every damned one of them. Hello? Put Rourke on the line."

IT WAS A ROLLER-COASTER ride for Winnie, who'd never dreamed that she'd be caught up in a murder investigation that put her own life on the line. It was exciting, just the same.

They landed at the Lawton-Fort Sill Regional Airport. Kilraven, too impatient to wait for one of the ranch hands to drive to town and get them, rented a Lincoln and they drove to the ranch at what she termed warp speeds, to Kilraven's amusement.

It was a surprise to Winnie, who was used to their own large ranch holdings. Now she understood why Kilraven found it so easy to fit in at society parties. The ranch, Raven's Pride, was built like a Spanish hacienda with many graceful arches sheltering a long, wide front porch. It was so big that it filled the horizon as they approached it. The pastures were fenced and those leading down the half mile of paved road to the ranch itself were white, spotless. On each side of the road, beautiful purebred Black Angus cattle grazed on fresh bales of hay. Their drinking water was in heated containers.

"It's amazing," Winnie said, staring out the window. "It makes our ranch look like a toy one!"

He chuckled. "It's been here for over a hundred and fifty years," he told her. "I'll tell you the history one day. It has to do with ravens who actually called wolves to sites of carrion, so they could get to the good parts after the wolves did the dirty work. Jon and I can't bear to part with it, although we don't spend much time here. We have a competent manager and submanagers in charge of routine operations."

"It's beautiful."

He smiled. "Cammy keeps the furnishings up to date. Oh, boy," he added with a grimace. "That's her car." It was a sleek Mercedes, gold and custom, parked at the front door.

"Not to worry," Winnie said easily. "My blades need sharpening before I attack anyone."

It took him a minute to get it, then he grinned. His wife was full of surprises.

He pulled up to the front porch and helped Winnie out. He threw the keys to a tall, lanky cowboy. "Bring the bags in, then put it in the garage, Rory."

"Yes, sir."

He led Winnie inside, where Cammy was waiting, her arms folded tight across her breasts.

"We're only here for a couple of days," Kilraven said at once.

"No problem, I was just leaving," Cammy said tautly.

"That might be best," he said. He bent and kissed her on the cheek. "We're about to stick our noses into a highly explosive situation with a senator's wife next door. She's the key to solving what happened to Melly."

Cammy dropped her haughty pose immediately. "Oh, no, you mustn't get yourself killed," she said worriedly.

"It's the only chance I have of breaking the case," he said gently.

Cammy looked past him at Winnie. "You're going to risk her life, too?" she asked uneasily. "You just got married!"

"It's not a real marriage," Winnie said quietly. "We had to convince the senator's wife that we had a legitimate reason to be in Nassau."

"But you're married," Cammy argued. She looked up at Kilraven, aghast. "She is a little chain saw," she said surprisingly, "but she's just what you need. You should keep her."

Winnie's jaw had dropped.

Cammy looked at her and shifted uncomfortably. "We're all difficult, in this family," she explained. "Both my sons are hard cases. You can't let them walk on you."

"No problem," Winnie said, recovering her poise. "My father didn't raise me to be a carpet."

Cammy actually smiled. "I've been talking to your mother," she said, surprising her. "A truly amazing woman." She looked up at Kilraven, who was also shocked. "She couldn't get you on your cell phone, so she called here. She says one of her contacts got word that Senator Sanders's brother was on his way to the Sanderses' home place, and he wasn't alone."

"When did she call?" Kilraven asked.

"About ten minutes ago."

He went to the gun case in the living room, unlocked it and started pulling out weapons. At the same time, he pulled out his cell phone, grimacing when he realized that he'd had it cut off, and activated it. He phoned the chief of police at the Lawton Police Department, a friend of his, and briefed him on the problem. He listened, his expression growing colder. He didn't reply to what he'd been advised to do, he simply hung up.

He started loading guns.

Winnie stood next to Cammy, uncertain.

"You're not going to wade in there shooting," Winnie said worriedly.

"Not unless somebody shoots at me first." He cocked the big .45 automatic and slid it into the shoulder holster he'd just put on. He reached for another weapon, which looked like a small automatic rifle.

Winnie stood straighter. "I'm going with you."

Cammy gaped at her. "No!"

"No!" Kilraven said at the same time.

"I can phone Pat and pretend that I'm taking her up on her invitation to visit," she said quickly. "You can hide in the back-seat. I'll let you out before I reach the house."

He frowned. This wasn't working out the way he'd planned. The idea of Winnie being in the line of fire was suddenly horrify-ing to him.

"I'm going alone," he gritted.

"No, you are not!" she returned. She grabbed him by both arms and actually shook him. "You're thinking with your heart, not your mind. You have to be logical. They'll be expecting you to walk in with guns blazing if they overheard Pat talking to me. You'll get yourself killed. What will that accomplish?"

He didn't reply. His eyes were glittering.

"You can let me wear a wire," she said. "I can get tape."

Now he did react, badly. "No. No way in hell."

"If you want a conviction, this is the only way, since all the witnesses are dead!"

He'd wanted nothing more than a conviction. Until right now, when he looked down at the slight figure of his wife. She was so young, so brave. He pictured her the way he'd last seen Monica, face up, mutilated by a shotgun blast. . .

"I won't let you," he said curtly. "I won't risk your life, not even for a conviction."

Winnie's eyebrows arched. "Well! I thought you didn't want to be handcuffed in a closet and kept as a sex slave!"

Cammy gasped and then burst out laughing at Kilraven's shocked expression.

"Sorry," Winnie told her. "It's a private joke." She let go of Kilraven's arms. "You have to let me do it. Too many people have died. It's time the perpetrators were stopped."

Kilraven hesitated.

"You have the equipment to do a wire, don't you?" she asked.

He nodded.

"Then let's go, before they kill Pat and get away with everything."

Cammy came forward. "She's right," she told him solemnly. "If she has courage enough to do this, you must have it, too."

The two women exchanged quiet glances.

"All right," Kilraven said. "But you'll do exactly as I say," he told Winnie firmly. "I've been doing this a hell of a lot longer than you have."

She saluted him.

He made a rough sound in the back of his throat and went to get the equipment.

"He'll take care of you," Cammy said gently.

Winnie smiled. "I know that. If I didn't trust him, I wouldn't have offered to go."

Cammy touched her blond hair gently. "Nice little chain saw," she cooed.

Winnie grinned. "You're just buttering me up because you know I can make homemade bread."

Cammy laughed.

KILRAVEN HAD HER wired and armed, with a small caliber pistol that fit nicely in her purse. He hoped that nobody at the old home place of Senator Sanders would search her. But if she played her part well, they might get away with it. Winnie had taken basic firearms training when she started working dispatch. She was a natural, Chief Grier had said.

He was going to exit the car within easy reach of the house while she drove up at the door. It was risky. He hated putting her in this position. But she was right. It was the only way they could bring the murderer to justice. Hank Sanders and his politician brother were going to do the time for what had happened to Melly and Monica and all the other victims.

They left Cammy in the house and walked out to the rental car together.

"Gosh, I hope it's insured for gun battles," Winnie thought out loud.

He winced. "Don't say that. The whole idea is not to get in one."

She sighed, turning to him as they reached the driver's seat. She looked up at him with a pert little smile. "Now, do try not to get shot. If you end up in the hospital, we would have to go weeks without sex."

He chuckled. She really was a little doll. As much as he desired her, he also liked her. Right now, he wasn't thinking about her misplaced birth control pills or a future without her or even a return to his stressed and dangerous lifestyle. He was only thinking of today. He sobered. "You sure you want to do this?"

She nodded.

He bent and brushed his mouth very gently over hers. It felt different. He smiled as he did it again. "You drive. I'll shoot," he whispered, recalling an old cop movie they'd both liked and talked about in the past.

She laughed. "That's a deal."

She got in under the wheel and he climbed into the backseat, armed to the teeth.

"You ready?" she asked without looking over her shoulder.

"You bet. Let's go."

WINNIE DIALED PAT'S cell number. It rang and rang. She gritted her teeth. Her perfect plan might have just gone over the falls if Hank Sanders was already at the ranch . . . !

Just when she was about to give up and panic, Pat's voice came on the line. It was flustered and quick. "Hello?"

"Hi! It's Winnie Sinclair!" she said merrily,

pretending that she didn't have a care in the world and that nobody was eavesdropping on the call. "You said to come over when you got back from Nassau, and I beat you here!"

"W-Winnie?"

"Yes. What's wrong?" she asked innocently. "You did invite me over to talk about that project of yours? You know, the hurricane fund, to be kept in escrow for Bahamians . . . ?" She was making it up as she went along.

"Oh. Oh! Yes, yes, I did, I'd forgotten."

"Isn't it convenient for me to come over now? I forgot to call. I'm already on the way."

There was a pause, voices murmuring. Pat came back on the line. "Is anybody with you?" she asked.

"With me? Who would be. . .oh, you mean my husband," she said in a harsh tone. "No, he's not with me. He went back to San Antonio on some case. And we're not speaking."

"I see."

"He can stay in San Antonio for all I care. I may go back down to Nassau. But that's my problem, not yours. I'd love to have coffee or tea or even water with you.

Just don't mention my husband to me," she added firmly.

Pat laughed nervously. "No. I won't. Certainly, you can come over. Uh, you'll need to park out front, okay? Do you know how to get here?"

"Of course," Winnie said smartly. "I did a Google search on your ranch and got directions." She laughed.

Pat laughed, too, but not with any humor. "Okay. I'll watch for you."

"See you shortly." Winnie hung up and let out a breath.

"Good job," Kilraven said quietly. "Very good."

"If we get through this, I'm lining up for a job at the FBI as a covert operative," she told him.

"Over my dead body," he muttered. "Okay, slow down when you get to the garage," he said, indicating a long, low building just below the house on the drive-way. "I'll jump out. You've got the gun. Can you use it, if you have to?"

"I can do whatever I need to do," she said between clenched teeth.

She felt a big hand on her shoulder. "Good to go."

She nodded. "Good to go."

She slowed down, just out of sight of the house, and he rolled out, closing the door gently behind him. She kept driving, her eyes on the sprawling ranch house ahead. She pulled up at the steps and cut off the engine.

As she picked up her purse and got out of the car, she noticed a big, white-headed man standing at the top of the steps. He was wearing an open-necked white shirt with dark slacks and he looked mean. Very mean.

"Hi," Winnie said with forced cheer. "I'm Winnie Sinclair. I came to see Pat."

"She's inside," the old man said in a surly tone. He jerked his head toward the front door and stepped to one side. But he gave her a look that made her skin crawl.

She nodded and walked ahead. Her knees were knocking, she knew they were. But Kilraven was out there somewhere. He would protect her.

Pat was waiting for her. "Come in," she said with forced brightness. "How nice of you to offer to help with my project! Let's talk in the living room."

Winnie felt herself being led toward a window where potted plants were sitting.

"Are you crazy?" Pat whispered frantically. "Copper made some calls before I got home. Hank's on his way up here right now. . .!"

"Don't worry," Winnie said softly. "It's all right."

"All right?" Pat ran a hand through her hair. "I overheard Copper tell his nephew that he was going to make sure I never told what I knew about that dead girl. He said he'd killed so many people that one more didn't matter, all because a stupid kid threatened to tell what Will did to her!"

Winnie's heart sank. She knew the wire was going to catch that statement. If she was caught wearing it, her life was over.

"I never thought you'd turn up here. Winnie, they'll kill us both!"

Winnie, who had learned to be calm under pressure from a job on which lives depended, put a soothing hand on her arm and smiled. "It will be all right," she said gently. "You have to trust me."

"What are you going to do?"

Winnie sighed. "You know, I have no

idea right now. But I'm sure something will come to me."

There were heavy footsteps and Jay Copper walked into the room with a younger man. They were both heavyset and un-smiling, and if death had a face, they were wearing it. Winnie clutched her purse. Her heart raced as she wondered if she'd have time to make a grab for the pistol.

Jay Copper smiled. "You think you're so smart," he drawled. "Like I don't know why you came rushing over here, after you'd just been with her in Nassau. You know too much, lady."

"My husband is a Fed," Winnie began, hiding her fear.

"Hell! Your husband is in San Antonio. I was listening when you were talking to Pat," he added, and Winnie pretended to be disturbed.

"We're not going to do both of them here, are we?" the younger man asked coolly. "Hank won't like it. His brother would be right in the middle of the scandal."

"Hank's on his way. He'll help us," Jay said easily.

Winnie felt sick. It was all going wrong. Kilraven was just one man. Even if he was right outside, these men were quick and smart and they were both wearing big automatic pistols. If she tried to shoot it out with them, she'd be killed and so would Pat. The pistol that had made her feel so secure ten minutes ago now felt like just added weight in her purse.

As if Jay knew that, he suddenly reached out and dragged the purse out of her hands, snapping it open. He burst out laughing as he drew it out. "What, did you think you'd hurt somebody with this peashooter?" he asked. "Piece of junk." He handed it to the younger man. "Better go and move her car, so nobody sees it." He tossed him the keys, which had been in the purse.

Before either man could move, there was the sound of another car approaching. Jay looked out the window and tensed until the car was in view, then he relaxed. "It's just Hank," he said. "Go on. Move the car."

"You bet, boss."

He walked out. Winnie and Pat exchanged worried glances.

A car door slammed, then another. There was a pause and an odd sound, and then footsteps coming rapidly up the steps. A tall, striking man walked into the house. He had jet-black hair and black eyes, with a prominent scar on one cheek. He was wearing a designer suit and shoes as polished as a mirror. He hesitated in the doorway and looked at Pat for a long moment. Only then did his eyes cut to Winnie and back to Jay Copper.

"What's going down?" he asked Copper.

"Just another little hiccup in a perfect plan. Nothing to worry you. Why'd you come? I told you I was going to handle this. I always handle problems for the senator." He grinned. "He's my boy. Your dad raised him, but I put him in your mother's belly. She was always keen on me, not that old rich man she married."

Hank hadn't smiled since he walked in. His dark eyes narrowed on the older man's face. "You're making problems for Will, not helping him."

"Oh, sure. Problems." His face darkened. "Where the hell were you when that stupid kid got high and enticed him into the bedroom? Where were you when she woke up naked and screamed and said her daddy's best friend was an anchorman in San Antonio and she was going to tell him everything! Where were you when Will cried his eyes out, scared to death, and begged me to fix it?" He cursed. "I've fixed everything for him since he was a teenager. I've always been around to do that. Nobody hurts my son as long as I'm alive!"

Winnie was standing frozen beside Pat, knowing that everything that horrible man was confessing was going right into a recording device. It would convict him. If she lived to testify about it.

"I was serving my country," Hank said quietly.

"Oh, yeah, serving your country. You're as bad as me," he scoffed. "You run one of the biggest illegal gambling syndicates in the state. How does that serve your country?"

Hank's eyes narrowed. "What are you planning?"

"Why don't you go back to San Antonio and just let me handle this?" Copper asked. "I know what I'm doing."

"You'll have Will hung."

"No, no, these are the last people who know anything about the case." He frowned. "Well, there's those detectives, but they don't have evidence of anything. And that minister has been told that his church will be burned down and his congregation barbequed if he talks to a cop again as long as he lives."

Hank moved closer to the man, smiling. "You've done so much already. I can do this for you. I've got Rourke out in the car. He's good with women."

Winnie felt sick to her stomach, even as she felt there was something familiar about that name, something she should remember. . .

16

While Winnie was trying to remember why that name sounded so familiar, Hank Sanders was waiting for an answer.

Jay Copper hesitated, but only for a minute. "No, Peppy can help me. He did Dan Jones and that woman who worked for Fowler," he drawled. "We got rid of everybody who could connect Will with the girl's death. I'm teaching Peppy. He's already a chip off the old block."

Hank moved even closer. He smiled. "Yeah. Just as stupid and just as gullible as you are. Uh-uh," he said quickly. His hand was close to the old man's stomach.

"You don't want to reach for that automatic. Know why?" His hand moved sharply toward the man. "Because this is a .40 caliber Glock and the clip is full. Besides that, there are two guns aimed right at your head. You make a move and you're as dead as your victims are."

Pat's mouth was open. So was Winnie's. The bad guy was turning against his own people?

The door flew open and Kilraven walked in with a tall, blond man with long hair who wore an eye patch over one eye. They were both carrying pistols.

Winnie almost fell with relief. "I got tape!" she exclaimed joyfully.

"Darling!" Rourke said with passion, approaching her.

"You touch her and you'll be shorter in one place than any man in your whole division," Kilraven gritted.

Rourke made a U-turn and went back toward Hank and Copper.

Hank shoved the old man toward Kilraven. "I hope you brought cuffs," he said. "Where's Peppy?"

"Sleeping soundly on the floor of the backseat of the rental car," Kilraven said, taking a breath of relief that Winnie was still in one piece and unharmed. Listening to her on the wire was the most terrifying few minutes of his life.

"Courtesy of yours truly," Rourke replied with a grin. "Trained him yourself, huh?" he asked Copper. "Very efficient."

"You go to hell," Copper said through his teeth as he was handcuffed. "You traitor!" he yelled at Hank. "You were working with the Feds all along?"

Hank handed the Glock to Rourke. "From the minute they found Dan Jones in the river in Jacobsville," he said shortly. "I never could prove you did the teenager, but I knew you did Dan Jones by the way he was killed and I thought we might just get enough evidence to convict you for that one. That was what you were in prison for, killing a man who cheated the mob in such a way that nobody else was tempted to cheat them. Did you think I'd forgotten?"

"Cop lover!" Copper spat at him. "I'll sell you out, if I have to do it from death row!"

Hank shrugged. "Try it," he said, and he looked every bit as menacing as the older man. "I've got friends on both sides of the law."

"He hasn't got that many on our side. I wouldn't worry too much," Rourke said sotto voce.

"Rourke," Kilraven growled.

Hank laughed. "Let him rail. He and his son can share adjoining cells."

"What do you mean?" Copper asked hesitantly.

"The Feds picked Will up for questioning about two hours ago," Hank said. "Denied him a phone call until I could get up here and save Pat." He glanced over his shoulder at her. "Will's been trying to call, to warn you, but he couldn't get past Copper."

"Nice of him," Pat said through her teeth. "He'll lose his senate seat."

"He'll lose a lot more than that," Hank said. He moved closer. His face tautened. "The girl whose father took a bribe to let Will off the hook for statutory rape, remember her?"

Pat nodded.

"Some San Antonio detective got her to press charges for it, belatedly."

Winnie smiled. She could imagine who that detective was.

"He'll go to prison, won't he, Hank?" Pat asked.

"Most likely." He drew in a long breath. "Going to stand by him, like the long-suffering, faithful little wife, and protect him from the media?" he asked harshly.

Goodness, Winnie thought, that was an odd remark. Then she got a look at his eyes and realized why he'd risked so much to save Pat.

Pat avoided looking at him. "I thought you were up to your neck in the crime syndicate."

"Oh, I am," he said bitterly. "I owed Garon Grier a favor, from another time, and I paid up. But I've never killed anybody, least of all a helpless young girl," he added, sniping at Copper, who glared at him from the next room, where Rourke had parked him temporarily. "Will knew Copper did it, and he kept it to himself until today. He told me, just before I came up here.He confessed the whole thing. My half brother, the accessory to the most horrendous murder I've ever heard about." He stared at Jay Copper with icy eyes. "I hope they hang you both! A man who'd condone doing that to a little girl deserves the same treatment!"

Hank went up in Kilraven's esteem. He'd

had a different view of the mobster. Until now.

"Will said she'd asked for it," Jay Copper scoffed. "Those young girls, they're tramps. They just lay in wait for older men who don't have no sense."

Kilraven was seeing his little girl on the floor, covered in blood, imagining if she'd been a few years older and that had happened to her.

Hank moved closer and put a hand on his shoulder. "I should have said something sooner. I had a hunch about the teenager, even your ex-wife's boyfriend. But I never believed my brother could be cold enough to condone the execution of a mother and child."

"Aw, the woman knew what I'd done! Her ex-boyfriend spilled his guts to her," Jay scoffed. "I did him myself."

Kilraven turned. His eyes were terrible. "It was you! You killed my daughter!"

Copper lifted a shoulder. "No. It was Dan Jones. I sent him to do your wife, after her ex-boyfriend spilled his guts to her. Dan was never supposed to hurt the kid, she just got in the way. They said that was why he got religion and started yapping about his evil past. His conscience hurt. He was going to tell that minister all about it." Jay smiled coldly. "But I got to him first."

"What about the thermos?" Winnie asked. "My uncle's thermos was found where the car was in the river."

Copper frowned. "What thermos? Oh, yeah, some guy loaned it to Dan when his got stolen. I had Peppy spike it. Dan was going to talk to a cop in Jacobsville about his past. We heard him say it on the phone talking to that girlfriend of his, so me and Peppy drove down to Jacobsville and ambushed him. He screamed like a little girl."

Little girl. Little girl. Melly, holding out her arms to him. Melly, laughing, saying, "I love you, Daddy! Always remember."

Kilraven took two quick steps toward the man.

Winnie moved right in front of him, very calm and self-assured, and put her hands on his chest. "No," she said softly. "The criminal justice system works. Just give it a chance. Don't give him the easy way out, after all he's done."

Kilraven looked down at her. He hesitated, while the forces inside him went to war. He wanted to kill the man with his bare hands. Melly had died because this fool wanted to protect his son from the law. But so many people had died already.

Winnie was staring up at him with soft, loving brown eyes. He calmed, just looking at her. She gave him comfort. She gave him peace. For the first time in years, he was pulling free of the black melancholy that sat on him from time to time. He drew in a deep breath. "Okay."

She smiled up at him.

"Nice girl," Hank mused, looking at Winnie. "Pity she married you when I'm still available."

"Hey, I'm available, too, and I'm not on the wrong side of the law!" Rourke piped in.

Kilraven shook his head. Rourke was incorrigible. He turned back to Hank. "You might go legit," he suggested. "It worked for Marcus Carrera."

"Who do you think he turned over his San Antonio holdings to in the first place?" he asked, aghast. But then he looked at Pat. "I don't know, though."

Pat looked back. Almost hopefully. Hank smiled. Pat flushed and looked away.

"Whatever I decide, right now I have to get back to San Antonio. Will's staff will be having hysterics, and there's the news media to handle. Thanks," Pat said, including Kilraven, Rourke and Winnie in her gratitude. "And you," she added to Hank. "I thought you were coming up to help him kill me," she said with helpless guilt.

He touched her cheek, very lightly. "I'm no ladykiller," he said with a faint grin.

"Well, I am," Rourke called from the next room. "Or I would be, if I could get past Kilraven there!"

Kilraven whirled, and he wasn't smiling. "She's my wife, damn you! And if you so much as smile at her, I'll make you into the world's first one-eyed soprano!"

Rourke stood up straight. "Yes, sir!"

Winnie was watching Kilraven with a very odd smile. That had sounded like jealousy. Of course, he could have been kidding. . .

He turned and looked at her. She blushed all the way down her neck. Oh, no. He wasn't kidding!

GARON GRIER TURNED up a few minutes later with a team of U.S. Marshals, whom Winnie found fascinating. She mentioned her great-grandfather to them, and beamed when one of them recognized the name from an honor roll he'd seen. Hank and Grier moved away to speak, after a fuming mad Jay Copper and his nephew had been taken away in handcuffs.

Pat was packing. Rourke was staying well clear of Winnie. Kilraven took her into an adjoining room and removed the wire.

"I'm proud of you," he said quietly, searching her eyes. "Very proud. You could have been killed."

She smiled. "Not likely, with you and your cohorts covering my back. Although I must admit that Hank Sanders came as a shock."

"To me, too, until your mother mentioned seeing him with Grier. Nobody in Texas would ever suspect Garon Grier of being hand in hand with organized crime. He's a real boy scout."

"A nice one," she agreed. She looked up at him. "What now?"

He'd been expecting that question. He drew in a long breath. "We take a breathing space. Just for a few weeks. I need time. . ."

"Yes." Time to heal, he meant. Time to grieve for his daughter. Maybe even for his wife. She smiled. "What about this?" She held up her wedding ring.

He looked uncomfortable. "I don't have time to see about things right now. We'll talk later."

Nice answer. Smooth. Very smooth. She leaned close. "Should I toss the hand-cuffs?"

He burst out laughing. The other men glanced at him curiously, but he just threw up a hand and walked out with Winnie.

Cammy almost hugged Winnie to death back at the house. "I was so afraid for you. For both of you," she added, hugging Kilraven, too. She hit him.

"What was that for?" he asked, ag-grieved.

"For scaring me! Don't you ever do that again!" she raged. And then she hugged him some more.

WINNIE WENT BACK TO work at the 911 center on the early morning to afternoon shift. She excused herself in the middle of a call for a wrecker, motioning to Shirley to fill in for her while she rushed into the restroom and threw up for five minutes. When she came back out, weak and pale and holding a wet paper towel to her face, Shirley turned around from her station and sang, softly, "Rock a bye baby. . .!"

Everybody around Winnie grinned.

She made a face. "And nobody tell Kilraven," she muttered, "or there will be trouble!"

"Terroristic threats and acts," Shirley whispered.

"That's right. I belong to the Jacobsville Barfing and Terrorism Society," she quipped.

The next day, Shirley presented her with a T-shirt with that logo. She took it home and wore it to supper.

"YOU SHOULD TELL HIM," Boone advised.

"Definitely," Clark added.

Matt gave her a long, sad look. "I miss playing video games with him."

"I miss arguing with him." Gail sighed, still nursing her gunshot wound, and on sick leave from her job in San Antonio.

"You should just tell him," Keely said gently.

"I am not telling him anything," Winnie said firmly. "He'd stay around out of guilt."

She sighed. "I haven't heard a word from him in three weeks. He might be talking to a divorce lawyer for all I know. He said he didn't want to get married again and he didn't want another child."

"Oh, sure, that shows," Clark mused, indicating his sister's growing little belly.

Winnie glared at him. "Sometimes things happen."

Everybody laughed except Matt, who looked perplexed.

"Don't worry, in about four years you'll understand a lot more than you do now," his mother said, patting him on the head.

Winnie laughed with them, but she was depressed. It was inevitable that someone was going to see her and tell him. Well, if they could find him. Winnie had no idea where he was. She only hoped that he hadn't gone overseas on some dangerous mission. What Jay Copper had said must have caused him some more pain.

The media was having a field day with Senator Will Sanders. He was in jail awaiting arraignment and there were satellite trucks all over the street where the detention center was located, not to mention all around the senator's home. Pat had escaped back to Nassau. Hank Sanders was also out of touch with his associates. Nobody knew where he was. Just like Kilraven, Winnie thought. She touched her belly and smiled. She loved being pregnant. Maybe she could go and live in Nassau, too, and have the baby and raise it there and Kilraven would never have to know. She pursed her lips. The Jacobsville Baby Hiding and Beachcombing Society. She burst out laughing. When she told them what she'd been thinking, so did they.

KILRAVEN HAD SPENT two weeks in his apartment, out of touch with the world, even with his brother, while he finally grieved for his little girl. He had videos of her that he'd never had the nerve to watch. Now, he took them out and savored every smile, every little laugh. There she was at her first birthday party, in a frilly dress, looking wide-eyed at the camera, walking and falling and picking up toys and putting them in her mouth. And laughing. Always laughing.

There she was at her second birthday party, with little friends, playing with the birthday cake while Monica fussed and Kilraven chuckled and got odd camera angles while he filmed her. Then it was her third birthday, and she was very pretty and wearing a scarlet dress with white hose. She ran to her daddy, knocking the camera. It lay on the ground, filming feet, while Kilraven picked her up and swung her around, and she was laughing, laughing, kissing his cheek and saying, "I love you, Daddy. Always remember."

"Always remember." He said it aloud, with her, and his eyes filled with tears. Until Winnie, he'd never shed a single one in seven years. He'd held the memory away, pushed it aside, ignored it, used his anger and rage to avoid facing what he faced now: the certainty that his child was dead and that he would never see her again in his lifetime. He would never watch her go on her first date, buy a pretty dress, go through the agony and ecstasy of adolescence, graduate from high school, go to college, have a career, get married and have a family. He'd miss all that. Now he sat in front of his big-screen television, staring at that beautiful little face that was so much like his, as if at a flower that had just blossomed and was cut down in the same instant. Melly was dead. Melly was dead.

He put his head in his hands and let the tears fall. They blinded him. They comforted him. They helped to heal him. After a few minutes, he forced himself to look at the screen. He pushed the start button. And there was Melly, still alive, still laughing, still saying, "I love you, Daddy. Always remember."

"I will, sweetheart," he said huskily. "Always. As long as I live."

Later, he found the framed pictures of her that he'd put away when she died. He took them out, dusted them and put them on the table next to the television.

"We got the man, Melly," he told her smiling face. "We got the man who ended your life. And he'll pay with his own. You can rest easy now, sweetheart. He didn't get away with it."

He touched the framed picture and managed a smile. "I love you. Always remember." His voice broke on the last word.

THREE MONTHS LATER, just back from an assignment to an African nation that he could never admit he'd visited in the line of duty, he walked into the 911 center as casually as if he was taking a tour of it, dressed in an expensive pair of slacks with a black turtleneck sweater and a cashmere jacket over it. Same polished shoes, same arrogant walk. But he wasn't quite as confident as he appeared. Especially when Winnie spotted him as she walked out of the canteen and stopped dead.

He didn't understand why she was so upset until he looked down and saw the evidence that her stomach gave to her condition. She was wearing the standard uniform that 911 personnel donned for the job, a navy blue shirt and dark slacks. But the shirt wasn't tucked in, and it was pulled fairly tight over that firm little mound. She looked very sexy, he thought.

She let out a sigh and looked resigned, as she realized the jig was up. She walked toward him and stopped. He was so tall. He towered over her. She looked up at him with resignation in her soft brown eyes and waited for him to blow up and walk away.

The last thing in the world she expected was for him to produce a small cloth grocery bag and hand it to her.

She frowned. "What is this?"

"Strawberry ice cream and dill pickles,"

he said smartly. He grinned. "I've been reading these books, and they say that pregnant women can't resist them."

She was still trying to adjust to the smile. The ice cream was freezing her hand. The pickle jar was heavy. Kilraven had lost his mind.

He bent and kissed her very gently. "Look deeper," he whispered.

Still frowning, she reached deep into the sack and felt metal. She stopped with her hand buried in the sack, gaping at him.

"Handcuffs," he whispered. He grinned wider.

She was aware that eyes were darting toward them from all the busy stations. She felt disquieted. He looked normal. She glanced into the bag. Handcuffs?

"You can't be a sex slave without handcuffs," he said, loud enough for people nearby to hear him.

"You animal!" she exclaimed, hitting him and laughing helplessly.

"You can borrow my handcuffs anytime you like, Winnie," one of the female operators who was also a Jacobsville police officer, offered as she rushed by.

"Mine, too," another officer chimed in.

"Nice coworkers." Kilraven beamed. "When can I take you home?" he added.

"I was just going off my shift," she stammered. "I have to get my coat and purse out of my locker."

He took the bag back. "I'll wait for you in the lobby," he whispered.

She just nodded. She walked to the back in a daze. She stayed in the daze past the grinning faces of her friends, all the way out the front door and into the Jaguar, while Kilraven held the door open for her.

She got in and put on her seat belt. She looked at him as he joined her. "Are you all right?"

He smiled. "I'm all right. I've had a rough few weeks, but I think I'm through the worst of it."

She smiled, too. "I guess you noticed that I'm pregnant."

He chuckled. "A lot of people noticed it," he said. "Marquez told me two weeks ago, but I'd just gotten back in from an overseas assignment and I had a lot of loose ends to tie up before I could come down here and start over with you."

"Start over?"

He nodded. He pulled out into the road. "An apartment is no place to raise a child. But we'll have to stay there while we look for a house. That okay with you?"

She was nodding blindly.

"Meanwhile, I've invited your family up for dinner. Jon's cooking. Cammy's going to be there, too." He chuckled. "So you have no excuse not to come with me. Right?"

She was beginning to feel like treasure. "Right."

"That's what I like. Docile agreement."

"Then you'd better divorce me and marry a doormat, Kilraven," she quipped.

He laughed. "No chance of that." He looked at her. "McKuen."

She hesitated. "McKuen," she said, making a caress of it.

He whistled. "Boy, does that do things to my blood pressure when you say it like that."

"Nice to know that I'm not totally unarmed in the war of the sexes."

He smiled and growled softly.

THEY ARRIVED AT HIS apartment to find her entire family in the lobby.

"We didn't have a key, and your brother Jon has to drive here from Dallas, so he's late getting here," Boone explained with a grin.

Kilraven laughed. "Sorry. I didn't think about the key. Never mind." He walked over to the security guard's station. "I have brought an entire family here for illicit purposes," he began loudly, while Boone's face stretched into utter disbelief.

Winnie laid her hand on Boone's arm. "It's okay," she whispered.

"I am having you drawn and quartered, Kilraven," the guard raged.

"No, no, no, I'm a person of noble birth," Kilraven lectured. "You have to have me beheaded."

The guard frowned. "Beheaded."

Kilraven nodded.

The guard pulled himself erect. "I will have you beheaded, Kilraven!"

"Much better." Kilraven grinned as he rejoined the others. Boone was giving him a cold look.

Kilraven turned back to the guard, pointing at Boone. "I am not taking him upstairs for any sort of illicit purposes," he called out.

"Oh, very good," the guard nodded.

"You married a lunatic," Boone whispered to Winnie.

"I heard that," Kilraven said as he led the way to the elevator. "Keep Trust!" he called to the guard.

The guard grinned. "Hold Fast!"

Kilraven saluted him and motioned the others into the elevator. "It's a Scots thing," he explained. "He's a McLeod. His family motto is 'hold fast.' My mother's people were Hepburns. Ours is 'keep trust.'"

"Another raving mad fan of sixteenth century Scots history," Winnie groaned.

"There, there," Kilraven said with a gentle smile. "You'll adapt."

She looked up at him with so much love in her eyes that he felt blinded by it. He slid an arm around her and pulled her close. "I'll adapt," she promised.

JON ARRIVED, TOO LATE to be presented to the security guard in his brother's usual outlandish fashion, with Cammy in tow. She was introduced to the Sinclairs, and she and Gail found a lot in common, including friends. Jon moved into the kitchen and started cooking, with some help from

Winnie and Keely. They sat down to a feast fit for an ancient monarch. Then they all had the courtesy to yawn and regret having to leave so soon, because they were so tired. But they ruined it by grinning outrageously as they said good-night at the door. Even Jon and Cammy.

Kilraven closed the door, shaking his head. "What a bunch. But they do blend seamlessly, don't you think? A good omen for the future."

Winnie was looking at the photos on the table beside the television. She turned to him and smiled gently. "She looked just like you."

He nodded. "She was a sweet child. It wasn't right, to hide her away like a guilty secret for so long."

"Yes."

He pulled her against him and touched her belly lightly. "Is it a boy or a girl? You have those skills, like your mother. Guess."

"We can have an ultrasound and know for sure," she said.

He made a face. "Takes all the fun and surprise out of it. Why don't we just wait until the baby comes?"

She smiled from ear to ear. "I was hoping

you might say that." She cocked her head up at him. "Are we getting the divorce before or after he's born?"

"He! You said he!"

She glowered. "Figure of speech. Answer the question."

"I suppose we could put it off for a few years. You know, until we're grandparents. Then we can talk about it."

She looked him up and down with soft appreciation. "I was just thinking. The doctor told me I ought to exercise. You know, to keep fit while I'm carrying the baby."

"He did?"

She nodded. She moved closer. She ran her fingers up his chest and over the buttons. His breathing quickened. "And I was thinking that some indoor exercises are every bit as good as walking or jogging and stuff."

"You were." His heart was slamming away.

"Yes. So I thought," she moved even closer and teased around a shirt button. His breathing was very heavy by now. "I thought we might get one of those Wii systems and that program called Wii Fit, so I can exercise indoors."

"Damn!"

She stared up at him. "Damn, what?"

He pulled her hips into his. "I've got a hard-on so bad that I could put it through a wall, and you're talking about a damned exercise machine?"

"Or," she said, breathless, "we could try that thing your buddy did, where he and his wiiiifeee. . .!"

TEN MINUTES LATER, they were sprawled on the carpet, shivering and sweating and gasping for breath.

"Thank God I don't have a sunken living room!" he exclaimed.

She laughed with pure delight. "It would still be worth a broken ankle," she pointed out.

He rolled over and kissed her with enthusiastic delight. "Two," he agreed, and kissed her again.

She tugged him down over her and nuzzled his face with hers. "I love you, McKuen," she whispered softly.

He lifted his head to look into her wide, gentle, dark eyes. She was a fighter, a lover, a mixer, a calm oasis in a storm. She could face down killers, juggle frantic calls and dispatch help with a flair, and in bed she was everything he could ever ask for. Besides all that, she loved him.

He brushed her nose with his, and glittery silver eyes stabbed into hers. "I love you, too."

She was surprised. "You do?" she asked blandly.

"Very much. Of course, I didn't know it until I let you walk into that bear pit wearing a wire." He sobered. "I thought, if she dies in there, they can just put me in the ground beside her. Because there won't be anything left on earth worth living for, if I lose her."

Tears burned her eyes, hot and wet. A sob escaped her throat.

He kissed the tears away. "Why are you crying?" he whispered.

"You were named for a poet," she whispered back. "Now I see why."

He grinned. "I can recite poetry," he told her. "Want to hear some?" He lifted his head. "The boy stood on the burning deck. . .!"

"Oh, for heaven's sake, not that sort of poetry!"

His eyebrows lifted. "Something more

suitable to our current situation, then?" he added, looking down at her pretty nude body with a grin. "There once was a man in Nantucket. . ."

She kissed him, laughing uproariously.

He kissed her back. "I suppose we should go to bed."

"I suppose."

He cuddled her close in his arms. "On the other hand," he murmured drowsily, "it's warm and cozy here. So what's wrong with the carpet, I always say."

"I always say that, myself," she agreed, and reached up to pull an afghan off the sofa to cover them with.

She closed her eyes and snuggled close to him, warm and loved and happier than she'd ever dreamed of being. He might be dangerous, she thought dreamily, but with courage like that to keep her and the baby safe, she had no more fear of the future. In fact, she could hardly wait to see it. Not that she lacked courage of her own. She was constantly amazed at her own part in their recent brush with death. Only a year ago, she couldn't have imagined herself doing something so bold. Kilraven had in-fluenced her, she thought, and so had her own mother. Perhaps courage was something that only presented itself when it was needed the most.

She glanced toward the photograph of Kilraven's little girl on the table and thought of her own child, lying soft and safe in her belly. This child would never replace Melly. But it would help to heal the old, deep wounds.

As she closed her eyes, far away, she imagined she could hear the sound of a child laughing, a silvery, soft, happy tone; the sound of a lovely little spirit who was, like her father, finally at peace.